MW01134903

Sweet Chemistry

September Roberts

Published by September Roberts, 2018.

Sweet Chemistry

Forbidden love has its sweet rewards, but is it worth risking everything?

After weeks of watching from a distance, Kate Rhodes meets James, igniting a desire neither of them has previously experienced. Kate, a senior at Bowman State University, is horrified the following Monday when she discovers James is her biochemistry professor.

James Baker has worked for nine years for his Ph.D. and has sacrificed a lot to get his position at the university. Just when he thinks he's found the woman of his dreams, his hopes are crushed when he realizes not only is she one of his students, but she is apparently already in a relationship; neither is enough to quell his desire to be with her.

Despite the issues keeping them apart, Kate and James cannot stay away from each other. Drawn together by fate and bound by passion, they are constantly reminded of the heavy price they will pay if their relationship is discovered.

James struggles to hold on to the life he's worked so hard for while Kate builds her future using her knowledge of food chemistry to open a bakery. Sweet Chemistry is a story filled with forbidden love and its sweet rewards, but can they find a way to be together without losing everything?

Copyright

This is a work of fiction. Names, places, characters, and events are either the product of the author's imagination or are used fictitiously, and any similarities to actual persons, living or dead, business establishments, events, or locales, are purely coincidental. Any trademarks, service marks, product names, or named features are assumed to be the property of their respective owners and are used only for reference. There is no implied endorsement if any of these terms are used. Except for review purposes, the reproduction of this book in whole or part, electronically or mechanically, constitutes a copyright violation.

SWEET CHEMISTRY
Newly published August 2018 edition
Copyright © 2018 SEPTEMBER ROBERTS
ISBN: 978-1723242007
Cover Art by Mae's Wicked Grafix

Dedication

I dedicate this book to Rich, my favorite chemist. He has given me years of sweet chemistry.

Acknowledgments

There are many people in my life who have given me their love and support. Cheyenne, I love you most of all for talking me down and encouraging me to keep writing. Thank you Laurie, Wendy, Monica, and Kendra for the countless hours of brainstorming and editing. I'm not sure how I will ever repay their kindness. Andrea, your real estate knowledge was beyond helpful. Thank you, Mae, for making this lovely cover. I'm so grateful for my RWA chapter and the support I've gotten from the League of Utah Writers. We all need cheerleaders and I have some great ones.

Chapter One

From his seat, James could see the majority of the club. Most people danced in spurts, stopping often to refuel at the bar and socialize with friends. But there was one person who stood out. She moved to the music as if she couldn't resist. As if nothing else mattered. He could tell she wasn't there to socialize. She was there to dance. What would it be like to be that free? Everything he did was carefully measured, perfectly planned, and judged by everyone.

Undergraduate school, graduate school, and a teaching assistant position. Nine years of work had gotten him the job he always wanted and, in a few weeks, he would start teaching at Bowman State University in sunny Southern California.

Preparing for the upcoming semester took most of his time, but he set aside the weekends to unwind, which is how he ended up at Addiction on Saturday night. Far enough away from the university to avoid anyone he might know, he sat at the bar and sipped his gin and tonic while he watched her.

When she left at the end of the night, he left too. He hadn't planned on staying that long, but she held him there. When he returned the following Saturday, the minutes passed slowly as he waited for her to appear. Seeing her again would be the highlight of his week. He didn't know her name or where she learned to move like that. All he knew was that she was the most beautiful woman he'd ever seen. Finally, she arrived.

Before heading to the dance floor, she stood at the other end of the bar and ordered a drink. Her friend said something and she laughed loud enough that he could feel it and it made him smile. At that moment she made eye contact with him. It was only for a few seconds, but it felt like an eternity. Somehow, in that crazy, noisy place, they connected. But just as quickly as it began, the connection ended when she blushed and looked away.

That was all it took. Week after week, he returned, waiting for another shared moment with her. There were plenty of nights where he almost talked to her but couldn't muster the courage to do it. Watching from his spot at the bar was safer. Was it just his imagination, or was she watching him, too? After another night of observing from a distance, she sauntered up to him and smiled and he knew it was his chance.

She slid onto the stool to his left and turned toward him.

Now or never. "Do you come here often?" Even as the words left his mouth he knew how lame they sounded. "Sorry, that was stupid. I'm a bit rusty."

The woman laughed and her blue eyes lit up. Before that moment, he couldn't figure out what color they were because she'd never been close enough for him to tell.

"Why don't I try?" She held out her hand. "I'm Kate."

"James." As he took her hand, a spark of electricity shot up his arm and she seemed to feel it, too. Neither of them made an attempt to pull away. "You look familiar."

"I get that a lot. I work at a couple of restaurants near Capistrano Beach." As she spoke she brushed her dark hair off her forehead and tucked it behind her ear. His gaze lingered on the lone strand of hair still out of place. It looked soft and he couldn't help but wonder what it would feel like running through his own fingers.

Snapping out of it in time to respond, he said, "Maybe that's why." Although he'd sampled most of the local cuisine, it didn't seem to be the reason he knew her face.

"Are you here alone?"

After a quick nod, he said, "You?"

"I'm with my friend, Meg, over there." As Kate pointed, Meg signaled for her to return. Kate held up her finger. "She's ready to go."

"Oh."

Kate pulled her hand away and stood next to him. "I'll be here next Saturday. In case you wanted to know. I get off work at eleven."

"Eleven," he repeated, smiling.

"WHAT'S THE PLAN?" MEG asked.

"I'm going to talk to him and get a feel for what he's after," Kate said.

"What are you after?"

"Sex. Maybe more. He seems like a nice guy, he might make a good boyfriend. But definitely sex. It's been too long."

"Sex is always good. Be safe."

"Always." The best part about going out together was that they had each other to ensure safety. "Will you give me feedback?" Kate could count on her best friend to be brutally honest and trusted her instincts implicitly.

"Of course."

When they walked into the club, Kate nodded toward the bar. "That's him."

Meg rubbed her hands together. "Let the feedback begin."

As they approached, James stood and smoothed his shirt, drawing Kate's eyes to the way the material hugged his lean, muscular body.

"You're here. With your friend." He couldn't seem to hide his disappointment.

"Don't worry, buddy. I'm not going to interfere. Much." Meg smiled. "How old are you?"

"Twenty-eight."

"Employed?"

James nodded.

"Do you have a personalized license plate?"

"No. Those are stupid."

"Three for three," she said to Kate. "You may proceed." When she pulled her friend into a hug she whispered, "If you need me, give me the signal."

"Thanks." After they parted, Kate smiled at James. "Sorry, just following protocol."

"Did she just vet me?"

"Sure did."

"And I passed?" Worry creased his forehead.

"With flying colors. Always nice to have a second opinion."

James relaxed. "Can I buy you a drink?"

"That would be nice. Lemon drop, please."

While he ordered, she took the opportunity to get a better look at him up close. Last week she'd been focused on his dark brown eyes and hadn't paid much attention to his short hair which was the color of raw chocolate, the same as his stubbly beard. His lips were gumball pink and looked soft and perfectly kissable. She realized a second too late he was talking to her. "What?"

"Your drink," he said and offered it to her.

"Thank you." She took a sip, closing her eyes as the alcohol slid down her throat, burning in the most delicious way. A hint of sweet and sour clung to her lips when she licked them. "Yum."

"Mm-hmm," he hummed, but he didn't seem to be paying attention. His eyes had glazed over and were unfocused.

"Do you live around here?"

James blinked and nodded. "Not far. You?"

"Close enough. Meg and I have been coming here for a year. The music is great." Time to kick her plan into motion. She took another long swallow to help steady her nerves. "Speaking of, would you like to dance with me?"

"I'm not, um, really—"

"Come on, it'll be fun." To give extra encouragement, she stuck out her bottom lip and pouted. "Please?"

With one eyebrow raised, he studied her for a moment. The anticipation was killing her.

"Pretty please?"

"Sure," he said with a smile.

That was her cue to finish her drink and hold out her hand. "Shall we?"

When they touched, she felt the same tingle of electricity pass between them. She'd been waiting all week to touch him again, and regret filled her when they reached the dance floor and she let go.

The music blurred into a never-ending loop of driving beats and pulsing electronica, moving them closer, but never quite touching until, by accident, Kate bumped into James. When she mouthed, "Sorry," he smiled and shrugged. While they were still touching, Kate started dancing again. That time, James danced with her. Their hands moved independently, but their legs rubbed together. They didn't talk. They just danced.

At the end of the night, they made plans to meet the following Saturday. Before leaving, she stood on her tiptoes and kissed his cheek, warming her entire body. She wondered if he could feel it, too. "See you next week." Kate was already looking forward to it.

THE NEXT NIGHT, JAMES stood next to his brother, washing dishes just like they always did after Sunday dinner. "Kate is so beautiful."

"You mentioned," David said, taking the clean pot out of his brother's hands and drying it. "You're sure she's coming back?"

"We planned on meeting." James stared out the window and smiled. Kate wanted to see him. Maybe they would get to dance again. Or better yet, maybe she would kiss him again. Her soft lips were enough to turn him into a pile of goo.

"What's the plan after that? Are you hooking up, or what?"

James shrugged. "I don't know. You're the one who told me to go out. I'm in uncharted territory." Going to a club to pick up women wasn't exactly his style.

David checked over his shoulder, probably making sure his wife was out of earshot. "Let me educate you. You meet someone, you buy them a drink, you ask them if they want to have sex, you have sex. End of story."

"It's not that easy."

"Yes, it is. How do you think I met Heather?" David nodded toward the front room.

"I'm not as charming as you are." Since they were kids, his brother had always known how to talk to girls. Confidence had always been easy for David.

"That's for damn sure, but you'll manage."

James turned the water off, faced his brother, and handed him the last pan. "You're a dick."

"Also true. Take it from me. She's interested in you. I don't know why, but she is."

"Hey," James protested.

"What you need to do is go to the store and buy yourself a box of condoms. Just in case. Then, next Sunday when you come over for dinner, you can tell me I was right and you were wrong. That I'm a genius and you're a dummy."

FINALLY, SATURDAY ARRIVED. Too impatient to wait, James arrived at Addiction early and sat at the bar. While he waited, he sipped gin and tonic and shredded one napkin after another. By eleven, he had calmed his nerves enough to relax. And then Kate showed up wearing an impossibly small tank top that hugged her breasts and exposed her lean stomach. Paired with skin-tight jeans, it was enough to turn his brain to mush.

"Hi."

James smiled but words wouldn't form.

Kate frowned. "Are you okay?"

"I'm happy to see you," he said eventually.

"Same here. How was your week?"

"Okay." What was there to tell about writing lessons, reviewing tenure requirements, and going over his class rosters for the hundredth time? "How about yours?"

"Long. I worked seventy hours again. I'm ready for a break."

"Wow. Do you need a drink?"

She shook her head and smiled. "Will you dance with me?"

"I'd love to." That time, he didn't hesitate to join her. When he took her hand, heat burned through his fingers and up his arm. The reacquaintance period passed quickly, giving rise to a familiar rhythm, the one they established last time. But it wasn't enough. "Is Meg here?" Talking was the perfect excuse to get closer. In order for her to hear over the music, he had to nearly touch his mouth to her ear. He was close enough to kiss her.

Kate nodded and pointed to an area across the room and then waved at her friend. Standing on her tip-toes she leaned up and said, "I'm glad you came." She wrapped her arms around his neck.

"I've been thinking about you." Only a few inches separated their bodies, and slowly but surely, he placed his hands on her hips and closed the gap.

"Me too." Her warm breath caressed the side of his face and then she kissed him. Not on his cheek that time. On his lips. Soft and sweet.

When he opened his mouth, she moaned and thrust her tongue inside. He tightened his grasp on her body and shuddered when she rubbed against his straining dick.

"Fuck," he whispered as he caressed her exposed back.

Kate looked into his face, breathing heavily. Her cheeks were flushed and her lips were swollen.

He wanted her more than anything in the world. "Do you want to go somewhere a little more private?"

She took a deep breath and nodded. "Yes. I'm going to tell Meg I'm leaving with you." Instead of walking away, she laced her fingers through his and dragged him across the room.

Unable to hear the conversation between Kate and Meg, he stood there, waiting. It was obvious they looked out for each other and for the second time, Meg must've given her approval because she was smiling when they left.

Once they were outside, James led the way to his car and unlocked the passenger door. When he turned around, Kate kissed him again. He gripped her ass and pulled her firmly against his body. They both moaned.

"This isn't much better." Kate panted as she looked around the crowded parking lot.

"Right. Sorry. Let's get out of here." James ushered her into the car and then slid into the seat next to her. "My apartment isn't too far."

In the twenty minutes it took him to get home, a dull ache had settled inside him. Want had turned into need. When he pulled into his parking spot, he turned the car off and looked at her. "Would you like to come up?"

"Yes, please," she said and got out.

They held hands as they walked up the stairs and kissed as they rounded the second flight. When he pulled away to breathe he pointed to his door. "We should go inside."

"Yes, we should."

A ball of excitement and nerves made his hands shake as he unlocked the door. "Here we are," he said as he stepped inside and flicked the lights on.

Kate closed the door behind her. "Here we are."

"YOU WERE RIGHT. YOU'RE a genius." James couldn't stop smiling. Waiting to tell David until after dinner nearly killed him, but he didn't want to talk about Kate in front of Heather.

"And?" David said.

"I was wrong and I'm a dummy."

"I'm glad you could finally admit it. What happened last night? Did she show up?"

James nodded. "We danced, we kissed, we went back to my place."

"Your apartment is a dump." David rolled up the towel he had been using and whipped James with it.

"No, it's not," James gripped the sprayer and gave his brother a quick squirt of water. "You helped me move in last month."

"Yes, it is. What kind of self-respecting professor lives across the street from the dorms? Those apartments are practically student housing. Besides, you don't even have a couch."

"We didn't need a couch. I have a bed." Tingles spread across his body at the thought of just how much they had used his bed.

David smiled. "It's about damn time. Are you going to see her again?"

"Yes. I got her number."

"Give it a few days before you call." David laughed. "Be cool, man."

"Be cool about what?" Heather asked from the doorway, their son Miles on her hip.

David wiggled his eyebrows up and down. "James and Kate hooked up. He likes her. A lot."

Heather ran across the kitchen and hugged James, making Miles giggle as she jostled him. "That's great. When do we get to meet her?"

"What the hell's wrong with you? He just met her." David shook his head.

"You told her about Kate?" The whole reason he'd been so careful about when he talked to his brother was to avoid conversations with Heather. She was forever trying to set him up on blind dates.

"Of course, he told me." Heather shrugged. "There's no harm in pursuing a person if you like them. Call her, James. Don't wait. Call her and tell her you want to see her again."

"Thanks, Heather. I will." He liked her advice more than his brother's, so he stuck his tongue out at him.

"How old is she anyway?" David asked.

James shrugged. "I don't know, early twenties."

David snorted. "Can't find anyone your own age? Gotta prey on the young?"

"She's not that much younger than me. Unless you forgot, I just turned twenty-eight. You make me sound like a perv." James scowled at his brother.

"If the shoe fits."

"Boys, play nice," Heather called over her shoulder as she left to put Miles to bed.

"Seriously though, I'm glad you met someone. It's about time you got over Tina."

James exhaled. "Tina was something." It was only in the last year James could say her name out loud without seething.

"Yeah, something bad. You didn't deserve what she did to you. You know that, right?" David frowned. "They're not all like her. I think taking Kate home was just what you needed."

"I want to see her again."

"I know, but you have to be cool. If she knows how pathetic you are, you'll never get the chance to bang her again."

James scoffed. "You're the worst. Remind me to stop talking to you about relationships."

The truth was James was envious of his brother's life. Not the part where David took over the family business running a construction company. James had that opportunity too, and the day he passed it up for graduate school was the day his father stopped being civil to him. James worked for Baker Construction plenty of summers as a teenager and had no desire to deal with lumberyards or contractors for the rest of his life. For as long as he could remember he wanted to be a professor, and he sacrificed a lot to make it happen. While James spent the last six years working on his Ph.D., his little brother got married, learned how to run a business, and had a kid. It seemed like no matter how hard James worked, he never got to the point where he got the whole package, and every time he saw his brother with his family, he knew wanted it too.

EARLY MONDAY MORNING James rode his bike to Hatch Hall, which housed the offices of the college of science faculty at Bowman State University. After tucking his bike against the wall in his office, he changed into a fresh shirt and visited the bathroom to fix his helmet hair. His first day was about to begin.

The department chair, Lloyd Moore, had been kind when he created James's schedule, allowing him time to adjust to the demands of his new teaching position. Introductory chemistry and biochemistry were his two main classes, and Lloyd padded the rest of his teaching credits with independent student research and thesis advising, both of which only had one student each.

Despite his relatively light load, his stomach churned as he faced a hundred students in his intro class. Student teaching hadn't prepared him for this, these were *his* students. The lecture hall sloped up and away from the projection board behind him, and even though he practiced last week, he couldn't get his laptop to sync with the equipment, so he ended up reading off of his computer screen. By the end of the hour, he had lost the attention of the students in the back rows, who were talking almost as loudly as he was.

As he ate his lunch alone in his office, he flipped through the Tenure Requirements package again. A knock on his office door pulled him away from the papers.

Lloyd walked in. "Doing a bit of light reading?"

James smiled around a mouthful of sandwich.

"Once you get settled, we'll get you on the right track for tenure." Lloyd frowned as he glanced around James's disheveled office.

James swallowed hard as a piece of sandwich got stuck in his throat. His desk was covered with books and lab manuals. Even though the semester had started, he was still putting his classes together. "How am I supposed to think about next semester?"

"It would serve you well to start thinking about how to stay on track. Excellence in teaching is only part of the requirements. I know from your teaching assistant position at UC Santa Barbara, you are no stranger to lab work, and I would like to make sure you have every opportunity to work on something meaningful here. Undergraduate research is a wonderful way to get your name on publications."

James nodded. "I was going to ask about lab space."

"You'll have to write grants for supplies and instruments if we don't have them already, but space is not an issue. We have a research lab in the basement where Alice and Sam are currently working on projects with students." Lloyd smiled and the wrinkles around his eyes deepened. "Sam is attending an undergraduate symposium in the spring, where he and two students are going to present their research."

James sighed. The information wasn't new to him. It was just another thing that made his head pound. Managing teaching and grading was enough to keep him busy every waking moment. Adding research and student symposiums to the mix would surely kill him.

"And of course," Lloyd went on, "we'll be sure to get you on the right committees. Being a tenured professor for Bowman State requires a certain amount of commitment. We need to know you'll be around for the long haul before we invest in your future." He nodded and his silver hair didn't move an inch. "It's all about give and take and making sure we're a good fit for you."

So far, the folder designed to hold his tenure package held his curriculum vitae and the Tenure Requirements document. Before he turned forty, this folder should be filled with syllabi, teaching evaluation data, awards he'd won, research publications, conference presentations, grants he'd been awarded, student research projects he'd supervised, committees he'd served on, letters from students and colleagues pointing out how great he was, and above all else, the statement, which would make his case for tenure. That was going to be the hardest part of all. When he wrote it, he planned to use excerpts from others to make his case. Now he just needed to start building relationships within the college so someone would say good things about him.

He skimmed through the pages in the packet without seeing them. How was he going to do any of those things, especially after the disaster with the projector this morning? If he couldn't manage to connect an HDMI cable properly, how was he supposed to attend conferences and give presentations on research?

"I won't disappoint you, Lloyd." James shook Lloyd's hand and hoped he was right.

WITH HER HEAD STILL in the clouds, Kate doodled in the margin of her notebook. The majors' room was filled with students, but she'd still managed to grab a table in the corner. When her friend Tim came in, they hugged briefly.

"Are those hearts?" He asked as he sat across from her.

"What? No." Kate scribbled across the picture. She'd been thinking of James. Again. Maybe she *had* been drawing hearts. If Meg saw, she'd never let her live it down.

"How was your summer?"

"The best. I met someone."

"And?"

Kate lowered her voice and leaned across the table. "We had the most amazing sex. Normally, it's so awkward the first time. Not with him. He was so—"

"Hot?" Tim said.

"For sure." The thought of his hands and mouth on her body was enough to turn up her internal thermostat. "Meg told me to wait to call him. She took my phone and wouldn't let me call him yesterday."

"Definitely wait. Make him come to you. You don't want to seem desperate, do you?"

"I am desperate. I can't stop thinking about him. I'm going to call him after school today."

Tim rolled his eyes. "Fine. Do what you want, but don't come crying to me when he doesn't answer."

DESPITE HIS LESS THAN smooth start that morning, James was looking forward to his biochemistry class. It only had fourteen students, most of which were majors. Better yet, he didn't need to use his computer so he wouldn't have to deal with connectivity issues. Perhaps he would find someone to start a research project with so he would be "on the right track" for tenure. Lloyd would be thrilled.

The classroom itself was much smaller, which did wonders for his nerves. "Welcome to Biochemistry 3630, my name is Dr. Baker." Calling himself doctor gave him a thrill he didn't think would wear off any time soon. He wrote his name and the class number on the whiteboard and turned toward the small group.

His face froze as his gaze fell on the dark-haired woman in the front row. Everything that happened Saturday came back in a rush. Longing got mixed with shame and ruined everything. No wonder Kate's face had looked vaguely familiar: she was his student. *Fuck my life.*

Chapter Two

Kate sat in the front row next to Tim and looked up at the sound of Dr. Baker's voice. "Holy shit."

Tim frowned. "What is it?"

Kate took quick shallow breaths. James seemed frozen too. How much time had passed? Could everyone in the classroom hear her pounding heart?

"Take a deep breath, Katie," Tim whispered out of the corner of his mouth.

Her cheeks burned and she broke her eyes away first, looking at the notebook on the desk in front of her. She wrote his name. James. She shook her head and added Dr. to the front and Baker to the end.

James finally started talking, turning his back to the class to write his contact information on the whiteboard.

"Are you okay?" Tim glanced at her paper. "Wait. How do you know his first name?"

"Shh, I'll tell you after." Kate's cheeks flushed again, prickling where his beard had rubbed her skin raw two days ago.

When he turned to face the class, Kate looked at his lips. She shivered and could almost taste his tongue in her mouth. This was going to be the hardest class she had ever taken.

At the end of the hour, as James packed his supplies, he looked at his roster and then to her. "Miss Rhodes, would you mind following me to my office? We need to discuss your enrollment."

Kate nodded quickly, hoping no one but Tim was close enough to see her jump when he said her name.

"See you later?" Tim asked, looking expectantly at her.

"Mm-hmm. Later, Tim." Kate couldn't look at James. She knew if she did, she would want to kiss him. And that would be bad. Wouldn't it?

The class dispersed and Kate followed James down the long hallway to his office. Once they were inside, he closed the door. A tall bike with skinny tires was wedged against the far wall, and a helmet and reflective shirt hung from the handlebars.

"What the hell? You're my student?"

His words stabbed through her. After fantasizing about him all day Sunday, it certainly wasn't the reunion she had hoped for. His anger made her defensive. "As if I knew who you were."

James covered his face with his hands. "If anyone found out." He shook his head. "I didn't know."

"Neither of us knew. It'll be all right."

His hands fell away from his face. "Oh. Will it?" he snapped. "What am I supposed to do?"

Kate's shoulders fell. "You're it. You're the only prof who teaches biochemistry. I'm a chemistry major and I need biochem to graduate." And she had to graduate to get the job Dr. Moore had lined up for her. It was all part of the plan. The plan that James could ruin in an instant.

"I have to spend fifteen weeks talking to you?" He squeezed his eyes shut and clenched his jaw.

Kate gripped the shoulder strap of her backpack, making her knuckles turn white. "Sorry to inconvenience you," she said, turning on her heel, jerking the door open, and storming out. He didn't stop her.

Tears welled in her eyes, and she ran as fast as she could out of the building so she wouldn't cry in front of her friends. She normally took the shuttle to the dorms, but not today. It was another perfect day, sunny and warm with bright white clouds filling the sky overhead. But she couldn't enjoy it. Not with a hole in her heart. He had used her and blamed her for everything. As she made the mile walk back to the dorms, she slowed and thought about everything that had happened.

Instead of going to her room, she went to see Meg, who was at her desk when Kate went in, dropped her backpack on the floor, and flopped face down on Meg's bed.

"Kate, what's wrong?" Meg sat down next to her.

"It's him," she said between sobs. "James is my biochem professor."

"Wait, wait, wait. James from Addiction?"

"That's the one. And he doesn't want anything to do with me."

"You mean he *can't* have anything to do with you. Do you know what happens to professors who have sex with their students? And what about you? Do you really want to be known as the student who slept her way to graduation?"

Kate sat up and faced her, wiping her cheeks. "That's not going to happen because I'm done with him." If he could move on, so could she. It was only one semester.

Meg sighed. "I'm sorry it didn't work out. Maybe you can give him a call after graduation."

Kate shook her head and tears welled in her eyes again. "I'm done." There was no way she was going to let herself get hurt again. The worst part was she honestly thought he liked her, but now it was obvious he had used her for sex and didn't want anything to do with her.

Later that night, while she was alone in her room, her phone vibrated. The screen lit up with James's name. Why? So he could tell her off again? He didn't leave a message.

When she went to work Tuesday, she hid in the back room. Normally, her part-time job as the chemistry department office assistant was a nice break in her day, but now, she was on the edge of her seat. What if she ran into James? What would she say to the office manager, Carrie?

Kate had started working with Carrie last year, and the job was perfect. It was flexible and stress-free, and unlike her seasonal jobs waitressing, bussing tables, and cleaning, she got to sit a lot. Plus, Carrie was a kind, motherly woman, which was comforting since her own mother was more than eight hundred miles away.

"You okay back here Kate?" Carrie called.

Kate tried to relax. "Yep, I'm just cleaning up this mess." The counter in the back office was covered with papers. "I meant to tell you, I can work on Tuesdays and Thursdays for a few hours at a time, or for an hour here and there the rest of the week if you need me."

Carrie smiled warmly. "I always need you. Just show up whenever you can and I'll put you to work. You know these professors, they can always use help getting their act together."

Kate smiled and went back to work. At the end of the day, she practically tiptoed out of the office. It was ridiculous but better than the alternative. At the same time that night, James called her. For the second night, she didn't answer, and he didn't leave a message.

Wednesday morning came with an excessive amount of dread. She had to see him three times a week. An hour might be manageable, but Friday was going to kill her. Biochem lab lasted for three hours, starting right after class ended. Four hours was a long time to have to spend with someone who didn't want you around.

Arriving early on Wednesday, she begged Angelica to switch seats so she was shielded in the second row.

Angelica didn't mind getting a little closer to the front of the class. "I could stare at Dr. B all day."

Bile rose in the back of Kate's throat.

When Tim came in, he sat in the second row with her. "Where'd you go? I waited in the majors' room, but you never came back."

"Long story. Coffee?"

Tim nodded.

James came in right on time, and after briefly glancing around the classroom, he began lecturing. Kate could feel his eyes on her whenever her head was down, but every time she looked up, he quickly focused his gaze somewhere else.

Kate took Tim's arm, leaving immediately for the coffee shop before James could say anything to stop her.

"No way." Tim squealed. "You and Dr. Baker?"

Kate nodded and frowned at the attention he was drawing. "He wasn't Dr. Baker when I met him. He was just James. You can't tell anyone. I'm serious, Tim." She leveled him with her gaze. "I'm sick about it. It really felt like we had a connection. I don't understand."

"You're a student. He's a professor. What is there to understand? It's bad news."

"Yeah, but he didn't have to be such a jerk. And why is he calling me?"

"I couldn't tell you. And it's true. He didn't have to be a jerk. Men are dogs. Believe me."

"Things aren't working out with Mark again?"

Tim shook his head. "He's hot and cold. One day we're fine, the next, not so much. When it's good, it's awesome. But when it's bad, it's awful."

Kate's stomach churned all morning Friday. Lecture and lab. Four hours of listening to James talk and being close enough to touch him without getting to. Four hours of watching his mouth move and not being able to kiss him. Four hours of trying to figure out why he had called her when he obviously didn't want anything to do with her.

The lab required students to pair up, so Kate and Tim claimed a bench near the back of the room. They were assigned lockers to keep the glassware they were renting, and everyone was required to keep a lab notebook.

Almost everyone had their own lab coat, but hers was the only one tie-dyed hot pink. Usually, she loved it, but for the first time in her career as a student, she wished her professor wouldn't notice her. Reluctantly, she pulled it on, snapping up the front and sliding her safety glasses over her eyes.

As the students worked, James made his rounds, checking on their progress. When he approached their bench, Tim saw him coming and stepped between them, putting his hands on his hips.

"I'm checking to see how your solution is coming." James peered around Tim, looking from Kate to the flask on the hotplate in front of her. "Looks perfect." He flashed a quick smile, revealing his perfectly straight teeth and pretty lips. "By the way, I love your lab coat, Miss Rhodes."

Kate frowned. "Thanks," she mumbled, remembering too late she shouldn't be staring at his mouth like that.

Tim took a step back, blocking Kate with most of his body, forming a barrier between her and James.

James's gaze followed Tim's movements. Something flashed across his face. Anger? Jealousy? At that moment, a beaker shattered in the corner of the room, breaking the odd tension between the three of them. James turned and walked away.

Two hours later, in the hall outside the lab, Kate sagged against the wall and sighed. She made it through her first week of classes.

KATE SPENT THE WEEKEND hanging out with Meg, who did a good job keeping her distracted. Thankfully, James had stopped calling.

The second week of class came and went. She kept her head down and avoided him like the plague. When she went to work, she stayed out of sight. James looked at her warily during lab, seemingly content to keep a distance as well.

The next week was filled with a flurry of excitement over the upcoming exam. The test was scheduled for the following Monday, and it was all anyone could talk about.

Friday after class, Angelica turned around in her seat to face Kate and Tim. "I'm hosting a study group Saturday afternoon around four. Just like last semester, bring something to share."

The lab that day was an enzyme assay. While Tim retrieved chemicals from the inventory shelves, Kate set up their glassware, pulling it from her locker. The laboratory was noisy and everyone bustled to get everything done in time.

When she turned, she squeaked and clutched her chest. James stood in front of her.

"Do you have everything you need?" His jaw was set in a firm line as he looked at her and then to Tim.

As she struggled to understand the meaning behind his hard stare, Tim came back with a tray full of brown glass bottles. "Come on, Katie, help me weigh these."

Without looking back, she walked away from James and set her sights on finishing her lab on time. Spending a minute more trying to understand him would have made her head explode.

KATE SPENT SATURDAY morning baking in the communal kitchen in her dorm. She danced around the large space, adding one ingredient after another to the raspberry cupcake batter. Once they had cooled, she frosted each with vanilla buttercream and topped them with a fresh raspberry. With a tray full of cupcakes in the back seat of her car, she picked up Tim and headed to Angelica's house.

The whole class was there, milling around and chatting quietly. Ever the gracious hostess, Angelica gathered everyone and opened her notes. Study group had begun.

About an hour in, Angelica was pulled away to answer the front door. The room filled with excited chatter when she returned with none other than Dr. James Baker.

Chapter Three

When Angelica came to James and asked if he would help at her study group Saturday afternoon, he said yes, and then began to notice the way she touched his arm and played with her hair while she talked to him. James's head spun. Did Angelica know about Kate and think he was the kind of professor who had sex with his students? It was too late to change his mind because he'd already said yes.

Joining the study group would be the perfect distraction. Angelica told him it started at four but warned him it always took a while before they got started. She also let him know it was a potluck, so he stopped for a few cases of soda on the way.

Angelica greeted him at the door and played with her hair again. Setting clear boundaries was his first priority, so when she offered to give him a tour of her house, he declined and made a point to be as short and gruff with her as possible.

Following her into the living room, he stifled a gasp when his gaze fell on Kate. Of course, she was there.

"Where should I put these?" James raised the cases of soda using it as an excuse to leave the room. He needed time to think.

Angelica turned to face him. "In the kitchen, it's on the right. I'll show you."

"No, I'll find it." James backed away and turned to the right, but Angelica must've meant her right because he found himself in a long hallway. Retracing his steps, he pushed open a swinging door to the kitchen.

Kate stood in front of the sink, drinking a glass of water. The sleek muscles of her neck moved as she swallowed. He wanted to trail kisses along her taut skin. The door slipped from his hand and swooshed shut behind him. Kate's eyes met his. If looks could kill, he'd be dead.

She opened her mouth and her venomous whisper paralyzed him. "What the hell are you doing here? This is a study group. For students." Her gaze focused on the swinging door. Was she waiting for someone? Of course, she was. She was waiting for Tim. The lucky bastard.

The sharp edge of the cardboard handles cut into his fingers. "I didn't know you'd be here. Angelica asked me to come. She said it would be helpful if the group ran into any problems." Why was he apologizing?

Her murderous glare returned. "I see you've moved on to the next student. I suppose you're married too." She clutched her glass with both hands.

How could she say something like that when it was obvious she and Tim were together? "Oh, you're one to talk."

"Dr. B, there you are," Angelica said sweetly. She looked at James, and then at Kate, and gripped James's arm possessively. "Sorry, I should've insisted on showing you where you should put the drinks. You're so nice to bring anything at all."

James shrugged and tried to pull out of her grasp, and only succeeded when the rest of the students came in to eat. As he backed away from the swarm around the table, he scanned the room. Where had Kate gone?

As he waited to fill his plate, James nibbled on a raspberry cupcake, which he managed to snag before the hoard of hungry students descended on the kitchen. His mouth watered. It was soft and delicious and melted against his tongue. He glanced at the tray and decided he would come back for another one after the line died down.

When he joined the study group, Tim and Kate sat together, whispering, and eating off the same plate. To make things worse, Tim put his hand on her knee and squeezed it.

James forced down the last bite of cupcake and turned to the group. "Thank you for the food. This raspberry cupcake is the best thing I've ever tasted."

"I know, right? Kate can seriously cook. Not that the rest of the food isn't delicious," Tim added quickly. "Angelica, this seven-layer dip is awesome."

Strike that. The cupcake was the second-best thing he'd tasted. Kate still held first place. He looked at her while he licked his fingers. Did she just shudder?

"Thanks for bringing soda, Dr. B." Angelica sat in the chair next to him and batted her eyelashes.

"So, how does this study group work?" he asked, hoping to redirect Angelica. A textbook sat open on the coffee table in front of him, so he picked it up and scanned the page.

Around the edge of the book, he could block out Tim and look at Kate. Why hadn't he taken things slower with her? If he had known he would only have one night with her, he would've worshiped every inch of her body.

James squeezed his eyes shut. He couldn't spend the next twelve weeks pining for a taken woman.

The pieces started to fall into place during the second week. Tim's hand on her shoulder, the protective stance he took when James tried to talk to her, and the way he walked everywhere with her. It was all the proof he needed Tim and Kate were together. He was familiar with this feeling of betrayal, but this time, she hadn't cheated on him, she had cheated with him.

And when Kate got up to leave and Tim followed, James's heart sank.

He went back to Addiction that night. Needing a distraction more than ever. He had been there every Saturday in the hopes of finding someone who would spark something inside him again, but no one did.

During Sunday dinner, David was a complete ass.

"It's not funny, David."

"No, not funny. Ironic. Leave it to my hermit brother to finally go out and find the *only* woman he can't have." David laughed.

"What am I supposed to do?"

"What do you want to do?"

"I want her. She's all I can think about."

"Well then, I guess you're fucked."

Heather put her fingers on her husband's lips. "James, don't give up on her. Have you actually asked her if she's dating Tim?"

"You told her?" James scowled at his brother.

Heather shook her head. "No, I asked him. You didn't come over last Sunday, so I knew something was up. Well? Have you asked her?"

"No," James admitted sadly. "She won't answer my phone calls, and now? You should see the way they are together. He calls her Katie and always seems to have his hand on her knee. It makes me sick." He shook his head. "I wonder if he knows."

"Knows what?" David peeled his mouth away from Heather's hand.

"That she cheated on him, with me."

"Bro, he's not your friend, you don't owe him anything. If she really was with him when you hooked up, she's not the kind of woman you should be wasting your time on." David dusted his hands together to emphasize his point.

"I know." James rested his forehead on the dining room table. Kate didn't seem like that kind of person, but his perception and reality were obviously miles apart.

JAMES'S BIOCHEMISTRY students were restless Monday afternoon, and when he passed out the exams, they all voiced the same question. "Where do we write our names?"

"No names. Student ID numbers." He beamed while they frowned. "They're on your ID cards. I like to keep an open mind while I grade."

The truth was, he was painfully aware of his bias toward Kate, so if he could grade his exams using ID numbers, it would be better for everyone.

Thirty minutes in, students started turning in exams. Most dropped them unceremoniously on his desk, but one person didn't. Kate. When he looked up at her she licked her lips and his heart skipped a beat. She had done that the night they were together. Flashes of memories came back. Soft skin, swollen lips, moans of pleasure. When he held his hand out to take her exam, she touched his fingers.

He was grateful for the position of his desk because it shielded his body, which cheerfully betrayed him. His eyes flicked to where Tim sat, to see if he was watching. He wasn't. Was she flirting with him? If she was, Tim was oblivious to it.

James cleared his throat. "Thank you, Miss Rhodes." He still couldn't bring himself to call her by her first name for fear his voice would betray his feelings. After putting her exam face-down on top of the others, he watched her walk away and adjusted his uncomfortably tight pants.

Grading took him two days. A few exams stood out from the rest, but because of his anonymous grading system, he had no idea who they belonged to. When the idea came to him, he updated his database for the class so that everything was filed by number, removing all traces of names and pictures. Until he submitted grades at the end of the semester, he wouldn't know anyone's scores.

Instead of handing the tests back, he left them stacked on his desk with only the number visible. "Feel free to collect your exams," he said before turning his back on the students and writing on the whiteboard. "If you want to discuss any particular questions in further detail, please see me after class." When he turned back around a few minutes later, the mood in the classroom was a mixture of excitement and disappointment, except for Kate, who seemed prepared for her score.

LIKE A FOOL, JAMES went to Addiction Saturday night. He sat at the bar in his spot and flagged down the bartender.

"Your usual?" the bartender asked pulling a glass out from under the counter.

James scoffed. He was nothing if not predictable.

The bartender opened a bottle of gin. "She's already here."

"Who?" His heart pounded against his chest.

The bartender's eyes glazed over as he turned toward the dance floor. "I think you're too late though, she and her friend came with a guy." He let out a low whistle. "I'd love to be in his shoes tonight. Lucky son of a bitch. Just imagine, mm."

James followed his line of sight, and there, on a platform on display for the whole world to see, was Kate, wearing a breathtaking dress that hugged her sensuous body like it was made for her. Tim was behind her, with his arms wrapped around her. Her friend was behind him, whipping her head back and forth to the beat of the music, dragging her long hair over his shoulders. James didn't want to imagine them together, but his mind went ahead without his permission. He could see their bodies sprawled on a large bed, limbs entwined, mouths open, tongues moving, Tim taking turns fucking them both.

His stomach lurched.

"Do you want me to make your gin and tonic?"

James shook his head while he balled his hands into fists. He needed to leave before she saw him.

Too late.

Their eyes locked and he bolted for the door. He fumbled with his keys, unlocked the car, and then slammed the door shut as Kate came out to the parking lot. Why had she followed him outside? His tires screeched against the asphalt as he pulled away.

On the way home, he stopped and bought a bottle of gin. Feeling numb was better than the alternative. At first, he drank in the kitchen, but eventually, he ended up in his bedroom. Because the bed still smelled like her, he'd been unable to wash his sheets. He buried his face in the soft material, surrounding himself with her lingering scent, and passed out.

When he woke the next morning, he struggled to open his eyes. His head spun and he was sure someone was squeezing the sides of his face with a vise. A vile film covered his teeth and as his tongue involuntarily moved back and forth, his stomach churned. He made it to the bathroom just in time, where he threw up until every muscle ached.

It took him the better part of the afternoon to recover. By the time he should have been having dinner with his brother, he was up to his neck grading exams for his intro class. There was no way he was going to get them back to his students on Wednesday like he promised. He called David and explained he needed to work, leaving out the half bottle of gin. The last thing he needed was his baby brother's pity. He had plenty of that for himself.

Chapter Four

"Wait," Kate shouted as she pushed open the heavy club doors leading to the parking lot. "James?" Their eyes met just before he took off. She leaned against the side of the building and stared at the ground. Maybe she should've avoided Addiction, just like she had been, but what right did James have to claim her favorite dance club? Her cheeks burned. Their night of celebration had turned into disaster.

The door opened and Meg poked her head outside. "You okay?"

Kate shook her head. "I don't know what to think. He was so mad. Why is he mad? I'm allowed to have a good time with my friends. Aren't I?"

Meg shrugged and sidled up next to her. "I don't know what to tell you."

"Why does it have to be so complicated? He either wants me, or he doesn't."

"Have you asked him?"

Kate's eyes filled with tears. "I don't need to." She laughed bitterly as tears streaked her cheeks. "I'm so stupid. I think about him all the time. But he acts like I'm diseased. That's why I never asked him."

"Oh, Kate. You're not stupid. You like him, you put yourself out there, and he stomped all over your heart. You don't deserve that. It's his loss, not yours."

"Thanks, Meg." Kate sniffed and wiped her face with the back of her hand. "Sorry to ruin our night out."

"You didn't ruin anything. I was getting tired anyway. I'll go get Tim." Meg slipped inside and came out a minute later with Tim.

"Honey, you okay?" Tim tilted his head and held her face between his hands so she would look at him.

"I'll be okay. You don't mind leaving?"

Tim and Meg shook their heads. "Nope, it's fine."

IN CLASS MONDAY, KATE couldn't take her eyes off James. But he refused to look at her, no matter how hard she tried to get his attention. Despite how much she wanted to talk to him, he clearly didn't want anything to do with her. No surprise there.

On Tuesday, Kate found Carrie frantically digging through a pile of papers threatening to fall off her desk. Carrie sighed. "I'm so glad to see you. I need help."

"I can see that. Where do you want me to start?" Kate dropped her backpack into the chair by the door.

"Well, I promised I'd help on two projects before I realized they'd both need me at the same time on the same day."

"Just tell me what you want me to do."

Carrie smiled at Kate. "Dr. Moore needs me to help him in his office with some paperwork for faculty senate," she paused and looked into the department chair's office, "so would you mind getting these tests sorted for intro chemistry?"

"I'm on it."

"You're a lifesaver, Kate. Oh, and if you have any questions, just ask Dr. Baker. They're for his class. He's in his office, although you'd never know it, he always has the door closed."

Kate swallowed hard. Shit. "Um, okay. Thanks, Carrie."

Carrie grabbed the other pile of papers and scurried into Dr. Moore's office.

Kate sorted through the tests on her desk and finally figured out the reason why Carrie had been so frustrated. Some of the forms were missing. The test had two parts: a written part, and a multiple-choice part, which was recorded on a form. It took Kate a while to go through the stack, matching the names on the forms to the names on the written pages. Finally, she had a stack of about twenty students missing their multiple-choice forms.

Kate took a deep breath and walked down the long hall with the tests clutched tightly against her body. She raised her hand to knock and noticed it was shaking. After taking a deep breath, she squared her shoulders and knocked three times.

The door jerked open. James looked as if he had been ready to ask a question, and just as promptly forgotten what it was. A frown creased his forehead and because he didn't seem like he was going to say anything, she did.

"You're missing multiple-choice forms," she blurted.

James shook his head. "What?"

"I work in the office with Carrie," Kate started.

"Of course, you do," James interrupted.

Kate ignored him. "Anyway, she asked me to help organize your exams so you could hand them back, and these are missing their forms."

"I gave them all to Carrie after I ran them through the machine." James crossed his arms over his chest.

"Why did you use the grading machine? Carrie always does that. I've helped her dozens of times."

"I didn't know, okay? I just thought I was supposed to do it. I fought that damn machine for an hour." James rubbed his temples and then took a deep breath. "I'll ask her to do it next time."

"That machine is awful. The tests get jammed if you load more than ten papers at a time."

"So that's why it wasn't working. I should've asked for help sooner."

"Well, now you know for next time, right?" Kate offered a tiny smile.

James stared at her and still hadn't produced the missing forms.

Kate cleared her throat. "So, are you sure you don't know where the other forms are?"

"Well, no. I'm not sure." He swept his hand into his office. Every surface was covered with papers, including most of the floor. "You should see my apartment." James closed his mouth and grimaced.

His apartment. She could visualize it perfectly: sparse furniture, spotless kitchen, and comfortable bed. Stop thinking about his bed. "Would you mind if I looked for them?" Before stepping inside, she paused. "Is there anything in here I'm not supposed to see?"

James looked at her like she was crazy.

"I mean anything biochem related?"

"Oh. No, this is all intro chemistry. Why did I assign so much homework?"

Confident it was okay, she pushed past him. "Because you're new? Give it twenty years and you'll barely show up to class." Kate laughed, not because it was funny, but because it happened during her last semester. "Do you mind?" she said as she touched a pile of papers.

"No. I don't mind. I need help. I need a lot of help." James frowned and opened his mouth to speak, but nothing came out.

Kate put the tests on a cabinet by the door and started sorting through piles of paperwork. She crawled around on the floor, shifting papers and opening folders, but still found nothing.

James sat at his desk and didn't seem to be having any luck either.

Once the floor papers had been thoroughly searched, she stood and checked the bookshelves. There was a picture of James and another man. They were probably brothers, featuring the same chocolaty hair, straight teeth, and full lips. He also had a collection of strange succulent plants, illuminated by a bright light clamped onto the shelf. Their leaves were glossy and plump. Kate gasped when she touched them. They were real.

"They have the most amazing photosynthetic pathway." James stood next to her.

Kate jumped slightly because she hadn't seen him move. Suddenly, his office was too crowded and she began to sweat.

"I'll bring them to class when I discuss it next week," he said in a soft voice.

Kate nodded numbly. Standing that close to him wasn't a good idea. If she breathed deeply, she could smell his skin. The skin she longed to touch. Focus on the tests. Forcing herself to step away from him, she searched the end of the shelf closest to the door. There, tucked against a textbook, was a stack of multiple-choice forms. "Oh. There they are." Time to get out before she said something wrong or did something unthinkable like kiss him or rip his shirt off and lick him all over. "I'm going to finish sorting." She backed out of his office and started down the hall.

"Um, Miss Rhodes?" James's voice called out from his open door.

Kate stopped mid-step but didn't go back to his office. "Yes?"

"Would you mind helping me organize this homework when you're done? I was going to ask Carrie."

How could she say no? It was her job, after all. Being away from him for a bit would be enough to get her libido in check. "I wouldn't mind. Give me a few minutes."

Back on Carrie's spacious desk, she finished collating the rest of the tests and left a note for Carrie telling her she would be working in Dr. Baker's office. Working. Nothing more. All she had to do was avoid looking at him, or touching him, or smelling him. Shit. Holding the finished tests carefully in her arms, she walked back down the hall.

"That was fast. Here, let me take those." James jumped up from behind his desk and took them out of her hands. When he put them down, he thumbed through the stack. "They're alphabetized."

"I hope that's okay, it's the way I usually do it for Dr. Moore," she said, kicking herself for not asking first.

"It's great. Can you help me put these assignments with those tests? That way I can hand them all back at once."

"Sure. Why don't you read the last name and hand them to me, and I'll file them?" Kate sat down on the floor and pulled the stack of tests into her lap. "Who's first?"

"Campbell."

"Beth or Andrew?" Kate asked immediately.

James gaped. "You memorized their names?"

"I sorted them ten minutes ago." Kate shrugged.

"There are nearly a hundred students in that pile."

"Beth or Andrew?" She held her hand open.

"Andrew."

Slipping the assignment in place, she said, "Next."

They went through the piles of paper covering his office over the next hour. The stack in her lap got too big to hold, so she split it in half.

When they were done, Kate looked around at the clean floor and desk. "Wow, it's like a new office."

"Thank you for your help."

"Do you want me to get you a box to put those in? It'll be easier to keep together." Kate couldn't stand the thought of leaving him yet. Just a few more minutes and maybe he'd forget about Angelica.

"Where are they?"

"Carrie keeps them in the supply closet. I'll show you."
Kate led James down the long hallway and into the main office

past Carrie's desk, and into the back room. The small supply closet stood open from where she'd gotten file folders earlier. "This is where Carrie keeps supplies. I always put boxes on the bottom, right here." Kate pointed to the tidy tower of boxes all perfectly nested together and lined up and stepped inside to pull them out. James followed her, filling the small room. Inches separated their bodies.

"Wow, I didn't even know about this. I used that space a lot before the semester started." James nodded his head toward the back room.

"So, you're the one who left the mess out here."

James shifted his eyes away sheepishly. "I was going to clean it up, but when I went back to do it, it was already clean."

"Yeah, Carrie and I tackled that the first week."

"So, I guess I need to thank you for that too."

"No need. It's my job."

"I insist. Thank you for helping me."

Kate stared at his lips again. She was in serious trouble.

Chapter Five

James had spent an hour hiding behind his desk while Kate crawled all over his office floor, and now they were standing inches apart. The walls closed in, pushing him toward her as the sweet scent of her skin called to him. She licked her lips. Surely, she wanted him too. Didn't she? Her hair covered her cheeks and he wanted to fix it, but his brain kicked in just in time and moved his hand away from her to a box of paperclips. "I need some of these." He focused his gaze on the supply shelf behind her.

"So, there are the boxes. Which one do you want?"

Kate's words jumbled together in his head.

"Yes. I'd like that."

She cocked her head and frowned.

Uh oh. Wrong answer.

Kate twisted and picked out a box. "Here, this one should work."

With the box in one hand and paperclips in the other, he stared at the shelf. In his attempt to block out thoughts of Kate, he completely zoned out and hadn't realized she had left. Following her to the main office, Carrie and Lloyd were discussing something with Kate, who was talking again but not to him. Lloyd said something.

James blinked. "What?"

Lloyd frowned. "I see you've met Kate."

"Yes, mm-hmm," James murmured.

Carrie started talking to Kate as James's focus blurred again. He couldn't take his eyes off Kate. And then Kate was talking to him and leaving. Why was she leaving, and why wasn't his brain working?

James stood in Carrie's office for a few seconds after Kate left, clutching the box like a mindless fool. "I, um, I'm going to finish up. In my office."

Carrie and Lloyd continued their discussion as he slipped back down the long hallway. Kate had not only left a tidy stack of tests on his desk, she'd also left the scent of her perfume. Leaning against his closed door, he groaned.

He was screwed.

JAMES MANAGED TO GET through the next two weeks without acting on his impulse to get Kate alone. He had finally started thesis research with one of the senior chemistry students, Michael, and the distraction was just what he needed. James worked with Michael in the research lab, and every time he was there, James became more familiar with what he had to work with. At one point, he even began writing down notes for a research project he could write a paper on. Being published in scientific journals was another huge step to getting tenure, which Lloyd was always happy to remind him of.

Michael was really talkative, and over the hours they spent together, James got a whole new perspective of the department, his colleagues, and the other chemistry students. Michael mentioned Kate once, and without trying to be too obvious, James asked whom she was doing her thesis with, only to find out she had already completed hers. James relaxed, but he kept his hands in his pockets to hide their sweatiness. While he was in the research lab, he never had to worry about running into her. Which was a good thing because biochemistry lab was bad enough.

Seeing James's interest in the lab, Lloyd assigned him a bench where he could keep his things, and James was happy to officially move in. The more time he spent at his bench, the more he got to know the two inorganic chemists Lloyd had praised so much: Alice White and Sam Bellevue. James had met all of his colleagues at one point or another, but he hadn't gotten to know any of them. Alice was a quiet woman in her mid-fifties, who was so focused on her work James had to make a point to talk to her so she would know he was there. Sam, on the other hand, was a loud man with a sharp New York accent. His bench was plastered with pictures of his kids.

"You're not married, are you?" Sam asked one day when it was just the two of them in the lab.

James shook his head and grimaced. "Almost. Years ago."

"Doesn't sound like it ended well." Sam laughed and pointed to a picture of a woman smiling and holding an infant. "I've been married sixteen years. Terri and I met when I was in graduate school. She was running the school clinic when I came in with a glass laceration. It was a side-arm flask incident." Sam paused and pointed to the inside of his right thumb. "She stitched me up, and we've been together ever since. She's a nurse at the worker's comp place now. We have two kids. Eleven and eight." Sam pointed to the two boys with matching cheesy grins and their dad's narrow face.

James smiled. "Happy kids." It was the same age gap between James and his brother.

"They get along most of the time. They have a good mom." Sam smiled and adjusted the picture. "Are you seeing anyone?"

James let out a bark of laughter, startling Sam. "No. I tried that. Didn't take."

Sam shrugged. "You're young. Give it time."

How Sam managed to be relaxed and pushy at the same time remained a mystery, and only added to James's list of reasons why they were friends. The hours they spent together in the lab were filled with laughter. He had finally made a friend at the university, and it had only taken him a month.

In biochemistry class, he reminded them their midterm was next Monday, and during lab on Friday, Angelica asked him if he would come to her study group again. Saturday at four o'clock, just like last time. He was going to decline, but everyone was looking at him expectantly. Apparently, her request got the attention of everyone in lab, including Kate. Her eyebrows were raised, forming a hopeful arch across her forehead. That was all he needed.

He nodded. "Count me in."

ON SATURDAY, WHILE he was getting ready, James called his brother. Perhaps he would talk some sense into him.

"What do you think you're doing?" David sighed.

"Helping my students?" Even James didn't believe it.

"Uh-huh. Sure you are. Anyone in particular?"

James groaned. "I don't know what's wrong with me. She's completely unavailable, but I can't stop thinking about her."

"I think what's happening here is you're pathetic and can't separate fantasy from reality. She was a one-night thing. You have to let it go. Plus, she's your student."

"I know. I know," James whispered.

In his fantasy, Kate was his girlfriend and he got to experience all kinds of pleasure with her. In reality, Kate was his student and dating Tim.

Right on time, James joined the study group. Kate and Tim arrived a few minutes later and when Kate picked her spot she chose the one next to James, making his pulse race.

Tim sat next to her and leaned around her to smile at James. "Thanks for coming to help us study again."

Now what was he supposed to think? "No problem." James gave him a cool nod. Two could play at that game.

Turning so Tim was at his back, James leaned in his seat and whispered, "What did you make?"

Kate blushed. "Lemon bars."

"Mm, my favorite," he said and wondered if he was noticeably drooling.

"Good to know." Kate looked away and opened her notes.

Angelica called the study group to order, and only after they had worked for an hour, did she direct them to the kitchen for a dinner break.

While the rest of the students filled their plates with lasagna and chips, James went straight for the desserts, where Kate had just finished cutting a solid golden mass into bars.

"Which piece do you want?"

James grinned. "Middle. I like the gooiness on top."

"Here you go." She pushed a lemon bar onto his plate, coating her thumb with lemon.

James gasped when she sucked her thumb into her mouth and licked it clean.

"Do you want anything else?" Kate swept her hands across the table.

You. James cleared his throat. "I can get it. You don't need to serve me."

"I don't mind," Kate said.

"Can you hand me two of those cookies?" He pointed to the container closest to her. "I should probably leave room for real food, though."

Kate shrugged. "Life's too short. You should always eat dessert first."

"Especially if you make it."

She blushed again.

"Hey Katie, can I have one too?" Tim leaned his chin onto her shoulder, making her jump.

James turned away as they started whispering to each other. Tim burst through his fantasy bubble, ruining the moment they just shared. Once his plate had a variety of food, he went back to his chair in the empty room. Kate came back soon after, by herself.

Saliva coated his tongue as he inhaled the scent of the lemon bar. As he bit into it, the cookie layer crumbled and the lemony goodness coated his teeth. "Oh shit, that's good."

Kate choked on her water. "Thanks."

"Seriously. You could open a bakery."

"That's what Tim is always telling me."

"Well, he's right." He tried to disguise the hurt in his voice by continuing to talk. "Do you only make desserts?"

She shook her head. "It's hard to do in the dorm kitchen, but I love to cook all kinds of things. Dessert is my favorite, though. It's like lab, only edible. And sweet. Sweet chemistry."

James laughed. "Does that mean I'm a horrible chemist? Because I can't cook?"

"I'm sure you can cook. You just don't. All you need is a little know-how. Guidance. I could show you," she added quietly.

"I would really like that." The rest of his words got stuck in his throat.

"Maybe next week? I have this big test on Monday. It's a real drag." Kate rolled her eyes and smiled.

When James laughed, he let out the breath he was holding.

Details. He needed details. When? Where? When? The last thing he wanted was to sound desperate, so he bit his tongue and waited for her to fill him in.

He had to wait five whole days.

Chapter Six

Their midterm was similar to the first exam. They all wrote their ID numbers instead of names. Kate was confident she had done well, and when she got it back on Wednesday, she grinned from ear to ear. Ninety-five percent. Tim shared the same score.

"Wanna go out and celebrate again at Addiction?" Tim asked.

Kate frowned. "That didn't work out so well. Maybe we should do something different this time."

Tim laughed. "We could watch a movie and get pizza."

"Sure. Saturday night?"

"Deal." Tim shook her hand.

Pride infused her steps as she walked up the stairs to the chemistry office to go to work on Thursday. She knew Carrie would be waiting to hear her score.

Carrie smiled. "Did you nail it?"

Kate nodded. "Ninety-five."

"Great job, Kate." Carrie handed her a pile of tests. "Would you mind taking these down to Dr. Baker?"

"Not at all."

That time, when she knocked on the door, her hand was steady. Ever since the afternoon she spent working with him weeks ago, things had gotten better. He had even been civil to

Tim during study group, which was a huge improvement over the puffed-out chests and biting comments.

When James opened the door, the corners of his mouth lifted as a smile spread across his face. "Hello, Miss Rhodes."

"Dr. Baker, here are your exams. I hope they're all here this time." They were still on a last name basis. That was safe.

James held his hands up. "Believe me, I learned my lesson. I'm also not going to make my intro students wait a week to get them back. I'm almost done grading."

"You need help?"

"Definitely." His smile grew.

"Hang on a sec." Ducking out into the hall, she called down to Carrie, "Hey, Carrie, do you mind if I help Dr. Baker for a while?"

"Go ahead, I have plenty I can do on my own," she said.

Kate appeared in James's office door and smiled. "I'm all yours." Open mouth and insert foot. "I mean, um, Carrie doesn't need my help for a while, so I can help you if you need me. If you need help." Heat spread across her cheeks.

The more she tried to explain, the more amused he looked. He seemed to like that he was making her so flustered.

Their conversation was degenerating quickly. "So, what do you need help with?"

Without getting up, he pointed to a large stack of papers on his desk. "This is the pile I've finished grading, so if you wouldn't mind alphabetizing, I would appreciate it."

"Sure thing." Just like last time, she dragged them onto the floor and systematically filed them all into order, adding the rest as he graded them. When the pile was done, she dusted her hands off.

"That would've taken me an hour."

"You're welcome." She chuckled and then stood. "I guess if we're done, I should get back to Carrie."

"Before you go—" James knit his eyebrows together and took a deep breath.

"Yes?" Kate's chest tightened.

"I was wondering," he paused and took another breath, "about you teaching me how to cook."

Kate sighed. It was too much to hope for more. Cooking lessons were miles away from what she really wanted. "How does Saturday afternoon sound? Around four?" She picked the time specifically so she would have a distraction that night with Tim, which was infinitely better than obsessing over every mistake she was sure to make while she was with James.

James smiled. "Great."

"What do you want to make?"

"Lemon bars?"

Kate laughed. "Do you have a mixer?"

"An old olive green handheld one. It belonged to my mom in the seventies."

"That'll work. I'll put together an ingredient list and get it to you tomorrow."

"Thanks for helping me again."

"You're welcome," Kate called over her shoulder and then got back to work in the main office.

Carrie looked at her over the rim of her reading glasses. "How was it?"

"How was what?" Kate cocked her head to the side.

"Working with Dr. Baker. I forgot to ask before."

"Fine." Kate's face flushed. Nothing happened. Absolutely nothing. And yet her heart was trying to jump right out of her chest. "Why do you ask?"

"That was only the second time he'd asked me for help. Honestly, I think he's a bit weird. He keeps to himself in his office all the time and doesn't talk to anyone much, but you two seem to get along."

Words failed her so she nodded.

Carrie narrowed her eyes. "Is he always weird?"

Kate shrugged. "I don't know. We organized his tests and homework. We didn't do much talking."

That was fine with her. Talking only made her want him more.

WHEN LAB ENDED ON FRIDAY, Kate handed James a list on her way out.

"What was that?" Tim nudged her shoulder.

"Just an ingredient list."

Tim smiled at her. "So, he actually wants to cook with you? I thought that was some kind of euphemism."

Kate sighed. "As much as I'd like 'making lemon bars' to mean something else, it is what it is."

She left her dorm a little early on Saturday, closing the door on the heap of clothes she tried on before settling on the outfit she was wearing. Even though it was already mid-October, she dressed in a tank top and board shorts and pulled a hoodie on for the walk home. San Clemente never got really cold, but the nights could get chilly.

Each step required a deep, calming breath. Her mind flooded with memories of the night she went home with him. The moment he stopped and kissed her as they rounded the second flight. His hands shaking as he unlocked the door. The way he moaned when she undressed him. Before she could knock, the door opened.

"You're early." James's cheeks were flushed.

"Sorry. I can wait if you're not ready."

"I was just cleaning up a little. More grading." He stepped aside. "Please come in."

Kate's eyes bulged. "You're not kidding." The living room was covered with papers. "Hey, you got a couch."

"My brother kept bringing it up. Telling me I needed a couch to be an adult."

"It seems like it's coming in handy for all those papers." Her mouth went dry. His bedroom door was open a few feet away: soft sheets, a cozy mattress, juniper and musk, and a nightstand full of condoms. She shivered.

James frowned. "I'm a little unorganized. But hey, the kitchen is clean and I went shopping." Showing her the list, he pointed to each and every ingredient, which spanned the length of the counter.

"I see that. Do you want to get started?"

James nodded and fidgeted.

Kate put her bag down and tugged the hoodie off her head. When she smoothed her hair out of her face, she noticed him staring.

James lunged, gripping the hoodie out of her hands. "Here, let me take that," he said before he darted out of the room.

Kate faced the counter and verified all the ingredients were present.

"Did I buy the right things?" he said, his voice incredibly close.

When she turned to face him, she nearly bumped into him. "Jeez, you scared me." Only a few inches separated her from his lips. His perfect, soft, delicious lips. Stop it. "Ready?" Kate didn't wait for him to respond. "Preheat your oven." When James didn't move, she added, "It's that knob. Three fifty."

It took longer than she expected to explain the process to James because he had no idea what he was doing. Instead of her typical approach to showing someone how to cook, she focused on the science behind baking.

"Okay. Lemon bars have two parts: a shortbread-like cookie on the bottom and lemon custard on top. Let's start with the cookie part."

Stepping back and letting him do it himself, she guided him as he opened packages of butter and attempted to measure sugar and flour.

James pressed his lips together. "Stop laughing at me. I don't laugh at you in lab."

"Yeah, because I'm not a complete dork. There's flour everywhere." Kate stifled another giggle when he glared at her. "You're right. I'm not being very professional. Carry on. Scoop the dough out of the bowl and pat it in place."

James showed her his palms, which were covered in sticky dough. "How am I supposed to get this into that pan?"

"Your hands are too warm, they're melting the butter," she said as she pulled a glob off him and patted it in place. "The trick is to work fast."

"I can't make my hands colder. I'm ruining it."

"You're not ruining anything." Kate held his wrist steady while she scraped the mixture off his skin. His pulse pounded against her fingers and he took quick, shallow breaths and relaxed into her grasp. After getting as much dough as she could, she instructed him to wash his hands. Direct contact made her lose focus and she had to take a deep breath to steady her nerves.

"Now what?" James came back with wet hands.

"Now you dry your hands. With a towel."

"Funny. I meant the pan."

"Now we bake, and while we wait, we make the custard. Here, put this in the oven, and set a timer for twenty minutes."

James followed the directions and then grabbed a tiny white timer off the side of his fridge.

"Did you steal that from school?"

James's eyes darted away. "I wouldn't do that. Stealing is wrong."

Kate chuckled. "Okay, now we're going to beat these eggs until the protein structure opens up, and as we add sugar gradually, the albumen will hold the sucrose in place."

James grinned. "This is my kind of baking."

"See? Just like lab, only delicious."

They assembled the rest of the ingredients just as the timer beeped. She mimed bewilderment. "Why do I feel like I should be getting something out of the water bath in lab?"

He seemed to appreciate her joke, even if it did point a finger at him "borrowing".

She guided him to pour the thick lemon custard on top of the hot cookie, and then put it back in the oven. "Now we wait."

"How long?" James fidgeted.

"Just long enough to clean up. I'll wash. You dry."

He came up next to her at the sink. "How long have you been cooking?"

"Since I was six. My mom caught me making eggs for myself one morning. She started giving me supervised lessons that day, worried I might catch the house on fire." She handed him the clean mixing bowl.

"Wow. No wonder you're so good."

"Thanks." Heat licked her cheeks. Her phone vibrated in her pocket. She dried her hands on her shorts, pulled it out, and huffed as she read the text.

"What is it?"

"So much for my plans later. Tim's blowing me off." She pushed her phone back into her pocket and faced the sink and growled. "Seriously? He's going to change his plans with me just because Mark wants to hang out. Stupid Mark."

"Who's Mark?"

"Tim's sort of boyfriend. What am I? Chopped liver?"

Chapter Seven

"Tim's boyfriend," James repeated. "Tim is with Mark." He was wrong about everything: Kate and Tim weren't together. Tim dated men.

"I guess they are right now. If you ask me, Tim deserves better than Mark. Honestly, what kind of a douche bag would string someone along like that?" She clenched her jaw and shoved a spatula into his hands. "Sorry. I'm done ranting."

James tilted his head. "So, you and Tim are friends."

"Yep."

"Just friends." He needed to be absolutely clear.

Kate gasped and her eyes went wide. "Wait. Did you think Tim and I were together?"

James shrugged and looked away. "Well, yeah."

She burst out laughing. "Meg always jokes that we would be perfect for each other. If only I had the right equipment." She gestured to her pants and then covered her mouth and continued to giggle. "I guess that's why he's settled on Mark. Because he can't have me." Her laughter stopped as soon as it had started. "Is that why you were so mad?"

"When was I mad?" James shrugged. Maybe she wouldn't remember.

Kate lifted a finger for each point she made. "Addiction, lab, and study group." She frowned. "That's what you meant when you said, 'you're one to talk.' You thought I was with him, didn't you? You thought I cheated on Tim that night with you."

"Yes." His stomach sank. Why did she have to ask all the wrong questions?

The death glare was back, only this time she started packing her things. "You thought I would do that?" She stopped and glared at him. "All this time, that's what you've been thinking about me?"

James wanted to deny it, but he couldn't. He'd spent the last seven weeks wallowing in a self-inflicted pool of pity and depression over a misunderstanding, and now it was ruining a perfectly good moment.

"I shouldn't be here." Tugging her bag over her shoulder, she pushed outside. He listened through the open door as her feet slapped against the stairs.

James closed the door and sagged against it. "Fuck."

When he realized she left her hoodie, he thought about calling her to let her know before she got too far. An image of her wiggling out of it popped into his head. When she had pulled it off, her tank top inched up, exposing her lean stomach. And then he buried his face in the material for the second time that night and knew he couldn't part with it yet.

"YOU MADE THESE?" DAVID mumbled with a mouth full of lemon bars. "You? My kitchen-phobic brother?"

"I'm not afraid of the kitchen. I wasn't interested." James looked away. "I may have forgotten to mention Kate came over and helped me."

"Oh, the truth comes out." David laughed and stuffed another one in his mouth.

"They're really good. Thanks for bringing them to dinner." Heather smiled at him. "Was it a date?"

James shook his head. "I wish. She's all business around me."

"Wait, I thought she was with what's-his-name. Your other student."

"I see what you're doing, David. I haven't forgotten she's my student, and I was wrong about Tim. Tim's gay."

Heather nodded. "So, you finally asked her?"

"No, he texted her while we were baking, and blew her off to be with his boyfriend. I feel like such an ass." James let his head fall on the table.

"You are an ass. A repugnant one." David laughed as he quoted James from several weeks ago.

"Thanks a lot."

"Well? What happened?" David asked.

"She figured out I thought she had cheated on Tim with me. She was so mad, and then she left." His words echoed off the table, sounding just as hollow as he felt.

Heather patted his shoulder and clicked her tongue. "Oh, James."

David nudged his shoulder. "Hey, what are you doing the weekend before Halloween? A buddy of mine is throwing a party. You make a great pirate."

James shrugged and gave his brother a weak smile. "I'll probably be grading."

"You should go out. Staying in that lonely apartment isn't good for you."

THERE WERE LOTS OF things that weren't good for James. Thinking about Kate on Monday was one of them. He had her hoodie folded on the edge of his desk and it pained him to give it back.

He paced his office for five minutes after class before there was a knock on his door.

"Can I have my hoodie back?" Kate asked without looking at him.

"Come in." James didn't know what he was going to say, but he couldn't stand the thought of her leaving.

When the door closed, she said, "This whole time? You thought I was a cheater this whole time?" Her face was pinched. "Why would you think that?"

"My ex-fiancée cheated on me," he whispered. The old wound bled a little as he admitted the truth about his past.

Kate froze. "Oh."

"I'm so sorry. I'm sorry for everything, okay? I shouldn't have been such a dick that first day after class, and I shouldn't have assumed the worst about you."

She took a deep breath. "What about Angelica?"

"What about her?" James remembered their argument in the first study group. "What? Me and her?"

Kate nodded.

"Never going to happen. Ever."

Her forehead smoothed and her shoulders relaxed.

Seizing his chance, he continued, "I had a really great time on Saturday. Until I screwed up. Thank you for showing me how to make lemon bars. My brother and his wife really enjoyed them." He nodded to the picture on his shelf.

Kate's gaze followed his and she smiled. "I'm surprised you had any left to share."

"Well, I did eat the other half. If you keep teaching me how to cook I'm going to need new pants." He chuckled. "Maybe next time we should make something that doesn't have a half pound of butter in it."

She blinked. "Next time?"

"If you're willing." He had never wanted anything so much in his life. "If you're free next weekend that would work for me."

"I, um, have plans."

"Right. Halloween parties and stuff."

"Yeah. I promised Meg."

His shoulders fell. "Maybe some other time."

Instead of answering, she put her hand on the doorknob.

"Don't forget your hoodie."

"Right." She tucked it inside her backpack, and then her footsteps echoed down the hall.

THE NEXT TIME JAMES went to the research lab, he noticed Sam's bench was decked out with Halloween-themed art projects and commented on it.

"You should see my office. It looks like a Halloween explosion. My kids keep giving me stuff. How many jack-o-lanterns do kids make in school these days?"

James laughed. "I like the fangs on that one."

"My eight-year-old is going as a vampire this year, so it's fitting. I love how warm it is here during Halloween. In the Bronx, where I grew up, it wasn't unusual for us to have to tromp through snow to trick-or-treat. Nothing ruins a costume faster than having to cover it up with a coat and moon boots. My kids don't understand what it was like." He shook his head. "What do kid-free adults do with themselves on Halloween? It's been too long for me to remember."

"I'll probably go to a bar over the weekend." Even though he had an invitation to David's friend's party, James would stay in town, just in case. When Kate mentioned her promise to go out with Meg, he hoped they would be going to the costume party at Addiction Saturday night, which is where he planned on being.

"Maybe you'll meet someone." Sam's eyebrows jumped up and down.

"Maybe." James wasn't interested in meeting someone. He was interested in making things right with Kate.

"Hey Dr. Baker, sorry I'm late," Michael called out as he wound his way through the lab. "Hi, Dr. Bellevue."

Sam pulled out his lab notebook and winked at James. "Let me know how it goes."

"Sure thing." James laughed. "Michael, are you ready to run your gels today?"

Michael nodded. "Let me get the microfuge tube out of the freezer."

With Halloween still fresh in his mind, James asked, "Hey, do professors dress up here for Halloween?" Everyone loves a pirate chemist, right?

Michael shook his head and Sam piped up, "The only faculty I've ever seen in costume are the ones from the theater department. But that's not exclusive to Halloween."

"Sometimes students dress up," Michael added.

The thought of Kate in a sexy costume sitting in front of him during class the following Wednesday was more than he would be able to handle.

Chapter Eight

Graduation was seven weeks away, and Kate couldn't stop thinking about what James said. Thanks to Dr. Moore's connections, she had a lab job lined up as soon as she walked, but all she could think about was opening a bakery. It wasn't the first time she'd been complimented. But it didn't matter how many times her friends had praised her cooking. They had to say nice things to her because that's what friends do. James wasn't her friend. And when James seemed to love everything she made, it led her to believe others would, too.

Spurred on by her obsession with the idea, she spent several hours researching supplies and what she would need to get a small business loan. It was crazy, and it made absolutely no sense to mention it to anyone, so she didn't. All her thoughts went into a notebook. On paper, she kept everything organized and safely out of her head, where they had been collecting and repeating on a constant loop.

On Thursday, Carrie didn't need her for long, so Kate ventured down campus and visited the college of business. The dean's secretary referred her to a professor who would be able to answer her questions about small businesses.

Kate knocked on the door. "Dr. Pullman?"

A gray head turned up from his desk. "Yes?"

"My name is Kate Rhodes. I have questions about starting a business and I hoped you might be able to help me."

He smiled at her. "Well, Kate, you've come to the right place."

Seated across from him, she handed him her notebook and held her breath. The most terrifying moment of sharing a secret dream is waiting for someone to laugh. That moment never came.

"Of course, I would suggest you complete an MBA from this fine college, but seeing as how you're about to graduate, I'm going to assume you don't intend to spend another two years here."

Kate grimaced. "Um, yeah. I'm ready to be done with school."

Dr. Pullman chuckled. "I remember that feeling. So, here's what you should do." He grabbed a pen and paper and started scribbling. "Read these books. They'll give you an idea about where to go next. You're well on your way." He pointed to her open notebook on the desk between them. "You have a really detailed business plan here."

"Well, I've had a few days to think about things, and I based the measurements on the kitchen in my dorm." Her focus on this new project had consumed every waking moment. It had to be perfect.

"Like I said, it's incredibly detailed. After you read those books, you should start pricing equipment. You'd be surprised how expensive everything is. Although sometimes, if you find a building that already has all the appliances, you don't even need to worry about it. You also might want to tour a few kitchens, talk to the chefs and get their feedback. I actually know the head chef for the kitchen here, on campus. I could call him and ask if you could meet with him if you'd like."

Kate smiled and nodded. "That would be great, thank you."

"I can also recommend a bank that might give you a loan."

"Actually, I'm going to try my credit union first. I have two accounts with them."

He stood and offered his hand. "It sounds like you're on your way."

When she left Dr. Pullman's office, she had an appointment to tour the campus kitchens on Monday right after biochemistry, a list of books to read, and confidence in her plan.

Slowly but surely, James shifted out of her focus, replaced by her passion to make her business plan a reality. It was certainly a healthier choice and involved absolutely no crying.

"WHAT WOULD I DO WITHOUT you?" Kate held a Cleopatra dress against her body. It was white, low-cut, and trimmed with gold.

"You wouldn't be a very good Cleopatra, that's for damn sure." Meg chuckled. "You're going to look great in it. Oh, and don't forget the headband and the arm cuffs."

Kate put them on and smiled at her reflection. "What time are we leaving?"

"I think the party starts at nine. How does ten sound?"

"Sounds like I have enough time to get my makeup done."

As Kate turned to leave Meg's room, Meg touched her shoulder. "It's good to see you smile."

Her secret plan was on the tip of her tongue, but she couldn't bring herself to tell her best friend just yet. "I've found a new focus."

"Good. See you in a couple of hours?"

Kate nodded and slung the white dress over her shoulder. When she got back to her room, she took her time putting her costume together. Once she changed into the dress, she turned her attention to accessories and makeup. She just happened to have a pair of sandals that perfectly matched the broad golden belt that hung straight between her legs.

The front of the dress had two slits, one up each leg, stopping mid-thigh, which would give her plenty of mobility. When she and Meg discussed Halloween, they both agreed their costumes would have to be suitable for the dance floor since that was where they were headed. Kate used a picture from the Internet as a guide for her makeup and then clamped the gold arm cuffs in place. As she walked to Meg's room, she enjoyed the way the material swished against her legs.

"Holy shit, how did you get your hair to do that?" Kate gaped at her friend who had a perfect beehive hairdo held in place with a white headband, which matched her knee-high white boots and her thick white vinyl belt. Meg's dress was covered with huge, brightly colored flowers, and barely concealed her ass.

"Hairspray and about a hundred bobby-pins." Meg grinned. "You like it?"

"Love it. You're the best go-go dancer I've seen."

Meg patted her fluffed hair. "Your makeup is perfect."

"Thanks. Shall we?" Kate held her arm out to Meg, and when they got to the parking lot, she pulled her keys out of her purse. "I'll drive tonight."

The Halloween party at Addiction was in full swing when they got there. They checked their purses at the coat check and Meg slipped the ticket in her bra, claiming it was the safest place. Out of habit, Kate walked by the bar first. No James. Splatters of blood decorated the bar, which fit with the bartender's zombie costume. He didn't try to hide his obvious pleasure at their outfit choices and stared openly at Kate's cleavage. "Where's your boyfriend, or did you two wear him out?"

"With his boyfriend." Kate pulled Meg away from him before he could say anything else.

The dance floor was more crowded and the music was louder than normal. Most of the women in the club were dressed like Meg, in sexy short costumes, which made Kate stick out like a sore thumb. As she scanned the room, her eyes fell on a gorgeous pirate, and when their eyes met, she sighed. James. Even in costume, she was attracted to him.

"He's here," Kate shouted.

Meg's gaze followed hers and she frowned. "Don't talk to him. He thought you were dating Tim while you had sex with him. Have you forgotten all the crying? I haven't. He's a dick, and you can't let him make you feel bad anymore."

Meg didn't know the whole truth. She didn't know about James's ex, and she certainly didn't know about their most recent conversation. James wasn't a dick. He had been hurt.

He was also her professor for seven more weeks.

After an hour of observation, Kate realized James had come alone. Talking required more confidence than she possessed, so Kate clung to Meg. Eventually, thirst overcame anxiety.

"I need water," Kate shouted to Meg and then moved through the crowd. As she stepped off the dance floor, she tripped and landed in strong arms. Someone rolled her body, cradling her waist and the back of her neck until she was face to face with the very same, devastatingly handsome pirate. "Hi."

"Ahoy." James smiled at her, making his eye patch lift off his cheek a little.

Kate giggled. "Thanks for catching me. I don't know what I slipped on." Kate pulled out of his grasp and straightened her dress as she looked around for the tripping hazard. Her heart was pounding. Falling off the stage and into his arms wasn't exactly the reconnection she was hoping for.

"T'was the alligator's tail." James pointed to a floppy foam tail thrashing around near the edge of the dance floor.

"Oh." Kate nodded. "I'm going to get a drink."

"Me's be goin' ta get more grog too."

"I like your accent. How long have you sailed the seven seas?"

"All me life."

She giggled again and led the way to the bar, looking carefully at the ground for more costume accessories. James was a step behind her the whole way. It was comforting to have him so close.

The bartender grinned and licked his lips as he made his way to where Kate was standing. "What can I get you?"

"Two glasses of water, please."

The bartender filled up two cups and put them down in front of her. "Are you sure you don't want anything else? I know I'm hungry, and I'd like to eat more than your brains." The bartender reached across the bar and gripped the band around Kate's arm.

"Belay that talk and git yer hooks off, ye scurvy bilge rat." James darted to the side and shoved the bartender's hand off her.

Her breath caught in her throat. "Yeah, what he said." She motioned to James, who was still scowling at the bartender.

"Hey, I was just playing around." The bartender skulked a few feet away.

Kate turned toward James, brushing her hand against his chest. The heat from his skin warmed her. "Thank you for sticking up for me. That guy's a creep."

"He needs a proper flogging." The muscles in James's jaw tightened as he stared at the bar behind her.

She sighed. It was time to be confident and in control. "Look, this is ridiculous. We're both adults, we should act like adults. I can control myself, and you can control yourself. Right?"

"Aye." James gave her a somber nod.

"So, can we just be here and have a good time without feeling awkward?" Awkward wasn't the right word. Anxious was more like it, but he didn't need to know she was a nervous wreck around him.

"Aye aye, Cap'n."

Kate smiled and handed him a cup of water. "I like your costume. What happened to your eye?" Her eyebrows knitted together in mock concern.

"Arr, t'was a most unfortunate accident with picric acid."

Kate snorted. "I almost believed the whole pirate thing, until you got all nerdy-chemist on me." She touched his arm and a pulse of electricity shot through her hand. Could he feel it too? If he did, he didn't let on. The feeling remained until she removed her hand.

James laughed. "Yer costume be amazing. Ye look a right saucy wench."

Even though she wasn't sure if it was a compliment, she brushed her hands down the sides of the dress. "Meg is a miracle worker. She's also a bit tipsy at the moment, so I should get back to her." She finished her drink. "Do you want to join us?"

"Aye. That I would."

Meg's eyes bulged when they returned, and before she could say anything, Kate leaned toward her and said, "It's cool. We had a talk." Meg scowled but didn't force the discussion at that moment either.

Kate and James spent the next hour dancing casually next to each other. James continued to talk like a pirate, making Kate laugh, especially when he called another pirate a "son of a biscuit eater." There were plenty of distractions, which was fortunate, since looking at James too long made her heart pound and her mouth dry. How could his costume make him even more attractive than usual? At one point, Meg got the attention of a very good-looking man dressed as a pimp, who was devoting all his time and attention to her. The last time Kate saw them, Meg and the pimp were at the bar and she was stroking the purple feather in his hat.

At the end of the night, as the club emptied, Kate tried to catch a glimpse of Meg but had no such luck. There were quite a few people lingering in the parking lot, and James stayed close as they searched for her. "I drove, but she has the ticket for my purse, which has my keys."

"Pr'haps she be at yer car." James scanned the dark parking lot.

"Maybe." She squinted, hoping to see the back corner of the parking lot without having to actually walk to her car alone. She and Meg had a rule about that. Parking lots were too dangerous to venture in solo.

Seeming to sense her hesitation, he slid the eye-patch to the top of his head and for the first time that night, he spoke normally. "I'll go with you."

Kate relaxed as they walked to her car together and smiled. "Thanks for keeping me company." The cool night air did nothing to quench the fire inside her.

"No problem."

"Here's my car and no Meg." She sighed. "I guess I should wait here for her."

"Probably best. It's like what they tell you when you get lost in the wilderness. Stay with your vehicle and rescue crews will find you."

"So, in this analogy, Meg is the rescue crew?" She leaned against the side of her car, distinctly aware of the distance between them.

"Don't forget her pimp escort."

"Riiight. How could I forget his huge purple feather?" She laughed and looked up at his face. The waxing moon bathed his forehead in cool silver light, hiding his mouth in shadow. It had been eight weeks since she'd kissed him. Eight long weeks.

All of a sudden, she needed to touch him. Her head swam and she couldn't fight her urges anymore. When her body collided with his, she wrapped her arms around his neck and sighed when her lips found his. As she pushed her tongue into his mouth, he moaned and touched the sides of her face.

Kate struggled to balance her need to breathe with her need to kiss him and fell back against her car, pulling him with her. The air left her lungs as his body pushed against hers.

Kate gasped for air. "Shiver me timbers."

James gave her a crooked smile and caressed her cheeks.

No matter how much she wanted him, it didn't change the fact that things were complicated between them and that making out with him wasn't a good idea.

"We shouldn't—"

Distant voices traveled toward the car. James tensed and took a step away from her, shoving his hands into his pockets. Meg stumbled through the rows of parked cars, being held upright by the pimp with the purple feather.

Kate's cheeks were hot and her lips were swollen. "There you are. We've been waiting for you. Did you get my purse?"

Meg winked and pushed both purses into her hands. "I'm sure you've been talking this whole time. That's why your lipstick is on his mouth, right?" She laughed.

James wiped at his mouth with the back of his hand, erasing the marks she'd left on him. He wouldn't look at her either. Did he regret what had just happened?

"This is Rob. He's a pimp. That makes me his ho. Right, Rob?"

"Whatever you say, sugar," the pimp said, groping her ass and kissing her.

Meg pulled away from him. "Wow. Rob has a really talented tongue."

The first indication Meg was on the verge of passing out from being drunk was her honesty. Well, that and not being able to stand up straight. "Come on, Meg, let's get you home. Thanks for bringing her, Rob."

Rob frowned. "I thought she was coming home with me."

"Are you interested in cleaning up vomit all night?" Kate lifted an eyebrow and waited for Rob to grimace. "Didn't think so. She needs to sleep it off. She'll call you tomorrow." James took a step toward Rob and stared at him until he released his grip on Meg's body. "In you go." While Kate unlocked the back door, James held Meg and then helped her crawl across the seat where she curled up in a ball.

"Party's over," James said with his arms crossed over his chest, threatening Rob just enough to make him leave.

"Thanks for your help." Kate tucked her hair behind her ear and looked at Meg in the back seat. "She can be a handful. It's a good thing I love her because it looks like I'm going to have a long night ahead of me." She sighed when Meg started moaning and holding her stomach. Tapping on the window, she said, "Don't throw up in my car Meg. You hear me?"

After opening the driver side door, she turned back to James one more time. "I have to go. Sorry about everything."

MEG LIVED ON THE FIRST floor, which was good because it meant Kate didn't have to drag her up the stairs, or worse, try to get her on an elevator. Meg managed to hold it in the entire ride home, but the moment she was in her dorm, she grabbed a bowl off the counter and started puking.

Kate took care of her for the rest of the night, leaving once to get pajamas from her room. They both fell asleep some time near sunrise and slept until late in the afternoon. It wasn't until late Sunday night when Kate realized there was a message on her phone.

From James.

Chapter Nine

James stood in the parking lot and watched Kate leave. As he drove home, his mind raced. What just happened? It had taken everything in his power to resist her for weeks, and then she kissed him. What did it mean? They needed to talk.

Before he could fall asleep, his body demanded release. He stretched out in his bed and squeezed his eyes shut. Images of Kate danced across his eyelids: her dress glowing in the dimly lit room and her body glittering with gold. She was the most beautiful Cleopatra he'd ever seen. He relived every moment, crushing her body under his, her soft lips impatient. Pretending she was there with him, he gripped his cock, moving across the slippery head the same way she touched him the night they were together. Her name was on his lips as he came.

JAMES WAITED UNTIL noon on Sunday to call Kate. When she didn't answer, his heart sank. He didn't regret their parking lot encounter, but maybe she did.

"Hey, it's me. I wanted to see how you were feeling today. I hope you got home safely, and I hope Meg is all right." He let out a long breath. "Listen, I want you to know I thoroughly enjoyed myself last night, and I hope you did too. Call me."

He kept his phone in his pocket the rest of the day, checking it frequently through dinner at his brother's. After Heather left to put Miles to bed, James leaned across the table toward his brother.

"I saw her again last night."

"So? You see her almost every day. She's your student."

"Shut up. I know she's my student." James exhaled. "Can you just be happy for me for a minute? We talked—"

"You just talked, huh?" David lifted an eyebrow.

"Well, maybe a little more." James pressed his lips together. "I want her more than ever. I tried calling her today, but she didn't answer." He spun his phone in his hand, checking for the hundredth time to see if he missed a call. He hadn't.

"Seriously bro, you're pathetic."

"Maybe. But I'm happy. Doesn't that count for something? She makes me happy. I guess I'll find out tomorrow how she feels about what happened."

"What happened?" David's eyebrows jumped up and down.

"We kissed, that's all." Not that he hadn't wanted more. He wanted so much more.

"Did she like your costume?"

"Yeah, and I talked like a pirate all night and made her laugh. Sorry I missed your friend's party."

"No big, it was pretty low key, and there weren't any pretty young girls there, so you would've been bored."

"She's not that young. Stop harassing me about it."

"Fine, just this once." David laughed. "I'm glad you're happy. You deserve it. Just be careful."

James took a deep breath. "I know it's still early for me to make any assumptions, but would it be all right if I invited her to come to dinner with me for Thanksgiving?"

David's mouth hung open. "I could give you so much shit right now."

"I know. I know. I'm not even sure I'll invite her." James held his hands up. "Well?"

"We'll have plenty of room. Mom and Dad aren't coming this year since they'll be on a cruise."

James relaxed. Not having to deal with his dad was always a bonus, especially if he was going to bring a girlfriend to a family function for the first time in years.

"I'll ask Heather." David got up from the table and made his way upstairs to Miles's bedroom. He came back a few minutes later. "Yes. Heather would be thrilled to meet her."

"And you?" James raised his eyebrows.

"I must admit I'm curious to meet the woman that has you so whipped."

"Shut up." James sulked. Why did his brother always have to be right?

BIOCHEMISTRY WAS ABOUT to start and that meant James would get to see Kate. Still sitting in the second row, she didn't avoid his eye contact like she used to. She even smiled a few times.

After class, he asked her if she would follow him to his office, but she said she couldn't.

"I have a meeting. I can't miss it. I'll stop by tomorrow morning." Kate gave him a quick smile and then darted out of the room.

His stomach churned and waiting twenty-four hours nearly killed him.

James paced his office Tuesday. He looked down the hall every time someone opened the door and became impatient until finally, Kate arrived. She stood outside Carrie's office but didn't go in. They made eye contact and she held up her finger.

What would she say? A minute later, she walked down the hall. The smile on her face helped put him at ease.

"Ahoy," he said in his best pirate accent.

"Hi." Kate closed the door behind her. "I'm sorry I didn't call you back. Meg was really needy."

"Is she okay?"

"Yes. Thanks for asking."

"Are *we* okay?" James held his breath as he waited for her to answer.

Kate laughed. "I'm such a hypocrite. Hey, let's be adults, oh wait I can't, let's make out."

"You don't hear me complaining, do you?"

"No." Kate's smile grew. "I'm not complaining either."

"Good. But you didn't answer me and I have to know. Are we okay?"

"Yes," she whispered and looked at the floor. Kate shifted and put her hand on the doorknob. "Um, I should probably go help Carrie. I'm here to work. I'll see you later?"

"Sure."

"Didn't you say you wanted to learn to cook something else?" Kate asked, turning back toward him. James nodded eagerly, "What did you have in mind?"

"Dinner?"

"Six?"

"Yes." His heart tried to pound its way out of his chest.

"I'll get you an ingredient list." She ducked out of his office and a half hour later, a piece of paper slipped under the door.

James picked it up and scanned the list. He smiled at the doodle of a pirate in the corner. He could hardly wait.

Once he got home from the store, he focused his nervous energy to get his apartment clean. For once, he was actually on top of his grading, so the couch and coffee table weren't covered with papers. Just in case, he made his bed and tidied the bedroom. His leg bounced while he watched the clock. Kate was early, just like last time.

When he opened the door, she held a large container in her hands and had a bag over her shoulder with a cookie sheet jutting out. James tilted his head to the side and stared at her.

"My contribution to dinner. I made bread dough, but I didn't have a chance to shape loaves or bake them. Do you mind?" Kate kicked her sandals off by the door and glanced toward his kitchen. Already in working mode, all he could do was get out of her way.

"Go ahead, I can move things if you want," he said as he touched the food that lined the counter.

"I'll work at the table. It's the right height if I stand," she said as she put her things down and washed her hands. Next, she pulled an apron out of her bag and tied it around her neck covering her soft pink T-shirt and jeans.

The table in the dining area only had two chairs, and he moved one of them out of the way and sat in the other.

Kate's fingers worked in a blur of speed as she folded, shaped, and pinched the dough into loaves, chattering about the process as she went. Just when he thought they were perfect, she sliced the tops of the bread and covered the loaves with a towel. Before moving on, she set the lab timer and put it on the table.

"While we wait for the bread to rise, we'll make dinner."

"What are we making?"

Kate stifled a laugh. "I thought it was pretty obvious. We're making spaghetti."

"The tomatoes make sense, but what about the veggies?"

Kate picked up the carrots, celery, and onion. "These are your aromatics. We are going to chop them. We start with the onion since a traditional *soffritto* is composed of the same amount of onion as the other two ingredients combined."

"Soffritto?"

"It's an Italian term used to describe the base for most sauces, soups, and stews." Kate pulled a large knife out of the block on the counter. "When you're holding a chef knife, you want to pinch the blade. It gives you more control." She demonstrated by cutting the onion down to size in less than a minute.

"We'll need two carrots and two stalks of celery," she said as she put the vegetables in his hand and pointed to the sink, directing him to clean, peel, and pare. "You don't want to get cut, so when you're working with anything that's round, cut it in half first, and then it won't roll around." She sliced the carrots lengthwise and then cut slits in the celery. "Here, you try."

She moved to the side and James took the position in front of the cutting board. Forgetting her earlier comment, he held the knife by the handle.

"Pinch the blade." She gripped his wrist and slid his fingers into position, moving her hand on top of his. "Relax, you can do this."

James chuckled. It wasn't the knife that was making him so nervous.

He followed her orders and held the stack of celery strips and chopped with surprising success.

Kate beamed at him. "Good job. Now the carrots."

When he was done, James looked at the piles of prepared veggies on the cutting board.

"See? Two parts onion, one part carrot, and one part celery. Now we cook. Do you have a sauté pan?"

"Um. I don't know." He pointed to the cupboard that held his pots and pans and hoped they weren't all covered with dust.

Kate squatted down and pulled out a large stockpot and a frying pan. "This will work, and the big pot will be perfect for the noodles. Preheat the pan over medium-low."

She grabbed the bottle of olive oil and splashed the pan. "It's shimmering already, so add your veg."

James did as he was told and stirred them. Kate added garlic at one point and complimented his attention to the veggies, which were turning a nice golden color.

"Where's the wine opener?"

"In the drawer to your left."

After she found it, Kate opened the bottle of wine and splashed the pan, turning the veggies a deep maroon. She put the cork back in the bottle. "The rest is for dinner," she said with a smile. "Do you have a balcony where I can chill this? I think it's the perfect temperature outside for red wine."

James pointed through the living room to the sliding door, which led to a private enclosed balcony.

"Damn," Kate called from outside. "I left my light on again." She was looking at the building facing his.

All this time, she lived across the street and he never knew. No wonder she had been able to get home so easily the first night they were together. He followed her finger, which was pointing to an illuminated window. Three stories up, fourth window from the right.

"Get back in the kitchen. A chef never leaves his pan," she chided.

James jumped and ran back to the stove, picking up the spatula and stirring the veggies again.

By the time they added the tomatoes and seasonings, the kitchen was filled with the most amazing aroma. Kate tasted the sauce. Her face puckered. "Too acidic. Now we need to neutralize with a base. Get the baking soda."

"How much?" He pulled the bright yellow box from the counter.

"We go by taste. It won't take much. Start with a pinch."

The sauce foamed and turned pink while he stirred, and when she tasted it again, she declared it fit for consumption.

While they waited for the water to boil, they preheated the oven and Kate set a new timer. James shook his head. "How did you do that?"

"Do what?"

"Make everything so it would finish all at the same time?"

"Timing is the most important part of making a meal." She smiled again. "The bread needs to cool slightly, to give the starch molecules a chance to solidify before we cut, which I know will take about ten minutes, and that is exactly how much time it takes to cook and drain spaghetti."

"I'm impressed. That's all."

Her cheeks flushed pink. "Thanks. Will you set the table?"

It had been a long time since he'd set a table for anyone but himself. He smiled as he arranged her plate next to his. He could get used to this.

When James took the first bite of his meal, he couldn't believe he'd helped make it. "This is amazing." Next, he bit into a piece of fluffy warm bread. "Damn, that's even better."

Kate grinned.

"Thank you for teaching me." The lesson had been great, but it was her company he enjoyed more than anything else, and this time, she wasn't leaving because of something stupid he'd said.

They carried their wine glasses into the living room after they finished eating and sat on the couch next to each other. Kate tucked her foot under her body and faced him.

"I really am sorry for not calling you sooner, after the first time I mean. My stupid brother." James shook his head.

"What does your brother have to do with anything?"

"He told me not to call you. He told me to play it cool."

Kate laughed. "Meg did the same thing. She took my phone."

James's shoulders relaxed.

"What would you have said?" Kate whispered.

"I can't stop thinking about you."

"Mm-hmm," she hummed, urging him to continue.

"I'm sorry for the misunderstanding about Tim."

"We've already discussed that. Anything else?" Kate's eyes burned into his.

"I've never wanted someone as much as I want you, and if you weren't my student—" He trailed off and tucked a strand of hair behind her ear. Did it really matter? What difference did it make if she was or wasn't his student? Clearly, his brain was no longer in charge and when he leaned toward her, she leaned, too. "If you weren't my student—"

"I won't always be your student," she said just before they kissed. His tongue urgently pushing her lips apart, seeking entrance. Her tongue joined his.

"You make me happy. Isn't that all that matters?" He kissed her sweetly. "Is this unwanted?" If she didn't want him, he needed to know now.

"What?"

"This." He gestured between their bodies. "Us. You and me."

"Wanted. Very wanted, but I don't want to be the kind of person who sleeps with her professor."

"And I don't want to be the kind of professor who sleeps with his student." He was sure he could keep her a secret for the next few weeks. It was the semester after that was going to kill him.

"We're not at school. Here, you're not Dr. Baker."

"And you're not Miss Rhodes."

"At school, everything is different. There, you're my professor and I'm your student."

His brain started to shut down. Nothing else mattered because no one was going to find out. "But here—" James kissed her again and their arms got tangled in an attempt to get closer to each other.

Kate crawled into his lap and put her arms around his neck. "Here, we can be together." Emphasizing the last word, she tilted her hips and rubbed against him. "I missed you so much," she said and kissed him while he lifted her shirt and tossed it onto the floor.

Smoothing her hair out of her face, he admired her beautiful flushed cheeks and her pink lacy bra. As much as he appreciated the prettiness of the garment, he was happier to see it join her shirt on the floor. He sighed and then rolled her nipples between his fingers as she continued to grind against him.

Her breath caught and then a low moan escaped her lips as her body shook, sending vibrations through his legs. A pink glow spread across her skin.

"Did you just come?"

She nodded. "I'm surprised it took that long."

"Would you like to go to my room?" he asked. Once she nodded, he kissed her again and held her tightly as he stood. She wrapped her legs around his waist, which only turned him on more. He growled and put her on the floor next to his low bed. "Is this okay?"

"Yes." Her breathy voice drove him wild. So did the feel of her fingers against his skin as she pulled his shirt off. Better yet, she kissed along his chest and flicked his nipples with her tongue. While her mouth moved, he kneaded her perfect ass and moved his fingers between her legs. Her whole body shuddered again.

The biggest regret he had from their first night together was not taking his time with her. This time would be different.

After pulling the blanket and top sheet down and out of the way, he kneeled in front of her, kissing her breasts while he opened her jeans. Mimicking her movements, he flicked her nipples with his tongue. She moaned and dug her fingers into his hair.

"Yes." The word made his dick twitch.

Trailing kisses down her stomach, he tugged on her jeans and groaned when he found matching pink lacy panties. While she wiggled her hips, he peeled her pants off and began kissing the edge of her remaining piece of clothing. More moans spilled out of her mouth when he pulled them off, too.

James kissed along an invisible line between her hips and blew on her sex. Kate grunted and arched her body. Taking the hint, he sat back on his heels and lifted her leg over his shoulder. Now he could kiss all along the inside of her thigh and down her other leg.

Kate twisted her fingers into his hair and whimpered. "More, please."

The heady scent of her arousal paired with her plea for more was all the encouragement he needed. Burying his face between her legs, he thrust his tongue inside her. At the initial contact, she moaned and writhed against him. Worried she might fall over, he wrapped an arm around her body, supporting her back while he fucked her with his mouth. With his free hand, he rubbed her clit.

It didn't take long for her to come again, shuddering against his lips and fingers. He licked her slit one last time before lowering her onto the edge of the bed. It took a minute for her breathing to even out and when she looked up at him through her eyelashes, she smiled.

"Your turn," she said as she rubbed against the bulge in his pants. Never breaking eye contact, she unbuttoned and unzipped his pants and pulled his cock out. When her lips made contact with the head, he let out a long, slow breath. She gripped his hips and pulled him closer, opening her mouth and taking him in inch by inch.

As she started sucking and swirling her tongue, he moaned. She did it again and again. Just when he thought he couldn't take anymore, she slowed her movements. Fast. Slow. Repeating this pattern over and over, he couldn't take his eyes off her.

"Are you going to be okay?" Kate asked with a wry smile, holding his cock and flicking her tongue across the head.

Words would not form in his dry mouth, so he nodded and handed her a condom from the nightstand. He wouldn't last long at this rate.

After ripping the package open with her teeth, she sucked him back into her mouth one final time and unrolled the condom onto his shiny dick.

"I need you," she said as she pulled him onto the bed between her legs. "Now." She kissed him hard and gripped his ass. When he tilted his hips and sank down, the head of his cock pushed inside her. They both moaned as she lifted to meet him, forcing him deeper.

"Oh, fuck," he whispered. "I missed you, Kate." Not Miss Rhodes. Not here. Here they could be together.

Kate took a deep breath. "I missed you too, James." Hearing his name on her lips felt almost as good as being inside her.

And then she kissed him again, sweet and slow as their bodies got reacquainted.

James pulled out of her almost all the way and slowly drove back into her. Kate moaned each time their bodies collided, and the sound of her obvious pleasure was more than he could resist. Even though he wanted the moment to last longer, he wanted to make her come more than anything else. He thrust harder and faster until the veins on Kate's neck bulged, and she screamed as she came. With one final thrust, he came with her, their mouths locked and limbs tangled. He leaned on his forearms while he caught his breath, admiring the sight of her flushed skin and happy face. He rolled away from her and shuddered at the loss of contact.

"I'll be right back." He threw the condom in the garbage and cleaned the sticky residue off his dick. When he got back to the bedroom, Kate had crawled under the covers making a perfect outline of her body. James didn't know if he should join her or get dressed, but when she patted the bed next to her, he knew what to do.

Next to her in the bed, he tucked his arm under his head and smiled when she snuggled closer and nuzzled her face against his chest.

"I love the way you smell," she said as she inhaled and moaned. "Why do you smell so good?"

James scoffed. "You're the one who smells good." The best part about having her over was knowing his sheets would smell like her again. "Believe me, it was painful to give your hoodie back to you."

"Maybe we should trade. I'll leave my shirt and take yours," she said while she drew lazy circles on his chest, which tickled in the most delicious way.

"Deal." Afraid she might think he wanted her to leave, he wrapped his arm around her and pulled her closer. "I had no idea you live across the street. Do you have a roommate?"

"Nope. I have a single. I waited three years for a single and I finally got one. Meg and I lived together for a while, but I do better with my own space. She has a little sister, so it's probably easier for her to share. Being an only child didn't give me any experience sharing with someone else."

"Do you see your parents often?"

Kate shook her head. "No. They live in Kemmerer, Wyoming, so I only see them for major holidays. How about you? Do you see your family?"

"Just David, my brother. I have dinner with his family on Sundays. It's nice. My parents and I aren't close. I don't think my dad ever got over the fact I didn't want to take over his business."

"What is your family business?"

"Construction. I worked there every summer when I was in high school. That was enough."

Kate looked up at him. "Do you still have your hard hat and tool belt? You could help me fulfill a fantasy or two." She smiled. "I'm teasing. Mostly. But I know the feeling. My mom and dad are jewelers and it bores me to tears. Luckily, they always knew I would never stay."

"I've never been to Wyoming. I'm a Californian, bred and raised." Now was his chance to ask what he wanted. "Are you going home for Thanksgiving?" His heart raced. Surely, she could feel it.

"Not this year."

"Do you think, maybe, you'd, um, like to come with me to David and Heather's?" It was a battle to get each word out of his mouth.

Kate pushed up onto her elbow and stared down at him, her face filled with shock. "James, are you inviting me to meet your family?"

"Yes. I know it's kind of early in our, um, relationship." They were in a relationship, weren't they? Asking her to meet his family was the perfect way to find out. "What do you think?" One of two things could happen. She could either say yes or no. And if she said no that meant she wasn't ready for a relationship with him. As the silence stretched between them, he got nervous. "My brother is cool and his wife is super nice. They have a baby, Miles and he's—"

She cut him off with a kiss. When she pulled away, she was smiling. "I'd love to."

"Really?"

"Really. Thanks for inviting me," she said, nuzzling against his chest again.

"I'll let them know you'll be coming."

"Are you making promises you intend to keep?" As she spoke, she slid her hand down his body and squeezed his dick. It responded immediately.

"I always keep my promises," he said and spent the next hour proving it.

Slick with sweat and smiling, Kate sprawled on the bed next to him. "Wow. You weren't kidding." When her breathing finally evened out, she glanced at the clock on his nightstand and groaned. "It's getting late."

"Can I see you tomorrow night?"

"I'd like that," she said as she got dressed. Standing in front of him in her jeans and bra, she chewed on her bottom lip like she did when she concentrated on something. "Um, can I still borrow a shirt?"

He sat up and pointed at his dresser. "Sure, I have some in the top drawer."

Kate shook her head. "I want it to smell like you." Instead of opening the dresser, she peered into his laundry hamper. "How about this one?"

"One of my favorites." Better yet, he hadn't worn it for a bike ride. His riding shirts could practically stand on their own.

"I can see why," she said caressing the material against her cheek and inhaled deeply. "I'll bring it back. Eventually."

"I trust you."

She smiled and tugged it over her head. It drowned her, but she didn't seem to mind. "Thank you." She picked up her pink shirt from the floor and tucked it under the pillow she had been lying on. "Now you'll have something to remember me by."

James laughed and leaned toward her for one last kiss. "As if I could ever forget you. Thank you for dinner."

"Thank you for after. I'll let myself out." Before leaving his room, she paused and said, "Good night, James."

"Good night, Kate."

The front door clicked shut and all he could hear was the faint echo of her footsteps. Just like that, everything went from uncertain to amazing. She was going to join him for Thanksgiving. All he had to do was ask.

Chapter Ten

Kate walked home in a daze. Dinner was amazing, and what happened after was spectacular. James was so sweet and hard all at once. She had never been with someone who knew how to read her like he did.

Getting an invitation to meet his family was the most mind-blowing part of the night. It meant they were together. No mistaking it. It was crazy how quickly the tides had shifted.

Being in his arms made her feel so good that she almost told him about her meeting. Almost. But she'd lost her nerve. How would it look if she admitted she was going to blow off Dr. Moore and all he had done to help her get a job in her field? Pretty bad. Plus, talking about her plans after graduation would only draw attention to the fact that she was still a student. When they were together, neither of them wanted to talk about school. It would be safer to tell him in a few weeks.

HALLOWEEN DIDN'T HOLD the same appeal it did when Kate was little. It used to be a day of costumes, candy, and fun. Now, it was just a Wednesday.

As Kate got ready for her morning classes, she parted her hair and tied a pair of horns to her head. They had been an impulse purchase at a craft fair a few years ago, but now they were her go-to for Halloween. The horns were burgundy and scaly-looking and the cord was black so when her hair fell back in place, it was hidden.

She had slept in James's shirt, and before she left, she tucked it under her pillow. She wanted her bed to smell like him.

Tim laughed when she came into class. "They look natural. Especially with that satisfied look on your face."

Kate held her finger to her lips and shook her head. "Shh."

"Coffee?"

"Fine."

James seemed to appreciate her horns too. He opened his mouth to say something, but then closed it. It was safer that way. After all, they agreed to be professional at school. She didn't linger after class, but she flashed James her phone as she left.

Kate was going to text him as soon as she and Tim were done having coffee.

"What happened?" Tim lifted his eyebrow and took a sip of his latte.

"What do you mean?" Kate batted her eyelashes at him.

"First of all, you never responded to my text a week and a half ago, and when I tried to talk to you about it, you were completely distracted. Second, it doesn't take a genius to see you're happy. You're glowing. Does a certain Dr. Baker have anything to do with that?"

Kate sighed. "Look. I was pissed you blew me off for Mark, okay? That's why I didn't respond to your text."

"And?"

Kate picked her words carefully. "And then Dr. Baker thought you and I were dating."

Tim snorted. "You're gorgeous, don't get me wrong. You're just not my type."

"I know, I know." She smiled at him and pushed on. "So, then I was mad at him because he thought I was cheating on you when he and I were together the first time."

"What?" Tim's shout got the attention of the students talking at the next table. He leaned forward and repeated himself in a lower tone. "What?"

"Yep. So, that sucked. And then I saw him at the Halloween party at Addiction."

Tim looked at his cup. "Yeah, about that. Sorry I didn't come."

Kate waved his guilt away. "Don't worry about it. If you want to waste your time with Mark you go right ahead."

"I'm not wasting my time with him." Tim crossed his arms over his chest and pouted.

"Anyway, he and I talked last weekend, and everything is all right."

"And that ridiculous smile you have plastered on your face?"

Kate blushed. "What? I'm happy. I'm allowed to be happy."

"Mm-hmm. There's something you're not telling me."

Kate pressed her lips together, which muffled her giggle.

"Fine. Keep your secrets."

"I will. And you need to keep them too."

Kate texted James as she rode the shuttle back to the dorms, asking when she should come over.

"Any time after 5," James texted back.

Kate worked on her business plan while she waited. The meeting on Monday was very informative. The head chef for the campus kitchens answered all her questions and offered information she didn't even know to ask about. He was willing to talk business with her, which was more than she could say for the chefs in the restaurants where she had worked all summer. By the time they were done, Kate had a thorough list of equipment she would need and a restaurant supply place in Los Angeles he frequented.

Kate ran into Meg as she was leaving the building. Unlike her go-go dancer costume, this time layers of black fabric hung from Meg's shoulders, hiding her body. Her skin had a faint green hue and a pointed black hat finished the look.

"Going trick-or-treating with your little sister?"

Meg nodded. "Emily always calls me a witch. Wait until she sees me. She looks forward to Halloween every year. Oh, to be a kid again." She laughed. "Where are you headed?"

Kate gripped the straps of her backpack. "Library." After all, James had a collection of books on shelves. It was pretty much the same as the library. Sober Meg wouldn't be as understanding as drunk Meg, so lying about where she was going seemed like the best choice.

Luckily, Meg didn't press her. "Thrilling. See you later."

Kate walked through the parking lot as if she were going to go back to campus, and then ducked over to James's apartment complex. She was out of breath by the time she reached his door.

"I ran into Meg, so I had to be sneaky and then I ran the rest of the way here." Her words came out between pants.

James nodded, welcomed her inside, and handed her a glass of water.

She swallowed it in two gulps. "Thanks. I—"

James pinned her against the door and kissed her. His tongue was impatient and hot, and when he pulled away, she was breathless all over again.

"I love your horns." James tapped the tip of one.

"Thanks. Where are yours?"

"I'm a different kind of horny." James lifted an eyebrow and kissed her again, slow and sweet.

Her body melted against his. "I can tell." She rubbed against his straining cock, and a shiver of pleasure worked its way through her body at the promise of what was to come.

They moved together toward his bedroom, kissing and tugging at clothes, leaving a trail of shoes, pants, and shirts along the way. Once he was against the bed, she pushed him backward making his long muscular legs dangle off the end. His boxers were covered with ghosts.

"Do they glow in the dark?" She traced the outline of a particularly large ghost. It moved under her fingers. Instead of answering, he lifted his hips so she could finish undressing him.

As she crawled up his body to retrieve a condom out of his nightstand, her breasts brushed against his face. This did not go unnoticed by James, who flicked her sensitive skin with his tongue before sucking on one of her hard nipples.

A moan escaped her throat when he moved to her other breast and pushed a finger inside her. Between his mouth and hand, she couldn't hold off any longer and screamed as she came, her arms shaking as she waited to catch her breath. She slid down his body and sat upright on his legs.

With the condom package wedged between her teeth, she locked her eyes on James, his dick glistening and jutting between their bodies. Coating her hand in a layer of precum, she stroked him with long, firm movements. It didn't take long before he squeezed his eyes shut and pressed his lips together.

His words came out in fragments. "I'm going to come if you keep doing that."

"What do you want?"

"You. Need to be in you."

Kate didn't waste any time. She ripped the package open and rolled it down his shaft with one fluid movement. The muscles on the inside of her thighs strained as she lifted her body and positioned the head of his cock at her slick opening. She exhaled slowly as she sank down.

James shuddered and gripped her hips, guiding her movements up and down as he thrust into her, their bodies meeting hard and fast.

She dug her fingernails into his chest and clenched every muscle in her body. A low moan filled the room as pleasure pulsed through her, but he never stopped, thrusting harder and faster, only drawing out the intensity of her orgasm.

When he finally came, she went with him, unsure about where one orgasm ended and the next began.

She collapsed on top of him and took long slow breaths. "How do you do that?"

"Do what?" James stroked her back.

"How do you know my body so well?" Trying to articulate exactly how mind-blowing sex with him was should probably be saved for a time when her brain functioned properly. At that moment, nothing functioned properly.

"I could say the same for you. No one has ever touched me the way you do."

Kate pushed away from his chest and looked down at his face. "It's like we were made for each other. Our bodies fit."

"Like an enzyme and a substrate."

Perfect analogy. She kissed him. "What's our product?"

"Pleasure." That time, he kissed her.

They froze mid-kiss when the doorbell rang.

"Are you expecting someone?" Kate whispered as she lifted off him. Her legs wobbled. Had someone seen her? She had been so careful.

James shook his head and sat up. The person knocked. James pulled his pants and shirt on as Kate made a mad dash for the bathroom, closing the door most of the way. Watching from a tiny gap, she couldn't help but notice the trail of clothes all over the floor. Whoever was at the door would surely notice that. Just as she was about to dart out and grab them, James turned the knob.

"Trick or treat," three little voices screamed in unison.

James's shoulders relaxed and he laughed as he pulled his wallet out of his back pocket.

"Thank you," they said as he closed the door and locked the deadbolt.

"I left the light on for you," he said as he flipped the switch. "I didn't even think about trick-or-treaters or buying candy."

Kate sighed. "Me either. I'm literally shaking. I can't believe how fast you got dressed."

"I didn't get dressed well. My shirt is on backward and I'm still wearing a condom."

"Trade me," she said as she sorted through the clothing on the floor and got dressed while he cleaned up in the bathroom.

"Do you like pizza?" he asked when he came out. That time, his shirt was on right.

Kate sat on the edge of his disheveled bed, still trying to get her hands to steady. "Who doesn't like pizza?"

"So, you'll stay for a while?" He lifted his eyebrows in a hopeful arch.

"I'd love to." Warmth crept through her body as he smiled at her.

James grinned and picked up his phone.

Kate tugged the sheets and blanket into place, smiling as she noticed her pink T-shirt still tucked under his pillow.

"James Baker. Yep. Okay. Thanks." When he ended the call, he joined her on the edge of the bed. "Pizza will be here in twenty minutes."

"You just ordered pizza with five words?"

"I order a lot of pizza." He gave her a sheepish smile.

"I guess so."

"I also have movies." James pulled Kate into the living room and pointed out a stack of Halloween-themed films.

It didn't take long to decide on an old black-and-white B-movie featuring an infestation of giant insects. They sat on the couch together, ate pizza, and laughed. It was the most fun she'd ever had on Halloween.

Still resting between his legs, she turned to face him while the credits rolled. "Do you need to be working?"

James shook his head and touched her cheek. "No, tonight is for us. Tomorrow, yes."

"Thanks for letting me come over. I couldn't wait to see you again." School didn't count.

"Me either," he said before he kissed her. "Will you teach me to cook something new Friday night?"

"Of course." Kate paused and frowned. "I'm worried someone is going to catch us." If Tim noticed, surely someone else would too.

"Especially if you keep smiling at me during lecture. It's distracting."

"Oh sure, blame me. You're the one talking the whole time, moving those pretty lips." While she talked, she touched his lips. "You have no idea how hard it is to resist kissing you."

James laughed. "My pretty lips are nothing compared to your cleavage. You have to stop wearing tank tops to class."

Kate scoffed. "If we're making a list of clothes that aren't allowed, you need to stop wearing tight pants like these. They make me want to rub up against you and grab your ass."

He lifted an eyebrow. "Really?"

She nodded. "I've been fighting it for weeks now. The way the material hugs your muscular thighs and your perfect ass might be more distracting than your lips." As she spoke she traced the seams on the inside of his legs and smiled when her fingers met and his body responded.

"Now I know your weakness." The words came out as a whisper. He touched her horns. "You probably shouldn't wear these to class again."

"Oh yeah, why's that?" She kissed him and rubbed against the growing bulge in his pants.

"Because I'll think of you riding me and the way your face flushes when you come." He tugged her shirt over her head and kissed along the side of her neck.

"We should get a—"

"There's one in my back pocket," he said as he unhooked her bra.

She nodded and then their mouths got too busy to talk.

Chapter Eleven

U p until Thursday, James had been able to avoid Sam and his inevitable comments about finding a girlfriend. Office hours meant he had to be available, even to his nosy friend.

"Well? How did it go?" Sam smiled. "You know, about meeting someone?"

James chuckled and invited him in, closing the door after. "I had a great time."

"What's her name?"

James fidgeted with a button on his shirt. "I'd rather not say."

Sam nodded. "I understand. Too early. You look happy though. That's always a good sign."

"It is, isn't it?" James grinned. If Sam noticed, someone else probably would, too. That meant he had to be extra careful in class Friday.

Lecture and lab meant seeing her for several hours and having to work extra hard to ignore the way her skirt swished when she walked. Even worse was trying not to notice how much of her legs were visible when she bent over. That was the final straw and as he walked to an empty bench, he tripped over his own feet and nearly fell, only catching himself at the last minute. Angelica took the opportunity to fawn all over him, but the last thing he needed was her attention. It took a few minutes to convince her he was fine, and he managed to keep a low profile for the rest of the lab.

His cooking lesson with Kate couldn't come fast enough. Just like last time, she arrived early with a bag of ingredients slung over her shoulder.

"I could've gone shopping." James closed the door behind her

Kate shrugged. "I already had everything. Are you ready to cook?"

"Almost." He took the bag off her shoulder, put it down on the counter, and then held her face while he kissed her. "I've been waiting two days to do that. Too bad we have that rule about behaving at school. Speaking of that. I have a new rule. You're not allowed to wear skirts this short. I almost tripped in lab."

"You did trip." She covered her mouth with her hand to hide her smile.

"Only because you bent over."

"Like this?" Mirroring the movement she'd made in lab, she bent across the dining room table. The back of her skirt hiked up, revealing the little birthmark she had on the back of her right thigh, which he caressed.

"It's very distracting," he said as his hands moved up.

"Notice anything else?" Kate leaned on her elbows and looked at him over her shoulder.

When his fingers found the curve of her ass, he noticed something was missing. Panties. "All day?"

She nodded and smiled.

"For me?"

Another nod.

If kissing her hadn't been enough to make him hard, the thought of her not wearing underwear all day was more than enough. "Fuck me," he whispered as he ran his thumb against her wet heat, focusing on her clit until she moaned.

"That was my plan."

That did it. In a series of frantic movements, he unzipped his pants, pushed his boxers out of the way and pulled his cock out. Thankfully, he had planned ahead again and didn't have to leave her to get a condom. Within seconds, he sheathed his dick and pressed it against her opening.

"Please." Her voice was a strained whisper, slightly muffled by the table. "Fuck me."

Holding her hips steady, he pushed into her and stilled his body. Being engulfed by her was the most satisfying feeling, and if he reveled in it too much, he would come too soon.

Kate gripped the edge of the table and pushed her chest up, like a cobra curving its delicate spine. He traced the chain of bones and noticed something else missing. He dipped his fingers inside the front of her shirt and moaned when her warm flesh filled his hands. She hadn't worn a bra either.

Cupping her breasts as he fucked her, he delivered one satiating thrust after another. He rolled her nipples between his fingers and a soft keening sound joined his guttural grunts.

"Yes," she screamed and her pussy contracted over and over, milking his dick until he cried out. Panting, she collapsed against the table, pinning his hands between her soft breasts and hard wood.

He leaned over her, molding his chest to her back and kissed the nape of her neck. Then he opened his mouth and sucked and nibbled at the exposed skin.

Kate's body spasmed and she moaned. "Mm. I like that. A lot."

Just another thing to add to the list of Kate turn-ons. His body protested as he pulled out of her, and his legs shook as he made the trip to the bathroom. After he cleaned himself up, he found Kate peering at the table he just bent her over.

"Shit, I'm sorry."

"What?"

"My belt scratched the table," she said as she traced a tiny mark on the surface.

James waved his hand. "Pft. That's nothing."

"It's right in the middle."

"And now, when I eat, I'll think about bending you over and fucking you. I can live with that. I promise," he said and trailed kisses up the side of her neck.

"Mm." She leaned her head to the side, giving him greater access. "I like that too. Come to think of it, I like everything you do."

James beamed at her. "That's very gratifying."

When her stomach growled, she held it. "We need to make dinner."

"Right. Now I'm ready for instructions. What are we making tonight?"

"Lentil soup," she said as she washed her hands.

"I'm sure it'll be delicious. What can I do?" He stood in front of his station at the cutting board and picked up the knife and pinched the blade, which made her smile.

"Since you're ready to chop, I'll wash veggies." A pile of produce grew next to him. "Start with the onion." Instead of telling him what to do, she leaned against the counter and com-plimented his attention to detail.

"Am I doing this right?" he asked when he had a pile of onion pieces on the cutting board.

"It's perfect. Just like you." She kissed him and added it to the pan. "You're a quick learner." Every time he chopped or measured an ingredient, she kissed him. It was the ultimate re-ward system. Kisses were much better than gold stars.

"You're a good teacher. You offer great incentives."

Kate smiled while she stirred, and by the time they were done cleaning the kitchen, the soup was ready.

As they ate dinner, Kate kept staring at the scratch on the surface.

"Please don't worry about it." To help ease her mind, he pointed out a huge scratch. "This one," he said as he ran his finger along a gouge near the edge of the table, "is from when David dropped it on a railing outside my apartment in Santa Barbara." The next closest dent was from when he threw his keys the night he came home and found Tina in their bed with another man, but he didn't want to share that story with her yet, so he moved to the next one. "And then I dropped it when I moved here. As you can see, this table has been through a lot. Getting a scratch from you is the best thing that's ever hap-pened to it, I promise." He smiled at her.

"What are you doing this weekend?" Kate asked just before she left.

He shrugged. "I have a little grading to do. Oh, and I need to write my intro exam. What do you have planned?"

"I, um, have a meeting tomorrow. It might last a while." When she opened her mouth to add something else, nothing came out. Instead, she smiled and said, "Call me when you need a break from grading."

He kissed her again before he let her go.

KATE WAS NERVOUS TO meet with the loan officer of her credit union Saturday despite how organized she was. The notebook with her business plan now contained cost estimates for everything she thought she might need. In addition, she had been scanning property listings online and had printed a stack of suitable properties for lease.

After introductions, Kate got down to business. Her hands shook as she handed Ms. Watts her stack of papers and her notebook. "I want to open a bakery, and I'll need a loan for supplies and possibly equipment."

Ms. Watts smiled at her and looked through her notebook. "You certainly came prepared," she said without looking up. "You've been saving for some time now, I see."

Kate nodded and took a deep breath and fidgeted in her seat while Ms. Watts looked over her work. Words gushed out of Kate's mouth. "I have worked for restaurants on and off for the past four years. I know how they work, and I know exactly what I want. I have researched every detail of my plan, and every moment I spend on it, I can feel, in my heart, that this is the right thing for me."

Ms. Watts chuckled. "I certainly appreciate your enthusiasm. Tell me about the properties."

"They're right there." Kate nodded to the pile.

"Yes, I can see a stack of properties, but which one do you like the most?"

Kate shrugged and then her shoulders sagged into the chair.

"Here's what I suggest you do. Before we go any further, go see a couple of properties. Talk to the landlords and get a feel for the neighborhoods. Then we'll talk. If you end up leasing a property that needs new equipment, the loan is going to be substantially higher, so until you decide which one you want, there's not much we can do."

"But I have a good chance of qualifying for a loan, right?" Her breath caught as she waited for her answer.

"I think everything will work out just fine." Ms. Watts stood up and offered her hand to Kate. "One step at a time."

"Right. Thank you." Kate shook her hand, grinning from ear to ear.

The soonest she could see properties was Tuesday and Thursday of the next week.

JAMES CALLED KATE TWICE on Saturday, but it went right to voicemail both times. In an attempt to distract himself, he wrote the first half of the intro chemistry test, which was enough to put him to sleep that night. Grading took up most of Sunday morning and by mid-afternoon, his head hurt.

That time, when James dialed Kate, she answered in a voice as smooth and sweet as honey. "Hello."

"I missed you yesterday."

"Me too."

"How was your meeting?" James wanted to know where she had been but didn't want to press her if she didn't want to tell him.

She didn't offer any information. "It was great. I'll tell you all about it. Someday. Soon. How's grading?"

James rubbed his temples. "Frustrating. I need a break."

"Go out on your balcony and look in the chair."

Waiting for him was a pair of binoculars. "Where did these come from?" He adjusted the width between the eyepieces and focused across the street. There she was; the third story up, fourth window from the right.

"They're a gift. Did you find me?" she said, waving.

"My shirt looks good on you."

"I'll take that as a yes."

"Can you see me?"

She squinted and shook her head. "Not really."

"I want you to come over."

"Can't. You're too busy grading."

"But I can't focus anymore," James whined.

"Sure, you can. You just need to blow off a little steam." She flashed her white teeth before she went on. "If I were there, I'd help with that."

"You're good at blowing."

Another smile. "Hang on." The phone clattered and a muffled sound came through his receiver.

He almost dropped his phone when he watched her peel his shirt off, leaving her completely naked in front of the window.

"Strip. And because I can't see you, I'm going to have to take your word for it."

James hesitated for a few seconds. "I can't hold the phone, binoculars, *and* strip. Wait a second, speakerphone." After putting the phone down near him, he dropped his pants and boxers and draped his shirt over the railing, shielding his naked body. "Okay."

"You're naked?"

"Yes."

"What do you want me to do?" Kate sat on the edge of a chair.

James took a deep breath. "Can you put the phone down, you're going to need both hands."

Kate grinned and propped the phone on her desk. "You're on speaker."

"Good. Touch your nipples until they're nice and hard."

"Like this?" Her hands moved in concentric circles.

James's focus was split between her face and her breasts. Her mouth was parted and her nipples were rigid. His throat was suddenly very dry. "Yes. Like that."

"Am I making you hard?"

"Very."

"Touch yourself and tell me what you want."

"I want you to suck your finger into your mouth." His cock jumped in his hand.

Following his command, she pushed her middle finger into her mouth and moaned as she sucked on it. Her eyes were closed, and she was still rubbing her nipples with her other hand.

James held his breath.

She leaned back in the chair.

"Open your legs." His head began to swim.

Kate complied and smiled, keeping her eyes closed.

"Now I want you to fuck yourself." He struggled to form words.

Her finger descended slowly, pausing before she made contact. "Take a breath."

James gasped, and Kate smiled again.

She pushed between the pink folds of her pussy. Each languid stroke of her slit made him shudder and was matched by his hand pumping his cock.

"You want me to *fuck* myself?" Her soft words licked at his ear. He growled. She pushed her finger inside and moaned as she pumped in and out. "Mm." Her mouth went slack and her breathing quickened. "I'm going to come. Come with me."

James grunted and squeezed his cock as he painted the balcony.

Her satisfied sigh filled his ear. "See? All better."

"Well, I don't know. Better. But not *all* better."

"I'll make it up to you in person."

"Promise?"

Kate nodded. "Grade. I'm going to work on homework."

"Okay. See you tomorrow?"

"One o'clock, just like every Monday."

Chapter Twelve

James finished grading just in time to make the drive to David and Heather's house.

Heather made a habit of putting Miles to bed right after dinner, which always gave David and James time to talk.

"She gave me a gift."

David leaned a little closer.

"Binoculars."

David rolled his eyes. "Are you going to go birding together? Nerd."

"She lives in the dorms across the street from me."

"Mm, slightly better than watching birds." David smiled. "The last time we talked, you were waiting for her to answer your call."

"She did."

"And?"

"She came over for dinner on Tuesday." James shook his head. "Wow, I can't believe how much has happened is less than a week."

"What happened?" David scoffed and stared at him.

"We came to an agreement. At school, she's Miss Rhodes. When she's with me, she's Kate. She's not going to tell anyone, and I won't either."

"Anyone besides me, you mean."

"Obviously."

"You had sex again?"

James grinned and nodded. "We scratched the kitchen table."

"Now you're just rubbing it in." David folded his arms over his chest.

"No." James waved his hands back and forth. "I'm not trying to rub it in. I'm trying to point out how good my life just got. She's amazing."

"She must be if she got you to have phone sex with her too."

"I never said that." Heat spread across his face.

"Not in so many words." David punched him lightly on the arm. "Your agreement, what does it change?"

James sighed. Nothing had changed between them except permission to give in to their carnal impulses.

"Are you seeing other people, or is this an exclusive secret relationship?"

James shrugged. "I don't know. We didn't discuss that."

"I suggest you do before someone gets hurt." David gave him a pointed look. "And by someone, I mean you."

KATE WAS HOPING TO see James Monday evening, but when she texted him, he was working with his thesis student and didn't know when he'd be free. Kate made dinner for Meg instead and got the full scoop on Meg's family, who lived nearby. Kate hadn't gone home with Meg since the fourth of July, and when Meg invited her to Thanksgiving dinner, Kate froze.

"I have plans." Kate played with her fork, unable to look at her friend.

"I thought you weren't going home this time."

"I'm not." Their eyes met for a split second.

"What plans?"

Kate blushed. "Well, um, I got an invitation to join some-one for dinner, so I'm going to do that."

Meg's mouth hung open. "Someone?" She stared at Kate until Kate looked away. "Is it James? Are you seeing James?"

Kate nodded slowly. "We just got back together and I wanted to tell you, but—"

"Kate, you don't need to worry about me. I won't tell any-one. I swear. I thought you were spending an awful lot of time at the library. Is he being nice?"

"Very." Kate's shoulders relaxed. "I was so worried you'd be mad at me. We kissed at the party at Addiction."

"I may have been drunk, but I still remember that little de-tail. I figured something was going on."

Kate sighed. "There's more."

Meg narrowed her eyes. "Well?"

Kate leaned across the table and looked her friend in the eye. "You promise not to laugh at me?"

"Promise." Meg's face was deadly serious.

"I'm going to open a bakery." The words spilled out, one af-ter another.

"Are you shitting me?"

Kate shook her head.

"What about your lab job?"

"I'm going to tell Dr. Moore I can't take it but only if every-thing falls into place."

"Why would I laugh? I think it's a brilliant idea. One I seemed to have heard before. I don't know how many times

Tim and I have suggested you open a restaurant." Meg stood and pulled her friend into a hug. "How far have you gotten? I want details."

Kate beamed. "I love you, you know that, right? Can I show you my business plan?"

Meg's enthusiasm for her bakery took the edge off Kate's nerves for her first day of seeing properties. Meg offered to go with her, but because Kate didn't know what to expect, she didn't want to drag Meg into it.

"I'll tell you what. If I find something worth seeing, I'll take you with me the next time."

"Deal."

"You can't tell anyone about that either. Promise me."

"If I were you, I'd be shouting from the rooftops." Meg was still looking through her notebook of sketches and price lists.

"I'm excited, but if something goes wrong, or it doesn't happen, I can't lose everything I've worked so hard for. You know?"

THE NEXT DAY, WHEN Kate was working in the back office, James poked his head in. No one was around.

"I've missed you," he whispered.

She smiled and stared at his lips, his soft, perfect lips. When she noticed him closing the gap between them, she shook her head, reminding them both not to be careless. "Not here. It's not safe."

"Right. Can I see you later?"

"I have stuff." She had no idea how long it would take her to look at three properties, but she didn't want to make plans and have to break them.

"Sounds mysterious."

"Kate? You still back there?" Carrie's voice called out as she neared the door.

Kate picked up the stapler in front of her and shoved it in James's hand. "Feel free to borrow it, but you have to bring it back."

James pulled his lips back over a tight smile and backed out of the office. "Thanks, Miss Rhodes."

Kate motioned to the door where he had just disappeared. "Dr. Baker's stapler jammed. I hope it's okay I loaned him the office one."

Carrie nodded. "Of course."

She sighed when Carrie seemed to believe it.

WHEN KATE SHOWED UP at the first property, she waited for nearly an hour for the realtor to show up. He moved in a flurry around the space, scanning the listing sheet to answer her questions. The restaurant was in a prime location and the appliances were all new. The price tag on the lease reflected both of those things and the more she walked around the space, the more she realized she would have to get a much bigger loan to make it work. The realtor didn't seem to care one way or another if she was interested in the property. After she thanked him, he locked the door and drove away without a backward glance.

Kate checked the clock in her car. Although she had planned the meetings an hour and a half apart, she didn't have enough time to get to the second property. She called the other realtor and pushed their meeting back by twenty minutes.

The two properties were like night and day. This time, the realtor didn't have to answer any questions because the rooms were not just empty, but barren. No tables, chairs, counters, stoves, ovens, or sinks. Gas and water lines were capped off at the wall, and as Kate looked around the kitchen, she started adding up the cost of appliances. It was even more than the other place.

As she sat in her car, she rested her head against the steering wheel. She had just wasted three hours and had nothing to show for it. She sighed as she drove to the next appointment.

If she was disappointed with the first two, the third was worse. The restaurant was part of a building that housed several other businesses, all of which were run down to the point it looked like the whole building had been condemned. She walked through anyway, and she only had one question. "How long has it been vacant?"

Five years. The building had been sitting there longer than she'd been in California. The grimy windows had five years of dust and cobwebs. The thought of getting it ready for customers was enough to sap the rest of her energy.

Kate drove home but couldn't get out of her car. If she went inside, she would end up complaining to Meg about how shitty her day had been. That was exactly why she hadn't planned to tell anyone about her business plan to begin with. No one needed to go through her frustrations with her. She looked in her rearview mirror and glanced up at James's apartment. The light was still on.

"Can I come over?" she texted.

"Please," he replied.

Too tired to walk, she drove across the street and parked. The three flights of stairs nearly wiped her out.

James greeted her with a smile, but it quickly turned into a frown. "Are you okay?"

Unable to answer, she shook her head.

He hugged her and rubbed her back. "Want a shower?"

Kate had to resist the urge to cry. It was perfect. *He* was perfect. A shower was just what she needed. "Yes, please."

While he started the shower, she got undressed.

"May I join you?"

Kate nodded and stepped inside. Within moments, he followed and began washing her tired body. As his fingers moved, the tension in her muscles eased away. Without having to ask, he massaged shampoo into her hair and rinsed it carefully. When he opened his arms, she happily fell into them.

She leaned her head against his chest and sighed. The disappointment and frustration from earlier washed down the drain.

"Can I stay for a while?"

"Of course."

When she was fully relaxed, he dried her off and carried her to his bed. It only took a few minutes of snuggling before she fell asleep.

Hours later, she woke and jerked upright. The sheets and blanket fell away, inviting the cool air to steal her heat. James stirred next to her, mumbling something in his sleep. The clock next to his bed told her it was after two in the morning. While they had discussed how to interact at school, they hadn't discussed sleeping over. That was next level relationship stuff and she didn't want to assume anything. As quietly as she could, she gathered her things and left.

When she woke up Wednesday morning, there was a text from James.

Where'd you go?

"Dorm," she replied. She wanted to tell him how much she appreciated him and how much the previous night had meant to her, but she didn't want to send it over text. It was a conversation that should be in person. Hoping to talk to him after biochem class, she asked if they could discuss last week's lab in his office, but he had meetings he couldn't miss, so she would have to wait. Waiting got harder and harder, but it came with the territory.

WEDNESDAY AFTER THEIR department meeting, James asked Sam if they could discuss tenure.

Whenever they were alone together, Sam made a point of trying to get information about James's mystery woman. Talking about tenure seemed to be the only subject worthy of distracting his curious friend.

As much as it pained him to miss a night with Kate, he buckled down and put his work first. Their meeting turned into dinner and drinks, and by the time they were done, his tenure track wasn't so intimidating anymore.

"There's only so much you can do," Sam said, as they got ready to go. "The rest is getting on the right committees and staying on the good side of the powers that be."

"Right, and that means sucking up to Lloyd. He's been busting my balls about staying on track, and I'm just trying to keep my head above water."

"Don't let him scare you. Lloyd means well, but he can be a bit overwhelming. I'm happy to help you out."

"Thanks, Sam."

"You know what else would help? Getting on the dean's good side, and it wouldn't hurt if you got to know the provost too. Eric's a really nice guy. We're playing racquetball tomorrow. You should come with me so I can introduce you."

"I haven't played racquetball in years."

"You should come."

James shrugged. "Why not?"

"I'll stop by your office to pick you up at eleven."

"Thanks for everything."

Sam nudged his shoulder. "That's what friends are for, right?"

"This is above and beyond being a friend. Really. Thank you."

JAMES WAS SURE HE WAS harboring a swarm of butterflies in his stomach as he and Sam walked across campus to the gym. It was only the second time James had visited the gym, and he was surprised to find a dozen racquetball courts. Six of them were enclosed with a glass wall and had an observation bench outside. Sitting on one of the benches was a man with a full head of salt and pepper hair. He was just finishing tying his shoes when Sam and James walked up.

"Eric." Sam smiled.

"Sam, I'm so glad you could make it." Eric stood and shook Sam's hand and then pulled him into a half hug.

James lagged behind, waiting for Sam to introduce him.

"Eric, this is our new biochemist, James Baker."

"Eric McKay." Eric nodded and shook James's hand. "I remember when we hired you. How are you liking the university so far?"

"It's beautiful."

"Well, James Baker, did you come to play?" Eric looked him square in the eye.

James nodded. "I'll wait until the two of you have a chance to play."

"Nonsense. I'm sure we can find someone to play doubles with us." Eric looked around and found a man coming out of a room next door. "Excuse me, young man, would you please join us for a game of doubles?"

"Sure. My name's Jon."

Eric held his hand out. "Jon, it's good to meet you. I'm Eric, this is Sam, and this is your partner, James."

When James shook Jon's hand, he laughed nervously. "You'll have to forgive me. I haven't played in years."

Jon leaned close to him. "Don't worry. I'm on the racquetball team. I'll cover you."

James sighed. Maybe this wouldn't be a disaster after all.

They were well into their second game before James got back into the groove of playing. Jon had picked up most of his slack, and even though they lost the first game, it hadn't been by much. Jon and James bumped chests when the tables turned and they claimed victory on the second game.

All four men were breathing hard and talking loudly when they exited the court.

Eric suggested they all go to lunch together, and when Jon agreed, James bought him a beer. Before too much longer, Jon had to go but promised if they ever needed a fourth, he was their man.

James, Sam, and Eric stayed and talked until Eric had to run to a meeting. "James, it was great to meet you, and Sam, always good to see you. Are you both coming next week?"

James agreed, and they shook on it.

Sam nudged James with his elbow after Eric had left. "Talk about good first impressions."

James shook his head. "Jon saved my ass out there."

"Maybe a little at first, but you really held your own. See? Eric's a great guy, and it doesn't hurt to be friends with the provost."

"Right you are. It also doesn't hurt to be friends with an inorganic chemist with connections."

"True. I'm glad you came, and I'm happy you're coming next Thursday."

"I'll be there."

Chapter Thirteen

Kate arranged Thursday off and after her morning class, she headed out with a fresh list of properties. Everything was on hold with her business plan until she found a place she liked. It all hinged on that one detail.

The first property was another disappointment. Only this time, the restaurant was too big. She couldn't imagine being able to fill twenty tables with customers. She thanked the realtor for her time and got in her car to see the next one on the list. One after another, she looked at properties that were too modern, too big, too small, or too scary. As she sat in her car waiting to see the last one on her list for the day, she opened her notebook to the sketches she'd made. Perhaps she had been too specific with her dream. Her expectations were so high nothing could please her.

With a heavy heart, she got out of her car and stared up at the unassuming building in front of her. The windows and door had been covered with brown paper with the words FOR LEASE printed across the door. The storefront was nestled between a used bookstore and a baby boutique.

"Are you Kate?" A woman with a blond bob and a perky smile held out her hand.

"Yes, Lisa?"

Lisa nodded. "Ready to see it?" She waited for Kate before she pulled out the key. "I talked to the landlord a few minutes ago, and he's happy to meet us here if you have any questions I can't answer."

Kate took a deep breath and followed Lisa inside. Her mouth hung open as she scanned the room.

The front of the restaurant had six tables, three on either side of the door, but the main focus of the room was a bar with highly polished wooden stools. The bar was made of the same wood and looked like it had just been wiped down. Kate couldn't speak. She imagined glass domes spanning the length of the counter, each one holding a different dessert.

Lisa rattled off details about square footage and utilities as Kate made her way into the kitchen. The appliances were a few years old but in decent condition. "Does the lease include the appliances?"

Lisa flipped through a stack of papers in the folder in her arms. "Yep, sure does."

"How long has it been on the market?"

"Six months. It's not big enough for most folks."

"I think it's perfect." Kate smiled and continued to poke around before she walked back out into the dining area and noticed a locked door next to the restrooms. "What's that?"

"There's an apartment upstairs."

Kate's eyes widened. "Is it available?" She only had her dorm reserved through the third week of December but hadn't started looking into finding a new place because it would need to be close to her bakery. Living above the bakery was about as close as you could get.

Lisa nodded. "They come as a package, which is another reason people have turned it down. The apartment doesn't have a street entrance, which was common when these older buildings were constructed, so when you lose the restaurant, you also lose the renter upstairs. Mr. Crane is offering a move-in special. Rent on the apartment and restaurant is half price for the first six months if you sign a two-year lease."

"Do you have a key?"

Lisa shrugged. "He gave me two, so maybe." The key slid into the lock and clicked. "Let's have a look."

Kate bounded up the stairs, which were steep and went straight back. The apartment consisted of a living area, a small kitchen connected to a dining area, and a bedroom with a bathroom attached to it. The living room and bedroom overlooked the sidewalk below. Light spilled into the rooms, covering the worn wooden floors with the slanting rays of the setting sun. She could almost see the ocean. The floor squeaked under her feet as she paced the living space again.

"I want it."

"That's great. I'll work with Mr. Crane, to draw up a lease agreement contract."

"I'll go talk to my credit union again as soon as possible." Kate was smiling so hard her cheeks hurt. "Can I come to see it again on Saturday with a friend?"

Lisa nodded. "Of course."

They locked up the apartment and Kate strolled through the kitchen one more time, checking off the supply list in her notebook. She made a list of the things she would still need to buy and was surprised by how small it was. It was as if this property was made for her.

She and Lisa shook hands again, but Kate didn't leave right away. She tucked her notebook under her arm and went into the bookstore next door. Getting a feel for the neighborhood had been one of Ms. Watt's suggestions. A bell chimed over her head and a friendly voice called from the back room, "I'll be right with you."

Kate scanned the room, noting that it was probably as big as the restaurant next door, only instead of being divided by tables and chairs, it was separated by towering bookshelves. A surfboard leaned against the wall next to the front door.

"Are you looking for something specific?" The woman behind the counter had a shock of purple in her hair and when she smiled, her right cheek dimpled.

"Actually, I'm looking at the restaurant next door, you know, to get it up and running." Saying the words out loud, even to a stranger, felt good.

"Great. We just love being here. Mr. Crane is a great landlord."

It was easy to smile after hearing that good news. "I'm Kate." She held her hand out, and the woman shifted a stack of books in her arms to shake it.

"Brandie. We knew the guy who ran the restaurant before."

"What happened?"

Brandie shook her head sadly. "His mom developed dementia, and he couldn't juggle taking care of her and the restaurant. It's a real shame too. He made the best gyros in town. What do you make?"

"Pastries and other stuff. I'm going to open a bakery."

Brandie scowled. "Great, now I'm going to have to try everything. If I get a fat ass, we're going to have words."

Kate laughed.

"Are you moving in upstairs too?" Brandie walked to a small table and put the books down.

Kate nodded and then scanned the room for the entrance to the apartment. "Do you live here?" Brandie nodded. "How do you like it?"

"It's great. There's a grocer around the corner that always has the freshest produce, we're close enough to the university to get plenty of foot traffic, and I hear there's going to be an amazing bakery on the block soon."

"I still need to talk to my credit union, but with any luck, there will be." Kate laughed again. "I hope it lives up to your expectations. See you around."

Brandie waved. "I look forward to it."

On her drive back to the dorms, Kate found herself in the parking lot of James's apartment. With her phone in her hand, she thought about calling him but decided to dash up the three flights of stairs and surprise him.

"Just a minute," James called through the door. When he opened it, he was holding twelve dollars. "That was fa—"

Kate beamed and then her mouth was on his. He wrapped his arms around her and dragged her inside his apartment.

When he pulled away from her, he had a silly grin on his face. "I thought you were the pizza guy."

Kate shook her head. "Nope, definitely not the pizza guy. Unless you let him kiss you too." She narrowed her eyes.

James laughed. "I missed you."

"I missed you too."

"Better day?"

"Yeah, about that—" Kate held his face between her hands. "I wanted to thank you. You were so wonderful."

"I'm glad I could help."

"You were very helpful. Sorry for bursting in on you. If you're busy, I can go, I just had to thank you."

"I'm taking a break from grading. Would you like to join me for dinner?"

Kate smiled. "That would be lovely. I won't stay too long."

James shrugged. "It wouldn't be the worst thing that could happen."

"No." Kate shook her head. "I'm not going to distract you while you grade. I have rules against that."

"Fine, be that way." James pouted.

Kate kissed him again, and James stopped pouting.

The next time James answered the door, it was the pizza guy, whom he paid twelve dollars, and did not kiss.

James talked about his day while they ate. Kate was quiet about her good news. Talking to Meg and a woman in a bookstore about her plans was one thing. Discussing them with James was something entirely different.

"So, Thanksgiving is just a couple weeks away. Are you still willing to come with me to David and Heather's?" His leg bounced under the table, making a muted tapping noise on the linoleum floor.

Kate smiled and touched his leg, which stopped bouncing. "Wouldn't miss it. Just tell me what you want me to make."

"I usually bring pie."

"What kind?"

"Pumpkin and pecan."

Kate nodded her head. "Done. Do they know I'm coming?"

James laughed. "Yes. I may have mentioned it once or twice." His leg started bouncing again.

"What's going on? I've never seen you so nervous."

He cleared his throat. "I thought, um, maybe after dinner with my family I could take you to a place in Santa Barbara for the long weekend. There's a vineyard I always wanted to tour and some really beautiful places on the beach to explore. If you're up to it," he added quickly.

Kate had just taken her last bite and nearly choked on it as she tried to swallow it in one piece. Her day just kept getting better and better. She nodded and held up her finger. When she was done coughing she smiled. "I'd love to."

James relaxed and smiled too. "Excellent. I'll take care of the plans. What are you doing this weekend?"

Kate shrugged. "I'm not sure yet." She planned to call Ms. Watts first thing in the morning to make another appointment to discuss her loan.

"Keep me posted?" His eyebrows rose, nearly meeting in the middle.

Kate nodded and pushed away from the table. "Thank you for dinner and thank you for the other night."

"Do you have to go?" James frowned.

"You have work to do. So do I. Good night."

Before she left, he kissed her long and hard.

"See you in class tomorrow."

KATE KNOCKED ON MEG'S door. "It's me."

"You look like you have good news. Do you have good news?" Meg was nodding and smiling.

"I found it. The perfect place."

Kate and Meg hugged and squealed. "When can I see it?"

"I'm going to go see it again Saturday and I was hoping you would want to go with me."

Meg nodded. "I'd love to. What time?"

"How's ten sound?"

"Great. I can't believe this is happening." Meg hugged her again. "I can't wait."

JAMES STRUGGLED TO focus on his work. Kate had said yes. They were going away together. Just the two of them in a city where they could be together, like a real couple. He got to work making reservations the minute she left because he couldn't get his mind back on grading until everything was planned for their weekend getaway.

His ride into work on Friday was perfect. The forecast called for rain, but the sky was clear, so he rode his bike the mile in. As he was pushing it down the hall to his office, Lloyd called out to him.

"James. Do you have a minute?"

"Sure, let me put this away." James parked his bike in his office and his cycling shoes clacked as he made his way down the hall. "What's up?"

Lloyd looked up from his desk, taking in the sight of James in his riding gear. "You could've changed first."

"I wasn't sure how long you'd be here, so I thought I'd see you first." James smiled.

Lloyd smiled back. "I wanted to tell you how impressed Provost McKay is with you. I had a meeting with him yesterday afternoon, and he pulled me aside to share his excitement over getting to know the new biochemist."

James chuckled. "Sam introduced us. We played racquetball yesterday. The provost is a great player."

"Yes, I've heard Sam has taken you under his wing. Seems like you're well on your way to learning the ropes around here."

James continued to smile. "Sam has been incredibly helpful. Thank you again for the space in the research lab. I have ideas for research projects I can do next semester."

Lloyd nodded. "It's not so difficult to plan for the future. I'm glad you're heeding my advice. That's all I wanted to say. Good job." He picked up his pen and turned his attention back to the papers on his desk.

"Thank you, Lloyd." James gave him one last smile before he went to his office. Even though Lloyd treated him like a good dog, James was still proud of getting his attention in such a positive way. He would have to tell Sam about it later. After he unwrapped his pant legs and changed his shirt and shoes, he cleaned up in the bathroom and went to his intro class with a stack of graded assignments.

Sometime during biochem lab, the dark clouds that had been gathering all afternoon ripped open. The rain came down in sheets, pelting against the window at the end of the hall. It was so noisy the entire biochemistry lab filed into the corridor and pressed their faces against the window. It was at that moment James realized he had forgotten his rain jacket at home.

"What's wrong?" Kate asked as they walked back into the lab.

"I forgot my rain jacket, and I rode my bike to work today." A mile in the rain meant a twenty-minute ride instead of five, not to mention the wetness.

"Take the shuttle. It picks up on the south side of the building every half hour."

Angelica piped up, "Oh, do you live close to campus?" She narrowed her eyes at Kate.

All the blood drained out of Kate's face.

"I bumped into Miss Rhodes on my way to the store one day. Turns out we're neighbors," James said quickly, trying to cover for Kate. "It's a small world."

"Mm-hmm, small world," Kate parroted.

"I have my car if you need a ride," Angelica offered.

James shook his head. "Thanks, but I think I'll just take the shuttle. Does it have a bike rack?" he asked the entire class.

Another student answered, "Yep, you'll want to get there early so you can load your bike as soon as the shuttle pulls up."

"Thanks for the info, class. Now let's finish this lab."

It took him twenty minutes to pack up his riding gear and get down to the shuttle pick up spot. He knew he was in the right place because Kate sat inside the bus shelter. James dashed through the rain, leaned his bike outside and ducked inside. Although they were alone, he propped his shoulder against the wall, carefully avoiding the spot next to her on the bench just in case someone was watching.

"I was hoping I'd catch you," Kate whispered.

"Why are you whispering? No one else is here."

Kate shrugged. "Thanks for covering for me. I didn't even realize she would hear me."

"Angelica doesn't miss anything. I don't think she thought much about it. Can you come over tonight? I want to see you."

"Doesn't this count?" A smile played across her lips.

James shook his head. "No. I had plans to see a lot more of you. In my bed."

"Believe me, I've been thinking about that for the last three hours, but don't you have grading to do?"

"It can wait until Saturday."

"I guess that settles it."

"So, you'll come?"

"You always make me come." Kate smiled and stood.

The bus pulled up, and in the two minutes it took James to hook his bike to the front, he got drenched. Kate stifled a laugh as he walked down the aisle and took a seat in front of her.

The bus driver turned to face them. "We'll give it another couple of minutes and then head out."

"No worries, Mac," Kate called out to him.

James turned to look at her through the crack between the seats. "You know him?"

Kate nodded. "I ride the shuttle all the time." She laughed again when water dripped down his face. "You should've just ridden your bike home with as wet as you already are."

James scoffed. "You think this is wet? After a mile in this rain, I would've been soaked to the bone."

"All of them?" Kate leaned forward.

He was about to respond when another wet person got on the bus and sat several seats ahead of him, forcing him to face forward. Mac and the other passenger started talking about the weather as Mac drove.

"There's only one bone I'm interested in," Kate murmured next to his ear. She pushed her delicate hand in the gap between the seats and pointed to his lap. "That one." She contorted her wrist to touch him, barely grazing the bulge in his pants.

James pressed his lips together and groaned. "I thought we were supposed to be careful in public," he whispered.

"I am being careful. Otherwise, I'd be in your lap right now." Kate's words stirred his dick even more.

"Don't tempt me," he ground out between clenched teeth.

The bus lurched around a corner forcing Kate back in her seat. After a few seconds, her breath was on his ear again. "I'd really like to get you out of those wet clothes."

"Me too."

"And then I'd really like to fuck you."

James groaned again. "You're killing me."

"I'd rather fuck you," she said, emphasizing the word "fuck" as if she knew how much it turned him on. "See you later." She sauntered down the aisle and stood just behind Mac's chair.

"Thanks for the ride, Mac. I hope you get back to the garage without any problems."

"Thanks, Kate. Have a good weekend," Mac replied as Kate got off the bus at the curb in front of the dorms.

As James struggled to free his bike, he lost sight of her. He peddled through the parking lot and across the street, and by the time he was climbing the steps to his apartment, his clothes were splattered with road grime. When he got to the third floor, he nearly dropped his bike when he noticed Kate dripping wet and leaning against his door.

"How did you get here so fast?"

Kate grinned. "It took you forever to unload your bike."

"I thought you were going to torture me and make me wait until later." James gripped the open flaps of her jacket and pulled her closer. His breath caught when he noticed how wet her shirt was. He could see her nipples through the creamy white material.

"I wouldn't dream of making you wait." Kate kissed him, pushing her tongue inside his mouth.

James tried to embrace her, but she pulled away and clicked her tongue.

"Not so fast. You're filthy and I'm wearing white." When she reached inside his pants pocket to retrieve his keys, she brushed against his hard cock. "Let's get you out of those wet clothes."

Kate unlocked the door and he eagerly followed her inside. "What are you going to do about your bike? It'll make your floor dirty."

"I have a blanket." Working as quickly as possible, he tugged the old stained blanket out of the coat closet and rolled his bike on top of it.

Kate dropped her jacket and backpack in the kitchen and bent over to help him straighten the blanket. Her teeth chattered.

"Shower." James pulled Kate into the bathroom with him and began undressing her. When he finally got her shirt off her head, it splattered the wall with water. Her bra was saturated and completely transparent. She unbuttoned his shirt and threw it in the sink. Once she had his pants off, she locked her lips on his. He peeled her jeans off and held them with his foot so she could step out. Their mouths never broke apart as they continued to undress. When their naked bodies finally touched, a jolt of pleasure washed through him.

The warm water was marvelous but having her in his arms was even better. Her hands were all over him, tugging and caressing and massaging. She pushed him against the back wall of the shower and bent over. He gasped when she sucked his dick into her mouth.

He marveled at how she could give him the most pleasure without making him come.

When she straightened her back, her cheeks were flushed. "I'm warm. How about you?"

James nodded.

"Good. Now I'm going to fuck you." Kate stepped out of the shower, wrapped herself in the towel, and went into the bedroom.

As James followed her, his legs shook.

"You forgot to dry off." Kate smiled as she unwrapped herself and used her towel to dry his skin.

She pulled the covers back and got a condom before she kneeled on his bed and crooked her finger. James walked to the edge of the bed and stopped. He was waiting for instructions. Instead of speaking, she sucked him back into her mouth, making his legs wobble again. Her mouth was replaced with a cool slippery ring of latex as she unrolled a condom on him.

"How do you want me?" His breath was quick and shallow.

"On your back. Right here." Kate pointed to the bed next to her. Once he was in position, she straddled his hips and reached between their bodies. "I've been waiting all week for this." She sighed as she lowered herself on his dick.

James moaned. He had been waiting all week too.

Kate rode him, rolling her hips and moving her body up and down. Her face contorted and her breathing quickened. Her mouth formed a perfect circle as she came.

He cupped her breasts and squeezed her nipples then pulled her down so he could kiss her. Her wet hair stuck to his face as her body molded to his. In this new position, he had more power. Holding her hips, he fucked her hard and fast, her wet, hot flesh yielding to him.

James flipped their bodies until he was staring down at her. Her dark hair glistened against the soft gray sheets, which were gradually becoming darker as the water diffused out of her hair. He sat back on his heels and gathered her legs against his chest. With his arms wrapped around her knees, he began to thrust again.

Kate gasped. "So good," she said and pushed against the wall meeting each thrust, and then she screamed.

That sound was more irresistible than any other and he grunted as he came. Vibrations worked through his body for a solid minute. He didn't want to pull out of her; he wanted to stay buried in her heat forever. As if she could read his mind, she wrapped her arms around his neck and her legs around his body, pulling him down for a kiss.

"Don't go yet," she said and then kissed him again.

He could wait a little longer. Finally, he pulled away from her, and when she protested again, he shook his head. "No sense in using condoms if they fall off, right?"

Kate let out a dry laugh. "Right."

While he was in the bathroom cleaning up, Kate said, "I'm sorry my hair got your bed all wet."

James brought a small towel to her and joined her on the bed. "Here, put this on it. It'll dry in no time."

"This is why I wanted to be on top."

James raised an eyebrow. "Is it?"

Kate grinned. "Well, one of them anyway. I've been called bossy before, and it probably applies to the bedroom too."

"I like a woman in control." He kissed her and then scooted her body until it was nestled against his.

Kate rested her head in the crook of his arm. "Thanks for warming me up."

"I'll warm you up any time."

"Sorry we're always here. My RA doesn't go for this sort of thing."

"You're not allowed to have guys in your room?"

"Not for sleepovers." Kate rolled her eyes. "That's what she calls it as if we're twelve."

James cleared his throat. "Have you had many, um, sleep-overs?"

Kate turned her face up to look at him. "No. Have you?"

James shook his head. "No."

"Besides your ex."

Her words hit him hard. He struggled to find his voice. "No one since her."

"How long?" Kate touched his face, smoothing out the crease of hurt on his forehead.

"Three years."

Kate smiled. "No wonder."

He couldn't help but smile too. "No wonder what?"

"You're so insatiable. And I thought I was having a dry spell."

"How long?" James tilted his head as he echoed her question.

"A little over a year."

"Ha. That's nothing."

"So how do you explain the big box of condoms you have in that drawer?" Kate nodded to the nightstand.

"After I saw you at Addiction the second time, I was hoping to get lucky." He squeezed her. "I did. Lots."

He took another deep breath. It was now or never to figure out what their relationship was. "So, are we together?"

"I don't know. Are we? I didn't want to assume," Kate whispered. Her breath tickled his chest.

James almost stopped breathing. "Do you want to see other people?"

"No."

It was the best word he'd ever heard. "I don't either," he offered before she had to ask.

"It's settled then. You're my secret boyfriend." Kate nuzzled into his chest.

It was too good to be true, and yet, there she was, in his arms. The word "secret" was the only part of her statement he didn't like. "I can't wait to get you away from here so we can be together in public. I want to be able to kiss you and hold your hand."

Kate slipped her hand inside of his. "This'll have to do for now. How was your week?"

As James recounted his very full week, Kate listened intently. Relief washed over him again as he explained how Sam had been helping him.

"He's mentoring you and introducing you to powerful people? Sounds like you need to make him cookies or something. That's what I would do. What do professors do for each other?"

James shrugged. "I'm not sure. He's my first friend at Bowman State."

Kate smiled gently. "I didn't know you played racquetball. I just thought your amazing legs were from riding your bike."

James laughed. "I need to practice. I'm playing again on Thursday."

"I could give you a run for your money."

"You play?"

"I took a class last year." Kate gave him a smug smile.

"I was going to ask Jon to practice with me, but I would much rather play with you."

Kate giggled. "I'm sure you would."

"Sunday?"

"Sure. How about eleven?"

"Sounds like a plan."

"Great. I'll reserve a court." Suddenly, she sat up and made her way to his dresser. "Can I borrow a shirt while we eat?"

"Do we have to?"

With a frown, she propped a hand on her hip. "Aren't you hungry?"

James nodded, taking in the sight of her slender wrist leading to her round hip. "Very hungry."

"I'm serious." She stomped her foot, and then her other hand was on her hip.

"I can see that. Pick whatever one you want." His eyes danced as he watched her pull a shirt on. It barely covered her ass. He imagined how much fun it would be to take it off her later.

By the time James pulled a pair of lounge pants on, Kate already had a box of macaroni and cheese opened and a pan of water boiling on the stove.

"You like mac and cheese?" James wrapped his arms around her waist as he came up behind her.

"Everyone likes mac and cheese. You make it sound like I'm some kind of weirdo."

"I didn't mean to offend you. It just seems strange that someone who makes their own bread also enjoys powdered cheese."

Kate shrugged. "Yeah, well, don't tell anyone, but I like packaged ramen too."

James covered his mouth in mock surprise and they both laughed.

Unfortunately, he never got a chance to undress her again, because she had to leave after they ate.

"I have plans with Meg in the morning, and you have grading. Works out well for both of us."

They had discussed enough serious relationship topics for the night and asking her to sleep over seemed like too much to hope for, even though he didn't want her to leave. He couldn't risk screwing things up. Not again.

Chapter Fourteen

Saturday morning, Kate tapped her foot as she waited for Meg to get her shoes on. "Are you ready? We need to be there by ten."

Meg rolled her eyes. "Hold your horses. I'm almost ready."

In no time, they were parked outside Kate's future bakery. Meg looked through the windshield at the paper-covered windows and frowned.

"I know it doesn't look like much but wait until you see inside." Kate stepped out of the car and shook hands with Lisa, who was waiting by the front door. "This is the friend I was telling you about. Meg this is Lisa."

Lisa smiled as she shook Meg's hand. "Good to meet you. Are you ready to go in?"

Kate and Meg both nodded. Warmth filled Kate's heart as she looked around for the second time. As Meg explored the kitchen, Kate opened her notebook and added more specific details about the position of the tables and how many stools there were in front of the bar. The only thing she needed to add was another oven.

"Oh Kate, I think it'll be perfect. Honestly, it's just what I imagined it would be like."

"Me too." Kate grinned at her. "It gets better."

"It does?"

"Lisa, can we see the apartment too?"

"Apartment?" Meg mouthed as Lisa pulled the keys out of her pocket.

Lisa let them go up alone, and once they were upstairs, Meg formed a square with her fingers and thumbs up as if she were framing a picture. "You could get a couch for right there, and that spot looks perfect for a little table. This is in your price range?"

Kate nodded. "The restaurant and apartment combined are less than I calculated for, so getting a loan shouldn't be a problem."

Meg gave her a serious look. "I know how you are when you get your mind set on something. I just hope it goes the way you want it to."

"You make me sound like a spoiled brat." Kate feigned mock hurt.

"No. Not a spoiled brat, just lucky. You always seem to get what you want."

"Luck has nothing to do with it. I work for it. You think I got a scholarship by accident? You think I like working three jobs every summer instead of lounging around the beach? I've been working to save for my future."

Meg put her hands up. "I didn't mean to get you all huffy. I just want to make sure you have realistic expectations."

Kate shook her head. "I know. I'm just anxious. If this doesn't work out, I have to start over."

"You just started looking." Meg stared at her.

"Yeah, but I'm done. I don't want to look anymore. I know this is right. I can see everything so clearly. This is the life I've been working toward."

Meg hugged her. "I'm so happy for you. You say the word and I'll help you move in."

"It's small but nice, isn't it?" Kate sat on the window ledge and looked across the empty room.

"How much space do you need? It's just you."

"Well, I was hoping, maybe, James might want—"

"What? Are you seriously talking about moving in together?" Meg's mouth gaped.

"Maybe? No. I don't know." Kate's shoulders fell.

"Have you talked about that with him?"

Kate shook her head. "No, we just barely discussed whether we're exclusive or not. Which we are," she added quickly. "In fact, he wants to take me away for Thanksgiving weekend."

"Wow."

"Yep, a whole weekend. It'll be just the two of us in Santa Barbara where we can hold hands and kiss in public. It's going to be like a real relationship. So far it's just been lots of secret sex."

"So, things are going well?" Meg grimaced.

"What's that face?"

Meg shrugged. "Realistic expectations. All I'm saying."

They both turned toward the stairs as Lisa ascended. "Well, do you still love it?" A tight smile was plastered on her face, but when Kate nodded, it softened. "Good."

As they left, Lisa told her she would be in touch when she had news from Kate's credit union.

"Thanks for going with me, and thanks for being honest." Kate nudged her friend's shoulder in the car.

"What are friends for, if not to try and crush your hopes and dreams?"

"No crushing, just a little reality check. Thanks to you, I'm calm and collected. Just in time for my meeting with Ms. Watts."

"Thanks for taking me to see it and for dropping me off." Meg got out in front of a coffee shop and leaned through the open passenger window. "Call me and let me know how it goes."

"You know I will."

Kate got to her appointment a few minutes early, just like last time, and waited anxiously outside Ms. Watts's office. Her calm façade was long gone and turned into worry about her plan falling apart again.

"You found something you like?"

Kate nodded. "Yes. I'll need an extra oven, but I have a contact that can help me get a used one. Other than that, it's perfect."

Ms. Watts smiled as she looked around her computer monitor. "Based on your account history and the property you've chosen, we can offer you a thirty-thousand-dollar loan, with a revolving line of credit for twenty thousand. That'll give you a running start."

It was happening. Kate was on her way to becoming a small business owner. Now all she had to do was wait for the contract to be drawn up and have an awkward conversation with the chemistry department chair.

Elation filled her body as she sat in her car outside the credit union. Her hands shook as she dialed Meg. "I got the loan." Her voice squeaked.

"Congrats Kate. Sounds like we need to celebrate. Does Tim know?" Meg was practically screaming into her phone.

"No, I need to tell him."

"Let's go to dinner, and you can break the news to both of us. I'll play along, and that way, Tim won't be the wiser about being left out."

"I can't think straight. Will you make the plans?"

"I'm on it. Be ready at six."

Kate stared at the paperwork in her hands. Her future was about to begin.

"WHAT ARE YOU GOING to name it?" Tim leaned toward Kate.

"Sweet Chemistry. And I thought it would be really cool to put the chemical formula for sucrose on T-shirts, aprons, and stuff to sell in the restaurant."

"Love it." Tim grinned.

Meg tried to disguise the word "nerd" in a cough.

Kate shrugged. "I have to put my chemistry degree to use somehow, right?"

"Don't listen to her, she doesn't know what she's talking about. I think it's perfect. Perfectly you."

Meg nodded. "Tim's right. It's perfect."

"Now I have to wait until all the paperwork is ready before I get the keys. It could take up to two weeks." She would also have to hire a part-time employee, but that could wait. Finding someone she could trust would be the hardest part.

"Don't worry, honey, I'm sure your classes will keep you preoccupied." Tim patted her hand.

"Mm-hmm, *classes*." Meg gave her a knowing smile.

"So, how are things with Mark?" Kate asked, ignoring Meg's comment. Of course, Kate asked about Mark knowing the conversation would be taken as far away from her and James as possible. It worked like a charm.

"UH," KATE SHOUTED AS she served. The sound echoed as the ball whizzed against the wall, bounced off the floor and hit the back.

"What the hell was that?" James stared at the ball still bouncing on the floor.

"Me giving you a run for your money." Kate winked at him. "Ready to try again?"

James narrowed his eyes, squared his shoulders, and held his racquet in front of him. "Ready."

Kate served again and the ball followed the same path, only this time James swung to hit it. His racquet clattered against the wall, filling the enclosed room with the sound of the collision and James swearing.

"You okay?" Kate smiled.

James shook his hand and then repositioned his hold on the handle. "Yes, I'm fine. Serve again."

"Uh." The ball knocked against the front wall and coasted by James. He hit the wall again, but not nearly as hard.

"Again."

"Uh." Kate waited for the sound of the racquet bashing into the wall but was surprised by the ball hitting her in the low back. "Ow." She contorted her arm and rubbed tiny circles over the tender spot.

"I'm so sorry. Are you okay?" he said as he came up behind her and touched her gently.

Kate nodded. "Good job returning it."

"I'm supposed to hit the front wall. Not you." James frowned. "That is a killer serve."

"I know. It's nearly impossible to return, and by the time your opponent figures it out, you're well ahead in points."

"Will you show me?"

Kate pointed to the square on the floor. "Stand there, bend your knees. You'll want to hit it underhand. Aim for that spot on the front wall. Watch." She moved him out of the way and demonstrated the serve in slow motion. "Now you try."

James mimicked her movements and hit the ball so hard it hit the back wall before it could touch the ground.

Kate came up behind him with a new ball and touched his hand holding the racquet. "Loosen your grip on the handle, it should be an extension of your arm. That's what my professor always told us." She stroked his arm and let her fingers glide down his hand and onto the handle. Within seconds, he relaxed and leaned into her. "Try again," she whispered as she put the ball in his left hand. As she took a step away from him, his body wavered.

As James swung his racquet, Kate could tell his serve was perfect. The ball bounced just behind her, and then it hit the back wall. "Excellent. Try again, and this time, I'll return it." Kate got into position with her foot propped against the side wall. "When you're expecting a serve like that, the trick is to lean against the side wall, but have your foot ready to push off in case they surprise you with a different serve. Ready."

James grunted and served perfectly. Kate returned it, sending the ball flying over his head to the front. She pushed away from the wall and stood ready in the center of the court. They volleyed the ball until they were both panting, and then James got in the path of the ball, where it connected squarely with his shoulder.

"Ow. I guess we're even." James smiled.

"Are you okay? Need me to kiss it better?"

James pouted and nodded, pulling his shirt down enough to expose the angry red welt on his shoulder. His eyes darted to the tiny door they had crawled through.

"Don't worry. We have the room reserved for another forty-five minutes. No one ever comes down here anyway since everyone wants the courts with a glass observation wall." Kate inhaled the masculine scent that lingered and kissed the circle of hot skin.

James wrapped his arm around her and tugged at the hem of her shirt. "I should kiss yours too. You know, to be fair." His pretty lips pulled back into a half smile, and then he was on his knees.

Kate's pulse quickened as his mouth moved along her belly and around to her back. He tugged the waistband of her shorts down and trailed kisses on every inch of exposed skin, his hot breath licking the curves of her hips and ass.

He turned her body until his mouth was nestled below her belly button again. "No one comes down here, huh?"

Kate shook her head and gave him a wicked grin. "That's why I reserved this court."

"You are so clever. Perhaps I could kiss a little more."

"I'd like that," she said, leaning against the wall.

He untied the drawstring of her shorts and nipped at the waistband of her panties.

She gasped and held onto his head.

He pushed her shorts and panties down to her ankles and while she stepped out of her clothes, he grazed her clit ever so slightly with his fingers. "Spread your legs."

As soon as she obliged, he buried his face between her legs and pushed his tongue inside her.

A moan echoed off the walls, surrounding them with the sounds of her pleasure.

It only took a few minutes before his talented mouth made her come, her moan intensifying and deafening her. Closing her eyes, she leaned heavily on the wall. Fabric moved and a package ripped open and then he was between her legs again, lifting her off the ground.

His cock nudged against her opening and all she had to do was sink down on him. Her moan filled his mouth as he thrust into her.

James gulped a breath of air and then dove back to her mouth, sucking and licking her lips as he fucked her, his tongue mirroring the movement of his dick.

Each time their bodies came together, Kate sighed. Her body filled with intense energy, and wanting James to come with her, she whispered, "I'm going to come, fuck me harder."

He latched his mouth onto her neck, muffling his groan of pleasure against her skin. His teeth scraped her pulsing flesh as his cock swelled inside her.

Kate screamed again.

"Oh shit. I'm sorry." James was kissing her neck where he had just bitten her.

"What?" Kate was still struggling to breathe.

"I gave you a hickey." His forehead was creased with worry.

Kate laughed. "I haven't had a hickey since high school."

James kissed it again and then put her on the ground. His body shuddered as he walked over to his duffle bag. He pulled a hand towel out and wrapped it around his dick.

"You're very prepared." Kate was still panting.

"Never know when I'm going to get lucky." He wiggled his eyebrows.

"Apparently that happens a lot when you're around me." The fact that their relationship included plenty of sex wasn't something she was about to complain about.

"Sorry again about the hickey." He stroked the side of her neck.

Kate shrugged. "I'm sure I'll be able to hide it." She finally gained control of her legs and got dressed. "Do you want to play a little more?"

James motioned for her to stand in the serving box. "Your serve."

As they were walking out of the gym and back to the dorms, Kate pulled her hood over her head, hiding her neck. The temptation to take his hand was almost too strong to resist, but school rules meant no touching in public. Never mind the fact that she'd just fucked him at the school gym. "When are you leaving for your brother's?"

James checked his phone. "In about an hour. Thanks for spending the morning and afternoon with me, and for everything else." He wiggled his eyebrows.

Kate smiled. "I'm sure your friends are going to be impressed by your serve. You have to promise not to kiss anything better if you hit one of them though, okay?"

James chuckled. "I'm not allowed to kiss my colleagues *or* the pizza guy? Jeez, you're so demanding."

"Remember, I've been called bossy before."

"You take orders pretty well for someone who's in charge."

Kate blushed. "Just because I like to be in control doesn't mean I don't enjoy sharing the power. It's all about give and take."

"Thank you for giving and taking."

"Have fun tonight. See you in class tomorrow."

James frowned. "Yes, tomorrow."

She turned, and went into the dorms, stopping at Meg's room.

"Can I make you dinner?"

Meg looked her up and down. "What have you been doing?"

"Playing racquetball. Well? Do you have plans?"

"If I had plans, I would cancel them. I'd be a fool to pass up that offer." Meg grinned at her.

"Give me twenty minutes and then meet me in the kitchen on the third floor."

After a quick shower and a scarf tied strategically around her neck, Kate gathered her supplies and went to the kitchen, where Meg was waiting.

"I'm really enjoying this situation." Meg scoffed when Kate gave her a blank stare. "You know, the one where you can't spend time with him so you make me dinner instead."

Kate pushed on her shoulder. "Jerk."

Meg smiled and nodded. "I'm not complaining. I was going to have a microwave meal for dinner."

"You still might."

Meg laughed. "Nice hickey, by the way."

Kate grimaced and touched her neck. "Can you see it?"

"Not right now, but when I saw you earlier I could. You think I was asking what you had been doing because you were wearing gym shorts?" Meg laughed. "That scarf is cute. I have a bunch you can borrow if you need them. Hey, have you told your parents yet? About the loan and bakery and all that?"

Kate shook her head.

"Did you tell him?"

She shook her head again. "I can't bring myself to. I guess I'm kind of nervous. Afraid he might judge me, you know?"

"Why would you think that?"

"Because I would be blowing off the job that Dr. Moore got me. Doesn't it make me look kind of flaky?" They'd had plenty of opportunities to discuss future plans, but she'd never had the nerve to tell him.

Meg shrugged. "He should know by now you're not flaky."

"I guess." They'd talked a few times, but how well did he really know her?

"You were just talking about moving in together, but you're not going to tell him about your bakery?"

Kate shook her head. "I haven't talked to him about that, either. I don't know what I'm doing. It's terrifying."

"I've never seen you so unsure before." Meg narrowed her eyes.

"I know what I want. I just don't know what he wants."

Chapter Fifteen

On Wednesday, when James reminded his class about the upcoming test in biochemistry, he was surprised when Angelica didn't ask him to join her study group. The surprise ended a few minutes after when she knocked on his office door.

"Angelica, did you forget something?" Unwilling to invite her in, he stood in the doorway and blocked her.

She batted her eyelashes at him. "I forgot to ask if you would come to my study group again."

James crossed his arms over his chest. "I would be glad to help. Four o'clock?"

"Thanks. You're the best." Angelica touched his arm and didn't pull her hand away.

James opened his mouth to reply, but his thoughts were interrupted by a noise down the hall. It was Lloyd, standing in the doorway to the main office. James cleared his throat. "Okay, Angelica. See you then."

"Thanks, Dr. B." She turned and walked down the hall, swishing her hips as she went.

James shook his head and stared at the papers on his desk. He had been working with Michael a lot lately, but despite their long hours, there was an issue with part of the project, and it took him the better part of the next afternoon to track down the source of the problem.

Thursday morning, Sam knocked on James's door. "Ready to play?"

James rubbed his temples. "Yeah, just give me a second." He made a few notes on Michael's paper.

"Everything okay?" Sam asked as they walked to the gym.

James shook his head. "No, Michael needs to repeat a part of his experiment. The results were a little too murky. He's not going to be happy."

Sam shrugged. "At least we have a break coming up, you could always work on it then."

"I have plans. With my family," he added quickly. "There might be time next week. I'll have to talk to him about it."

When the four men met at the racquetball court, they divided into new teams. Jon and Sam played together while James and Eric paired up. As James got in position to serve, he knew no one would be able to return it. Eric high-fived him between serves. They scored several points before Jon switched positions with Sam and started returning the wicked serve.

After the game, Jon shook hands with everyone again. "Where'd you learn that serve?"

"I have a source." James chuckled.

"Are you friends with Coach Winters? He's a great professor and that's his signature serve."

James frowned. "I haven't met him."

"Did your secret girlfriend teach you?" Sam teased.

James's cheeks burned. Just like that, he was fourteen again, getting teased by his friend for liking a girl. He took a deep breath and reminded himself he was an adult now, and this friend was a good guy.

"Secret girlfriend?" Eric smiled.

Sam piped up, "He won't say anything, no matter how much I pry."

James cleared his throat. "Oh, Eric, I wanted to thank you for putting in a good word for me with Lloyd Moore."

"Don't mention it, James. Lloyd's a tough nut to crack, so I figured it couldn't hurt." Eric patted him on the back. "Since next week is Thanksgiving, are we on for the week after?"

Jon nodded. "You can count on me."

Sam and James both murmured agreement.

"See you in two weeks." Eric slung his bag over his shoulder and he and Jon both left.

Sam tightened the laces on his shoes. "You're a sly guy."

James shrugged.

"I hope you know I'm just giving you a hard time." Sam straightened his back and added, "Although I must admit the more you won't talk about her, the more curious I am."

"Good thing you're not a cat." A smile cracked James's serious face, and then they both laughed.

"ARE YOU COMING TO ANGELICA'S on Saturday?" Kate asked between lecture and lab on Friday. All the other students had left to get their lab supplies set up, but she followed him to his office.

"Yes, are you?" James sat on his desk, resisting every urge to grab her and kiss her.

"Only if you are." She grinned and it made his stomach flip. "Can I see you tonight?"

"Can't. Michael and I need to work on his research project."

Kate pouted. "But it's the weekend."

James shrugged. "He wanted to work on it over Thanksgiving break, and because I already have plans, he suggested we work on it tonight, Monday, and Tuesday."

"Okay, fine. I'll just make dinner for Meg again."

Now it was James who pouted. "What are you bringing tomorrow?"

"What do you want?"

James thought for a second. "Pumpkin cookies."

Kate laughed. "You really like fruity desserts, don't you?"

"Almost as much as I like you." Before he could kiss her, she took a step backward.

"We can't. Rules, remember?" He hated the panic in her voice and the fear in her eyes.

"I know." He touched her neck. "It's almost gone."

"I heal fast." Kate smiled and pulled her lab notebook out of her backpack and turned the doorknob. "Thank you for answering that question, Dr. Baker."

Even though he had worked for years for that title, he hated hearing her say it. By the time he got to the lab, everyone had already started working, including Kate, who didn't so much as acknowledge him. It was driving him crazy to be that close to her without being able to touch her.

Usually, James looked forward to lab, because it meant the beginning of the weekend, but this Friday, it only meant more work. After everyone else went home, James went down to the research lab.

"Hi, Michael. I'm going to be over here grading while you work. Feel free to interrupt if you have questions though, okay?"

Michael nodded. "I wish I had waited to take biochem so I could've taken it from you. I bet you're a really good professor."

James smiled and shifted uncomfortably. "Thanks, Michael."

Over the next three hours, James finished grading and Michael got to a stopping point where he could easily start on Monday. The ride back to his apartment was dark, and he was grateful for the tiny headlight he strapped on the front of his bike. He glanced up at Kate's window. The light was still on. He stopped outside her dorm and called her.

"What are you doing?"

"Writing a paper. Are you done?" Kate yawned.

"I'm outside."

Kate appeared in her window. "I can't see you."

James shined his headlight at her window and covered it with his hand so it would appear to flash. "Now can you see me?"

"Sure can. Well, I can see a flashing light."

"It's been a long week." James sighed and then added, "I miss you."

"I miss you too," she said in a soft voice as she touched the glass.

He started breathing hard and his throat tightened. "Will you come over?"

"It's kind of late."

He had to force the next words out of his mouth. "I meant to stay over."

The longer Kate paused, the more he regretted saying anything. When she finally answered, he could hear her smile. "I'd love to. Give me a minute?"

James sat on the curb in the empty parking lot and propped his bike against his leg while he waited for her. His leg bounced the entire time. When she came through the door, he jumped up. "Hi."

"Hi." Kate smiled at him and adjusted the strap of her backpack.

"Do you want a ride on my handlebars?" James joked.

Kate laughed. "What am I, ten?" She shook her head. "No, I'll just walk next to you."

At the bottom of the steps, Kate looked at his bike. "Is it heavy?"

"No, it's a carbon-fiber road bike. It weighs eighteen pounds."

"The whole bike?" Kate's mouth hung open.

James nodded. "It also cost more than my first car, which is why I keep it in my office."

"I can see why. Can I carry your bag while you haul your bike up three flights of stairs?"

"It's probably heavier than my bike since my laptop is in there." James handed his bag to her. "You sure you don't mind?"

"I'm sure."

Once they were inside his apartment, they stared at each other for a few seconds. "Here's your bag."

"Thanks." He pointed to the table in the living room. "You can put your stuff down."

"Have you eaten?"

James shook his head. As if on cue, his stomach growled.

Kate grinned at him and retrieved a container from her backpack. "I thought that might be your answer."

"What's that?"

"Dinner."

Words wouldn't form in his mouth and he couldn't move to take it from her. Kate pushed past him and went into the kitchen. A minute later the microwave dinged. Kate set a spot at the table for him.

"Come and eat it while it's warm." Kate pointed to the seat, and when he still didn't move, she tugged him by his hand.

"Thank you." His words were quiet and sounded small. He wanted to say so much more, but nothing came out. Instead, he sat and ate. "That was delicious."

"You should've tried it fresh. It doesn't taste the same when it's reheated."

"I'm sure Meg appreciated it."

Kate nodded. "Yes, she did."

Their normally easy conversation was stifled by the tension between them. James's throat started to squeeze tight again. "I didn't mean to make you uncomfortable, I just really wanted to see you. You certainly didn't have to make me dinner or clean up after me."

Kate moved away from the sink and stepped between his legs. "I didn't have to. I wanted to. I was hoping I would see you when you were done, and I'm glad you called. I'm even more grateful for the invitation to spend the night. I wasn't sure—"

"Me either. I, um, don't know what I'm doing," James stammered.

"That makes two of us," she said as she wrapped her arms around his neck.

Because he was still sitting, he was the perfect height to nuzzle into her breasts. Within seconds, her nipples hardened.

Kate sighed. "I promise I have some control over my body. At least I used to. Before I met you. It's pathetic, my nipples get hard if I even think about you."

"I'm in a similar situation, only it's not my nipples that get hard." He glanced down.

"Maybe we should go to your bedroom," she said as she pulled him up and off his chair.

"That's a great idea."

Knowing she wasn't going to leave gave him time to worship her body and give her as many orgasms as he could. When he finally came with her, the sounds of their pleasure erupted out of them, filling the room with bliss that hung heavily in the air like the fragrance of summer flowers at night.

Leaving the bed was the most difficult thing he'd done all night. After visiting the bathroom, he stood over Kate and looked at her peaceful face. With her arms bent and her hands tucked under her head, she looked vulnerable and happy. The sheet moved with each breath and when he joined her in bed, she opened her eyes and smiled.

"Hi," she said in a drowsy voice while her eyes closed slowly.

"Hi." Wiggling under the sheet next to her, he traced the contour of her smooth inner arm, stopping when his fingers fell on a ridge under the skin covering her bicep. "What's this?"

Kate opened one eye and looked at his fingers then closed them again. "It's my implant. Got it last year."

"What kind of implant?"

Kate smiled but didn't open her eyes. "The birth control kind. It was more cost-effective than the pill, so I got it. It lasts for four years. I also got tested. All negative. Just in case you were wondering."

Getting tested for sexually transmitted infections was the first thing he did after he left Tina. "Me too. All clear." Waiting for results had been a painful reminder that she had cheated on him. Even now, years later, it still hurt and he didn't want to think about Tina anymore. Caressing the implant in Kate's arm lightly, he said, "Does it hurt?"

Kate shook her head slowly. "Never seen one before?"

"No, I've never even heard of them."

Kate's eyes opened slightly. "You need to spend more time in the Student Health Services building. Oh, and have a uterus and ovaries."

James laughed. "I'll get right on that." He kissed her and turned the light out. "See you in the morning."

Kate mumbled something and rolled her body, draping an arm and leg over him. She was warm and soft and her deep, even breathing lulled him to sleep almost immediately.

The next time he opened his eyes, the windows were bright. Too bright to be in bed still. For a minute, his disoriented brain thought he was late to class, and then he remembered it was Saturday. Not just any Saturday. Kate had stayed over, but the bed next to him was cold and no one answered when he called out. She was gone, just like last time.

Chapter Sixteen

The sky was just beginning to lighten when Kate woke. As she stretched she nearly punched James in the head because she wasn't used to sleeping with anyone. That changed last night. For a few minutes, she looked at his peaceful face. Without the worry that normally etched his forehead, he looked younger. Almost boyish, which made her wonder what he was like as a kid. Maybe she'd ask his brother on Thanksgiving.

After a quick trip to the bathroom, she got dressed and tiptoed into the kitchen. Staying over gave her an opportunity to do something she hadn't done before, make him breakfast in bed.

The fridge contained a few eggs, a box of pizza, and a door full of condiments. The cupboards didn't have much more. Breakfast in bed would require more ingredients. Ingredients she happened to have at her dorm.

As Kate stood in front of the locked door, she couldn't decide what to do. Should she leave it unlocked while she ran to her dorm or take his keys? He hadn't given her permission to take his keys, but a horrifying image of someone coming into his apartment and hurting him while he was sleeping was enough to encourage her to dig through his pockets until she found them. After writing a quick note and sticking it to the fridge, she pulled the door closed behind her and locked it.

While she gathered supplies, she couldn't decide what to make him. They'd never had breakfast together, so she took everything and hoped he wasn't too picky.

The first thing she noticed when she unlocked the door was James sitting on the edge of the bed, cradling his face in his hands. Disappointed that she'd missed the opportunity to surprise him, she walked into his room.

"Hi." Her words got his attention, but his gaze was unfocused and sad. "Sorry, I was hoping to surprise you." When he didn't respond, her heart started to pound. "Are you mad at me for taking your keys? I'm sorry. I should've asked. But you were sleeping so soundly and I just had this crazy thought someone was going to break in or something while I was gone."

He looked up at her with stormy eyes. "What?" He shook his head as if he was trying to knock her words into place.

"Are you mad because I borrowed your keys?" Kate repeated.

"Why would I be mad about that? I thought you left."

Kate shook her head and touched his scruffy cheek. "Just for a minute. I wanted to make you breakfast, but your fridge is empty. I brought stuff." She opened her bag and showed him the groceries poking out. "Do you like pancakes, French toast, omelets, biscuits and gravy, or—"

"Yes. All of the above." The creases of worry on his face melted into a smile. James closed his hand around her wrist and pulled her between his legs. "Good morning." He buried his face against her chest and gripped her shirt.

She stroked and then kissed the top of his head. "Good morning. What'll you have?"

"I usually eat cereal or instant oatmeal. You don't have to make me anything."

"I don't have to do anything. What'll you have?" she repeated.

"French toast."

"French toast it is," she said, ignoring the rest of his comment and got to work in his kitchen. While she cooked, James made coffee.

"Coffee?" James offered her a mug.

"I'll have a little. Too much and I'll be wired for the rest of the day." Kate took the cup out of his hands. "Thank you for inviting me to stay over. I'm sorry I wasn't here when you woke up."

James came up behind her and wrapped his arms around her waist. "I'm sorry I panicked."

Kate rested her head against his chest and smiled. "Will you set the table? Breakfast is almost ready."

Before pulling away, he stroked her neck.

James closed his eyes while he ate, moaning with each bite. "You've ruined me."

Kate laughed. "I'm glad you like it."

"It's amazing. Is there more?" He looked into the kitchen at the empty pan.

"In the microwave."

"This is a real treat. Can you teach me how to make it?" he asked as he loaded his plate.

Kate grinned. "Gladly."

James stretched out on his bed after breakfast and groaned. "I ate too much." He patted his belly. "I'm sleepy again."

"Five pieces of French toast will do that to you. If you're tired, you should sleep." Maybe this was her cue to leave.

"What are you going to do?"

"Make cookies for study group. I need to go shopping. I don't have any pumpkin." She paused long enough to get the courage to ask her next question. "Can I make them here?"

James nodded. "I'd like that."

"Okay then. I'll go shopping while you rest, and then I'll bake." Happiness flooded her.

"Take my keys so you can let yourself in." James closed his eyes. He obviously trusted her, which made her happier than the invitation alone.

"See you soon."

James was in the same position when Kate returned.

She moved as quietly as possible, unloading the groceries on the counter and jumped when she heard his voice behind her.

"What's that?"

Kate clutched her chest. "I thought you were sleeping. I hope I didn't wake you." When she kissed him, he smiled. "That is a Queensland blue winter squash. It's my favorite variety for making cookies and pies."

"How are you going to make cookies out of that?" James tilted his head as he looked at the squash.

"I roast it, scoop it, blend it, and then I combine it with flour, spices, and other stuff and *voilà*, cookies."

James frowned. "I didn't mean to pick something that was going to be so much work."

"I need to roast a pumpkin for Thanksgiving pies anyway, so this will be perfect. Don't worry about it. Now, I need to break it open." She picked up the squash, opened the front door, lifted it over her head, and threw it on the concrete. When it bounced toward the railing, James jumped.

"The trick is to hit it until it just barely cracks open. Don't look at me like that. Do you have a kitchen saw?" The blank stare on his face was all the answer she needed. "Didn't think so. Now stand back so I don't hit your feet." She heaved the pumpkin onto the concrete, and that time the flesh split open. "Perfect. Now I wash and roast."

An hour later, Kate sat at the table and scooped the cooked pumpkin into a bowl.

"This seems like a lot of work."

"It's worth it. Believe me. Plus, there's enough here for several pies, lots of cookies and pancakes too. I'll freeze it. Do you mind if I store it here? The fridge and freezer in my dorm is kind of tiny." It was the one thing Kate hated about living in the dorm since it limited her ability to cook and bake in bulk. Soon enough, she would have a walk-in freezer.

"I'll have to rearrange the ice cream and gin, but I'm sure it'll fit."

Kate stifled a laugh. He definitely lived like a bachelor. "I like cooking here. Don't get me wrong, the dorm kitchen is nice, and it has four ovens, but there's nothing like having your own space, you know? Plus, there aren't random students popping in to 'help' taste everything."

"You're welcome to make the Thanksgiving pies here, too. If you want."

"I was planning on doing that on Wednesday. I'm sure you'll be busy."

James shrugged. "I may, but that doesn't matter. I have a spare key. You can just let yourself in."

Kate stared at him with her mouth hanging open. "Okay." It was pretty clear how he felt about her and she couldn't be happier.

James looked away and stuffed his hands in his pocket. "Does this mean I can't taste the cookies?"

Kate tried to figure out what he was talking about and then laughed. "You're not some random student. Eat as many cookies as you want. I made them for you. In fact, the first batch should be done right now." Seconds later, the timer beeped.

"They're hot," she warned as James hovered over the cookie sheet.

James broke one open and licked a string of melted chocolate that dripped on his hand. He blew on the pieces for a second and then shoved it in his mouth. "Damn that's good. When you open your hypothetical bakery, you need to make these."

A lump formed in her throat. Another perfect opportunity to tell him, but she couldn't bring herself to do it. It wasn't final yet. When she signed the lease and had a set of keys, then it would be final. "Yeah, okay. Anything else you think should be on the menu?" she asked as if she were playing along.

"Lemon bars."

"Obviously."

"Oh, and apple pie. I love apple pie. And raspberry cupcakes, and pumpkin pie, and I could go on for hours."

Kate laughed. "Want another cookie?"

James nodded and put one in his mouth whole. "Ow," he mumbled. "Still hot."

Kate fixed lunch before James filled up on cookies, and as they were cleaning up the kitchen, she split the remaining cookies into two containers. "One for study group. One for you." She pushed one of the containers into his hands.

"Do you have to go?"

"I think Angelica might notice if we showed up together." Kate rolled her eyes.

"Thanks for staying, and thanks for the cookies." He put the container down and dug in the drawer next to the stove and pulled out a spare key. "Here, take this for Wednesday."

Kate smiled as she took it. Warmth spread through her body as she added it to her key ring. "Thank you. I'll get it back to you."

He stared at the floor again. "No rush. Do you want to shower before you leave?"

Kate nodded. "I'd love to. Would you care to join me?"

"I wouldn't miss it for the world."

They embraced under the warm water, and the only thing that pulled them apart was the knowledge that they needed to leave for study group.

Kate kissed him one more time before she left. "See you soon." She hated to leave. Sure, she would see him in less than an hour, but it wasn't the same as the moments they shared alone, and it might be days before she got to be with him like that again.

She picked Tim up on the way to Angelica's house. James must have gotten there early and had time alone with Angelica since she was holding his arm when they arrived.

"Dr. Baker? Can I ask you a question about the lecture yesterday?" Tim pulled his notebook out of his backpack.

James gave him a grateful smile, pulled his arm out of Angelica's grasp, and sat next to him.

Once study group officially started, Kate leaned toward Tim and whispered, "Did you really not understand what he said about protein extraction techniques?"

Tim shook his head and smiled. "It looked like Dr. Baker needed rescuing. So, I helped him." He elbowed her. "And you too, it would seem."

Kate looked away.

As soon as she and Tim got in her car after study group, she asked, "Is it obvious?"

"Only because I know your past with him. Although, I have a sneaking suspicion that Angelica knows something is going on too because she's turned up the charm." He tossed imaginary hair over his shoulders. "Oh Dr. B, you're so funny." The impersonation was spot on, right down to her giggle.

Kate laughed.

"How often are you seeing each other?"

Kate stared at the road. "Depends on our schedules. You can't say anything, Tim."

"As if I would." Tim folded his arms over his chest.

"Sorry, I don't mean to imply anything, but I have to be careful."

"Is that where you got your hickey?"

"Yes." She pressed her lips together. Apparently, she hadn't done as good a job of covering up as she thought.

"Have you had sex in Hatch Hall?"

Kate scoffed. "No. School is off limits." Tim didn't need to know that she'd technically been at school when she got the hickey. "We have rules."

"None of this?" Tim mimed jerking someone off and Kate slapped his hand.

"Stop it. Speaking of, how's Mark?"

"Don't use him to change the subject."

If that didn't work, maybe something else would. "Do you want to see the outside of my future bakery?"

Tim sat up straight in his seat. "Now that is tempting. Are we close?"

"I've been headed that direction for a few minutes now. I'm surprised you didn't notice."

"I was too busy trying to get you to spill details about Dr. Hottie." Tim elbowed her.

Based on how warm her cheeks were, she was sure she was blushing. "No more talking. We're here." Kate got out and tugged Tim over to one of the paper-covered windows. "I wish you could see it. It's going to be so perfect."

As they talked about the font for the sign, a stout muscular man came up next to them. "Can I help you?" His words were clipped and even, just like his gray hair.

Kate smiled. "Um, I was just showing my friend the restaurant."

"I'd show it to you, but it's under contract."

"Under contract?" Kate's mouth went dry and her heart began to pound. Her dream was trying to slip through her fingers.

"Yeah, my realtor is drawing up a contract to get a bakery in here."

Kate sighed as she got a firm hold on her dream again. "Are you Mr. Crane?"

The man nodded slowly and narrowed his eyes. "And you are?"

"Kate Rhodes, the woman who's going to open a bakery here." Kate held her hand out and smiled as he shook it.

"Philip Crane. A pleasure to meet you. I guess I can show you inside if you and your friend are interested."

Kate looked at Tim, who nodded. "Sorry, where are my manners? Mr. Crane, this is Tim."

The two men shook hands.

"Please call me Philip." He pulled his keys out of his pocket and let them into the building. "If you'll excuse me, I was just coming down to check a water leak next door."

Kate gasped. "At Brandie's place?"

Philip nodded.

Kate shook her head. "Water leaks and books are not a good mix."

"I've been told, which is why I'm here on a Saturday. It shouldn't take me more than a few minutes. I'll be back to check on you."

"Philip?" Kate called as he turned away. "Before you go, can you unlock the apartment too?"

He gave her a smile and unlocked the door leading upstairs.

"Thank you, we won't stay long." Kate pulled Tim in behind her.

Tim gave his stamp of approval and made Kate promise she would take him shopping to pick out plates and flatware. Mr. Crane came back and sat at the bar next to them.

"Philip, how long do you think it'll be? I've never done this before, and I don't know how long it takes to get a contract drawn up and signed." Kate fidgeted with the zipper on her hoodie.

"The holidays are going to push things back a little, but I bet you'll hear something the week after." Philip touched her shoulder gently. "Don't worry. Golden Realty does a good job. Lisa represents several of my properties, and she always takes care of everything."

Kate's shoulders relaxed. "Thanks. I really appreciate everything. It was really great to meet you."

Philip shook her hand, and then Tim's, thanking them both before he drove away.

"I don't know how you can concentrate on school with everything else going on right now," Tim said.

"I'm balancing it all so far. I can't do anything with my bakery yet, so the distraction is welcome."

Tim laughed. "No one else I know considers their final semester of college a distraction."

Chapter Seventeen

Even though James had set aside most of Sunday to write the biochemistry exam, he still couldn't get it finished by the time he should've been leaving for David and Heather's for dinner.

James dialed his brother. "Sorry, but I have to bail on you again. I thought I'd be done by now."

"No big. See you on Thursday. I'm looking forward to meeting Kate."

"Thanks, David. See you then."

The words on his laptop screen blurred as Kate popped into his head for the hundredth time that day.

His heart raced. They were in a relationship; one that made him so happy he questioned whether he deserved it. Why, out of everyone, had Kate picked him?

The night she stayed over changed something between them. For the first time in years, he was content, but he couldn't ignore the guilt that was always present with her. Separating Miss Rhodes from Kate became harder with each passing day and the fear of switching the two at the wrong time created an ever-present worry.

The following weekend would be their first opportunity to act like a real couple. All he had to do was get to know her well enough to make the trip special. He still couldn't believe she'd agreed to go with him.

James shook his head. Biochemistry. It was time to get back to the grind. After it was done, he would have four whole days with Kate. He only had to work a little longer.

Monday morning, Carrie didn't seem to mind being under a time constraint to make copies of the biochemistry exam for him. She already had his intro exam copied and ready to go, since he had left it with her last week. When he got back from class, he handed her the complete multiple-choice forms and picked up the exams for biochem.

"I'll get these done today, and I'll have Kate sort them tomorrow if you can wait that long."

James nodded. "That'll be perfect. Thank you, Carrie." Planning for exams and making time to grade had gotten easier with each passing test.

His biochemistry class faced him with a mixture of confidence and nerves. "You have one hour."

Kate was focused on the test in front of her, looking up occasionally to meet his gaze. It was going to take every ounce of self-control to keep his eyes to himself. The intro exams were the perfect distraction. Work now. Play later.

He made a sizable dent in the intro class pile, and by the time Michael started to clean up that night, he was all but done.

James stayed in his office until he had a tidy stack of graded exams. Grading the biochemistry tests would have to wait until tomorrow. The cool night air cleared his head as he rode home. He stopped outside of the dorms. Kate's light was off. He sighed and finished the trip to his apartment.

The first thing he noticed when he opened his apartment was the smell of something delicious, and then he saw his table was set and there was a note between a fork and knife.

Dinner is in the fridge. XOXO Kate

He scanned the apartment to see if she was still there, but she wasn't. When he opened the fridge, he found a covered plate with a note stuck to it.

I made you spaghetti. The other container is for tomorrow night. XOXO

James stood in front of the fridge for a few seconds staring at the plate of food. His throat tightened. "Why are you so good to me?" he whispered to her note.

JAMES TOOK HIS TIME getting to work Tuesday morning. It was going to be another long day. By the time he got in, Carrie was already buried in a pile of papers.

"Do you have the multiple-choice forms graded?"

Carrie nodded and leaned back in her chair. "Kate? Will you help Dr. Baker collate his intro exams when you're done alphabetizing them?"

"I'm almost done," Kate called out. "I'll be down in a second."

"Thank you," James replied.

Carrie smiled.

James was in the middle of changing out of his riding shirt when someone knocked on his door. He slipped a clean shirt over his head and opened it to Kate's beaming face.

"Here are your exams, Dr. Baker." Kate pushed into his office while he closed the door quietly behind her.

"Thank you for dinner last night," he whispered.

"I don't want you to get the wrong idea or anything. I'm not trying to sway you while you're grading our exams or make you biased in some way, I just thought you might be hungry after such a long day." Kate still held the stack of sorted tests in her hands.

James laughed. "That ship sailed a long time ago but I have no idea what grade you're getting so how could I be biased? And by the way, it was delicious."

Kate smiled. "I'm glad." She cleared her throat. "Okay. I'm here to work. Put me to work."

"Hmm, tempting." He wanted nothing more than to put her to work all over his office. Naked.

Kate scoffed. "Organizing your exams."

"Oh." James let out a heavy sigh. "I guess that'll do."

Kate sat on the floor of his office, just as she had done in the past, and alphabetized the other part of the exams. "I'll do this while you go fix your hair. It's all dented. Oh, and your pants are still wrapped up." She pointed to the elastic strap around his ankles.

James tugged the straps off his pants and rubbed his hands against his head. "There. Is that better?"

Kate peered at his hair. "Not even a little bit."

"I'll do it in a minute. I don't want to leave while you're here."

Kate blushed and got back to work.

James sat at his desk and opened his backpack, carefully hiding the biochemistry exams from Kate when she announced she was done. "How can you be done so quickly?"

She shrugged and leaned over his desk. Because of how she was bending, he could see right down her V-neck shirt. His pants were suddenly very tight.

"I like your shirt."

Kate looked down at her chest and shook her head. "You know the rules."

"What? I said I liked your shirt. I kept the part about wanting to take it off you and fuck you on my desk to myself," he whispered.

The blush spread across her chest. "I'm on the clock."

"What if I hired you?"

She shook her head again. "I'm not for hire. I already have a job. Remember?"

"That's a real shame. I would give you a good bonus."

Kate snorted. "I'm sure you would." She swiped the stapler off his desk and then opened the door and spoke loudly, "Of course I'll take the stapler back to the main office. Glad I could help."

Reminding him of the rules didn't make him want her less. If anything, it made him want her more.

"THANKS FOR WORKING on this with me again, Dr. Baker." Michael handed him the vial containing the newly collected protein concentrate.

"I'm sorry we got as far as we did without having much to show for it."

Michael shrugged. "The good news is, I know what I'm doing now since I've done it before, so it shouldn't take me as long. I just appreciate you taking the time to be here with me."

"It's not a problem. I like it down here. Plus, I got all my grading done. I would've just been holed up in my office or apartment anyway, so it's really not a problem."

"I know it's already late, but would you mind if I got some things prepped for tomorrow so I can work again before the break?"

"I'll help you." James stashed the graded biochemistry exams inside his backpack and started getting supplies out for Michael.

On Wednesday he handed out exams. His intro students were all pleased he had graded them so quickly, except for the ones who had bombed the test, which was easily ten percent of the class. In biochem, he arranged the tests on the front table like last time and turned away to start writing his lesson on the whiteboard. "After today, there are only two more weeks of class. Your lab notebooks are due at the end of your last lab, and your final exam will be in this room on Monday, December tenth. Now, let's get back to enzyme kinetics."

The students groaned but pulled out their notes and gave him their attention.

He spent the afternoon with Michael again, and because he had finished grading, they worked together. They got done earlier than James anticipated, and the sun was just setting on his ride home.

A trace of cinnamon wafted out from James's apartment. When he opened the door, the fragrance of freshly baked pies made him salivate. The counter in his kitchen was covered with mixing bowls, a blender, and ingredients as far as he could see. Kate was working on the table.

"Hi," Kate called out to him as she rolled out a piecrust.

"I could definitely get used to this. My apartment has never smelled so good," he added. The best part about coming home wasn't the smell of pie, it was seeing her waiting there.

Kate grinned. "That's the pumpkin pies. They're almost done."

"They? As in more than one?"

Kate nodded and lifted the piecrust into a pan.

"What are those for?" James pointed to the two pie pans in front of her.

Kate turned the pan in her hands, crimping the crust as it moved. "This one will be pecan, and that one will be apple."

"You're making apple too?" His stomach growled.

"You mentioned you liked apple—"

"When we were making a fake menu, I didn't mean for you to make one for tomorrow."

Kate cleared her throat. "As I was saying, you mentioned you liked apple pie, so I decided to make one too."

"Kate, it's too much work for you."

"If that's how you feel, you can help." She turned to face him and it was the first time he noticed her apron. It was hot pink and with the formula for sucrose on it.

James grinned. "I love your apron. Where did you get it?"

Kate blushed. "I had it made. I'm glad you like it because I have one for you too." She washed her hands and reached into her bag and pulled out a matching black apron.

James smiled as he read it. "$C_{12}H_{22}O_{11}$. It's perfect and almost as sweet as you." Before putting the apron on, he pulled her into a kiss, which was sweeter than usual. When he pulled away, she sighed and smiled. "All right, tell me what I need to do."

"You are going to make the pecan pie filling. I toasted the nuts earlier, so now all you need to do is combine those ingredients," she pointed to them on the counter, "and pour them into this shell."

"Sounds easy enough." He looked into the mixing bowl in front of her and inhaled. "Can I have a piece of apple before I start?"

Kate scrunched up her nose. "It has flour in it, so it'll taste sort of starchy, but if you really want to try it, go right ahead."

"Mm, cinnamon and what is that?"

"Nutmeg, freshly grated." She nodded to the brown lump sitting next to the grater.

"It's delicious. Now I'm ready to work."

Kate gave him directions, which he followed step by step, and as he was filling the pie shell with gooey pecans, he smiled. "This is the first pie I've ever made."

"Congratulations. Now, before we can bake it, I need to check on the pumpkin pies." Kate poked the surface of the pies with a paring knife and then announced they were done. She turned the oven temperature knob up a little. "Okay, put your pie in and set a timer for forty minutes."

"Now what?"

"Now we make a lattice top for the apple pie."

By the time he got the crust cut into strips and put in place, the timer went off. "Seriously? It took me forty minutes to roll out and cut crust?"

Kate smiled. "You're learning. It's bound to take you longer."

"Go on, make fun of me."

She gasped. "I would never." She kissed his cheek and helped him finish making the pie.

When the last pie came out of the oven, Kate took off her apron and put it inside her bag. "I hate to bake and run, but I have a date with the Laundromat I can't miss."

James's shoulders fell. He was hoping she would stay the night again but consoled himself with the thought that she would be spending the next three nights with him.

"What time should I be here tomorrow?"

"I like to be there by noon, so if you get here at ten, that would leave us plenty of time to pack the car and get there. We'll probably run into traffic. They live in Thousand Oaks, so we'll already be part of the way to Santa Barbara."

"I'm so excited, and nervous. What if your brother and his wife don't like me?"

"What's not to like?" James pulled her into a hug.

Kate shrugged. "I don't know. I'm anxious. I know how much he means to you, so if I don't get his approval, I worry about what that means for me."

He squeezed her again. "Stop worrying. Be here at ten."

Kate sighed. "Okay. See you in the morning." She kissed him one last time before she left.

As James packed the next morning, he called David. "Do you need us to pick up anything on the way?"

"It's so weird to hear you say *us*." David cleared his throat. "You're bringing pie still, right?"

James grinned. "Yep, I even helped make them."

David chuckled into the phone. "I can't wait to meet the woman who has persuaded you to cook."

"She gave me an apron. It's really awesome. It has the chemical formula for sucrose on it." James could practically hear his brother rolling his eyes.

"Nerd."

James shrugged. "I've been a nerd my whole life, and I've finally found someone who can appreciate it. She's amazing. You'll see." David was going to like her, that's all there was to it. Kate had nothing to worry about.

"Heather says to bring cream for the pies."

"I'm on it. Anything else?"

The receiver squeaked as David covered it with his hand to ask Heather. "Nope. Just pie and cream. See you soon."

A few minutes later, Kate knocked on his door. She was wearing a dress that hugged her breasts and took his breath away. Her backpack was over her shoulder and was bulging at the seams.

She put it down on the floor and said, "I don't own luggage."

"Me either." James nodded to his backpack, which had clothes spilling out of the top. "How are we supposed to transport the pies?"

Kate pointed to the counter. "I left pie boxes here last night."

James laughed. "I'm so observant."

Kate showed him how to fold the cardboard.

"These look store bought, except for my lattice on the apple pie."

"You have to start somewhere. I'm sure it'll taste delicious. Are you ready?"

James nodded and picked up their backpacks and the two pumpkin pies, but Kate stopped him.

"One of them is for you. I don't think we need four pies tonight."

James only hesitated for a second, and then put the pie back in his fridge. "You're right. Three pies will be plenty for the four of us." Once they got to the door, one of the pies nearly slid out of his hands as he tried to lock the door.

"I'll lock it." Kate pulled her keys out and shook them, balancing a pie in her other hand.

Kate was quiet for most of the time it took them to get to Thousand Oaks, and when he pulled into the parking lot of a grocery store, she frowned at him.

"We need to get a can of whipped cream."

"I can't believe they're open. That's something I haven't gotten used to yet. Back home, nothing would be open on Thanksgiving."

Once they were inside the store, Kate took his hand and entwined her fingers in his. James grinned. "We should come shopping here more often."

Chapter Eighteen

As they sat in the car outside David and Heather's house, Kate smoothed her dress one too many times. James noticed.

"Don't worry. It's going to be great."

She bit her lip. "I hope so."

Kate stifled a gasp when David opened the door. She had seen pictures of him with James, but nothing could've prepared her for how similar they were in person. The only noticeable difference was that David's face was clean-shaven.

David was also holding a baby, which was something she hadn't seen James do. "Please come in. You can put the food down before we are properly introduced." He led them inside where the scents of turkey, stuffing, and mashed potatoes welcomed them.

The front room joined to the dining room, making one large open area, connected by a beautiful arch. Another arch led to the kitchen on the right while a hall led to the bedrooms on the left. The closer they got to the kitchen, the stronger the aromas became.

Once they were in the kitchen, James smiled. "David and Heather, this is Kate, and that little boy my brother is holding is Miles." James grabbed Miles's chubby little arm and nibbled it, making him squeal.

Kate put the pies down and offered her hand. "Nice to meet you both, I've heard so much about you. James didn't tell me how beautiful Miles is." She smiled at him, and Miles smiled back. "Heather, he looks just like you."

"You think? Everyone always tells me he looks like David." Heather smiled.

Kate looked between the three of them. "He has your eyes."

"Yes, but he got my devastating good looks," David added, making them all laugh.

"Heather, can I help you with anything?" Kate looked at the stove, which was covered with pots.

Heather nodded. "Sure, there are a few things to take care of before dinner is ready. Boys, will you set the table?"

James and David turned and left them alone in the kitchen.

Kate looked around her. "I really love your house. It's so warm and inviting."

Heather beamed at her. "Thanks. It's an old house, so we had to do a lot of work when we bought it, but I really love it too. It's nice to have a husband in construction." Heather was staring at her. "I'm so glad you could come. James has been talking about you for months now. It's nice to finally put a face to the name."

"Months?"

"I've known about you since August." Heather's eyes sparkled. "We heard all about James's dark-haired woman."

"Is that what he called me?" He must've been watching her, just like she had been watching him. Heather didn't need to know she had a name for him too.

"Until he learned your name." Heather laughed. "And then when he found out you're his student, it nearly killed him. Not to mention the whole Tim misunderstanding." Heather shook her head. "For the record, I told him to ask you about Tim, and he wouldn't listen to me."

Kate's heart started pounding. James had told them everything. "I wish he had."

Heather gave her a warm smile. "I'm glad you worked it all out. He's been much more pleasant to be around."

"Believe me, that was rough for both of us." Kate sighed and changed the subject. "How long have you lived here?"

"A couple of years. David and I had been living in an apartment for a while before we got married, but I didn't want to raise a baby in an apartment. I wanted him to have a home and a yard to play in." Heather looked out the window over the kitchen sink, overlooking the backyard.

Kate came up next to her. "It's perfect."

"The best part about living here is the business is only a few miles away."

"Baker Construction, right?"

Heather nodded. "Their dad retired last year, and now David runs it, which is great because he makes enough that I get to stay home with Miles."

"That must be nice. My mom stayed home with me until I went to kindergarten, and then she went to work with my dad."

Heather smiled. "Why don't we get the food on the table?"

When they pushed through the swinging door into the dining room with bowls of food, the table still had not been set. Heather put the mashed potatoes down and scowled at David and James who were sitting on the floor playing with Miles.

"I thought I asked you to set the table."

David jumped up. "Sorry babe, I'm on it." He tapped James in the leg with his foot. "Come on, bro."

They moved in a flurry and had the table set before Heather and Kate brought out the next round of food.

David carved the turkey while Heather got Miles in his highchair. Kate sat next to James, across from Heather and David.

Kate filled her mouth and smiled. It had been a while since someone had cooked for her. "Heather, this is all so delicious."

"Thank you, Kate. I had help." She nodded toward her husband.

David grinned. "I opened the bag of green beans."

Kate covered her spoon with gravy and licked it and then nodded. "Definitely the best gravy I've ever had."

Heather blushed. "That's kind of you to say, especially after how much James has raved about your cooking. James, feel free to bring Kate to dinner as often as you want."

James laughed. "I like that idea."

"No wonder Miles is such a good eater." Kate grinned at him just as he smeared a handful of mashed potatoes across his face and into his hair.

David snorted. "Is that what you call it?"

Kate laughed as Heather wiped Miles off.

"So, Kate, have you always lived in California?" David took a bite of turkey and leaned toward her.

"No, only for the last four years. I got a scholarship to Bowman State through the chemistry department, which is why I'm here and not in Wyoming."

"Must've been a big change," Heather added.

Kate laughed. "You could say that. I was shocked the first winter I spent here. Back home, it seems like it's always snowing because the wind blows so much. I had also never seen so many flowers in spring. I love it here."

Heather tilted her head. "You must miss your family."

"The first year was the hardest. Luckily, I have a great friend who shares her family with me."

"Meg?" James asked.

Kate nodded. "Whenever I can't make it home, Meg always offers to take me with her. Her mom and dad are awesome, and I absolutely love her little sister."

"Were you supposed to go there today?" James touched her hand.

Kate's face burned. "She invited me, so I had to explain I had other plans. I hope that's okay. She promised not to say anything." Technically, Tim knew about them too, but she hadn't told him, he had guessed.

"Hey, don't worry. If you trust her, that's good enough for me." James smiled.

Kate exhaled, letting her shoulders relax.

David cleared his throat. "What do you do besides school? Do you have a job or something?"

"I work for the chemistry department part-time during the school year, and during summer break, I work at a couple of restaurants near the beach and then an office cleaning service at night."

"Wow. That doesn't sound like much of a break." Heather gaped at her.

"I know, right? School is a piece of cake compared to that." Kate laughed.

"Is that where you learned to cook?" David asked.

James piped up. "No, she's been cooking since she was six."

Kate squeezed his leg under the table and grinned at him.

It took them an hour to finish eating, and when Kate offered to help clean up, James shooed her from the kitchen. "This is our job."

Kate joined Heather in the front room, where Miles was pulling himself up on the couch in front of his mom. "I swear this kid is going to be walking before I know it. I can't believe he's going to be one next month."

Kate sat on the couch next to Heather and when Miles started inching toward her, she held her hand out to him. Miles gripped her finger and wobbled as he continued to move toward her. He bumped into her knees and moved past her, making his way to the other couch.

Miles didn't release his grip on her finger, and when he moved farther than she could reach, she moved with him. Before too much longer, she was walking back and forth between the two couches, helping steady him.

Heather smiled. "He likes you. You seem like you've done that before. Do you have siblings?"

Kate shook her head. "I used to babysit."

"Do you want kids?"

"Yeah, I do." Her words came out of her mouth before she had a chance to filter herself. It was true. She did want kids. "Someday."

"James would be a good dad."

Kate blushed and looked down at Miles.

"Someday," Heather added.

Miles stopped walking and rubbed his eyes. Kate picked him up and put him on her lap. "He looks like he's ready for a nap."

Heather nodded. "Right on time. I'll be back in a few."

Kate walked around the silent room, looking at the family pictures on the walls. There was a collage of David and Heather's wedding, one of them featuring a younger beardless James. He was smiling, but his eyes were sad.

James came up behind her and wrapped his arms around her. Kate leaned against him. "Why do you look so sad in this picture?"

"I was a little envious of my baby brother."

David came up next to them. "Some of us are better at picking partners than others." David directed his next comment at Kate. "Looks like luck is on his side now though. Except for the whole teacher-student thing."

James tensed.

"Our circumstances are temporary." Kate turned to face James, tilted her face up, and wrapped her arms around his neck. "I think we both got pretty lucky."

James's face softened, and when David left the room to check on Heather, he whispered, "Thank you."

When she kissed him, he relaxed and tightened his hold around her waist.

David cleared his throat. "I don't mean to interrupt, but do you want to play a game or something? Heather just got Miles to sleep."

Kate nodded and they followed David into the dining room, where Heather was setting up a game. Kate grinned. "I love tile rummy."

They finished four games before the conversation turned to pie. Kate pushed away from the table. "I'll get it."

Kate was standing in front of the fridge when James joined her.

"I came to help."

"How am I doing out there?" Even though she thought things were going well, it didn't hurt to ask.

"Amazing. Just like I said."

"Really?"

"Really. David said you were too good for me. I punched him."

Kate laughed and kissed him. "Will you take the plates, forks, and whipped cream to the dining room while I cut the pies?"

He nodded and came back into the kitchen a moment later and picked up the pie she just cut. Kate carried the other two into the dining room where she was greeted with cheers.

They all opted for a slice of each, loaded with a generous pile of whipped cream.

"This is amazing," Heather mumbled around a mouthful of pumpkin pie.

"Kate and I made them. She's going to open a bakery." James winked at her.

Heather smiled. "Just another thing to add to your some-day list, right Kate?"

Both men looked at them and then shrugged.

"Yeah, someday." Kate smiled and took a bite of pie.

"You know how I told you I like apple pie?" James had a bite on his fork, hovering in front of his mouth.

Kate nodded.

"This is the best pie I've ever had."

She beamed at him.

"I second that. Although the pumpkin is my favorite." David stuffed another fork-full in his mouth.

Kate smiled. "I think the pecan pie is the best."

Heather took her last bite and then disappeared down the hall. Miles was happy and rosy-cheeked when they came to the table. "It wasn't a long nap, but at least he's happy." Heather bounced him on her knee as James and David cleaned up the dessert plates.

Miles turned toward Kate and reached his arms out to her. "Is it okay if I hold him?"

Heather laughed. "Please. Be my guest. Sometimes my arms ache from holding him so long."

Once Miles was on her lap, Kate shook her hair over her eyes and played peek-a-boo with him. Miles squealed and giggled every time her face reappeared. At one point, she caught a glimpse of James, leaning in the doorway, watching her. She flashed him a smile and got back to her game with Miles.

Eventually, James and David joined them at the table. James cleared his throat. "I hate to be the one to break up the party, but we should probably go soon. It's getting dark."

Heather got up and loaded a few containers with leftovers. Kate insisted she keep the pies, but Heather put the apple pie with their stack of food. "I don't want James to throw a tantrum."

Kate laughed. "Good idea."

Kate and Heather hugged before they left. "Thank you for the wonderful food and company. It was lovely to meet your family."

Heather smiled. "I'm so glad you came, and now I can see why James is so crazy about you. Don't be a stranger."

Kate hugged David and Miles at the same time. "Thank you again."

James hugged them all too and then whisked Kate to the car.

"Now do you believe me? They like you."

"You think?"

"I know. You have nothing to worry about." James patted her leg.

"Miles is such a cutie. I just love his laugh."

"I've never been able to get him to giggle like that."

Kate shrugged. "Kids like me, what can I say?"

"I like you too."

"Good. How about your brother? What else did he say?"

James laughed quietly. "A lot."

Kate snorted. "Heather had a lot to say as well. I really like her."

"I'm glad." James wound his fingers through hers.

They rode in silence for a while, and eventually, they were driving right next to the ocean. The black water lapped silently at the gray sand as they sped by.

"We're here," James announced as they pulled up in front of a large house overlooking the beach. It was decorated with bright white Christmas lights.

"We're staying on the beach?"

"Almost. The beach is just across the street. Hang on a second. I'll go get our key." He got out of the car, ran to the main office, and was back before Kate could get the trunk open. "We're in number seven." James nodded down the row.

"We have our own bungalow?"

He grinned. "Yes, I thought it would be nice to have a little privacy."

They grabbed their backpacks and the Thanksgiving leftovers and followed the path past the main house to bungalow number seven.

The cool night air surrounded them, and the soft sound of the water lapping filled her ears. She took a deep breath and looked out toward the sea. "I love the ocean."

"Good. We'll go exploring tomorrow." James turned down the walkway between two bungalows, pulled the key out of his pocket, and opened the door.

The main focus of the room was a large bed. A fire crackled in the fireplace in the corner of the room with a soft couch positioned in front of it. A small kitchen was tucked off to the left and a bathroom was across from it. Kate walked over to the sliding glass door and opened it. Just past the empty street, she could see the shadowy ocean. Cool salty air filled the room. She closed the door, put her backpack down, and walked into the little kitchen. A welcome basket of fruit, coffee, tea, and sweet bread waited on the counter. "Good thing there's a fridge here, otherwise, we'd have to eat all these leftovers tonight."

James shook his head. "That would be terrible. Then I'd be forced to eat more apple pie."

Kate laughed and looked around again. "James, it's so beautiful."

He touched her face. "You are beautiful."

"Did you look in the bathroom? There's a jetted tub."

James nodded. "Did you look over there? There's a bed."

Kate ran and dove onto it, landing with a giggle. "Yes, it's really comfortable too."

"I think you would be even more comfortable if you were naked." James pulled the curtain over the windows, and then came back to the edge of the bed. "How do you get that thing off?"

Kate slid off the edge of the bed, pulling the bedding down with her and twirled around until she was facing away from him. "Zipper."

James turned the light off and then slid the zipper down and pushed the material over her shoulders. Her dress dropped on the floor around her feet. He unhooked her bra and then gripped her arms and kissed her neck. His breath tickled her spine as he sank to his knees behind her.

She turned to face him. The glow from the fire illuminated the room. His eyes were dark and heavy.

He leaned over and reached into his backpack to retrieve a condom. Kate put her hand on his shoulder to stop him.

"Don't. I want you. Only you."

James frowned. "But—"

"We're safe. Please?"

James dropped the condom and pushed her onto the bed.

Chapter Nineteen

While James got undressed, Kate wiggled out of her panties. His hands shook as he opened his pants and then he was between her legs, kissing and licking her swollen skin. Something changed when she said she wanted him. Only him. It was like getting to be with her for the first time all over again. But no matter how much he wanted to bury himself inside her, he was determined to get her off first. It didn't take long before she writhed on the bed and filled the room with her moans.

He sat up between her legs, stroking her slit until his hand was shiny, and leaned back on his heels and stroked his cock. "Are you sure?" he whispered.

Kate nodded and licked her lips and watched him manipulate his dick. "I've never been so sure of anything in my life." She scooted her body closer to him until his knuckles rubbed against her sex.

James sighed and his cock jumped when their bodies touched. Kate lifted her hips off the bed, getting even closer to him, forcing the head just inside.

"Fuck." James sighed and then pushed into her all the way. Her slick walls engulfed him, and he struggled not to come. "You feel so good."

Kate nodded and closed her eyes. "So. Good." Her pussy contracted around him, squeezing him as she came.

He pulled out almost all the way, and his body shuddered for a moment, and then he slammed into her quivering flesh. Kate gasped. He reached between their bodies and rubbed her swollen clit and drove into her over and over again, extending her orgasm.

Kate's body went limp, and she was panting.

James stilled his hips. "Are you okay?"

Kate nodded. "More than okay. Do that again."

"What?"

"All of it. Fuck me again. Don't stop." Her words came out between gasps as he started moving again.

James propped her legs up on his chest, held them in place, and complied with her request.

"Oh yes. Right there. Yes. Yes," Kate screamed again, and that time, James couldn't hold back. His cock swelled inside her and his hips jerked when he came.

He moved her legs so he could lie down next to her, and when he shifted his body, Kate moaned again.

"Don't pull out." She threw a leg over his, holding it firmly in place.

James dropped onto the bed next to her, legs entwined.

She laced her fingers through his and smiled. "That was amazing. Why haven't we tried that before?"

"I didn't know we could." James brushed a strand of hair out of her face.

Within minutes, she closed her eyes and her breathing evened out. Still inside her, he let the sound of her breath and the crackling fire lull him to sleep.

IN HIS DREAM, JAMES was surrounded by something warm and soft, and his entire body tingled as pleasure washed over him. When he moved, he knew it was more than a dream and his brain engaged.

Gray, early morning light came in through the window and illuminated Kate riding him and gripping his chest. Even though her body was moving, her eyes were closed. When she moaned as she came, it was a low, sleepy sound.

As she coasted down, her eyes fluttered open and she seemed to be registering the reality of what was happening. Fully awake, she looked down at him. "Is this okay?"

"Don't stop," he said before sucking a nipple into his mouth.

She moaned again and then fucked him hard and fast. "Come with me." Her words went straight to his cock. After another powerful thrust, they came together.

Kate collapsed against his chest. Only when her breathing became less ragged did she sit up again and look at him. "Did I start that or was it you?"

James shrugged. "Either way, you won't hear me protesting."

"That's never happened to me before."

"Me either."

"What a lovely way to wake up."

"Do you want to watch the sunrise?"

Kate nodded and pulled away from him. "I'm all sticky. We need to shower first."

James chuckled. "I'm usually the sticky one."

Kate's legs wobbled as she stood next to the bed. "Small price to pay for orgasms like that."

He tried to help her but found his legs to be just as ineffective as hers, so they held onto each other and bumped into the walls as they made their way to the shower. James was tempted to fill the tub but knew they wouldn't have enough time to get outside before the sun came up if they had a bath.

Wrapped in warm clothes, they grabbed the basket of food and went outside. The cold air made Kate shiver so she pulled her hoodie over her wet hair.

"Hang on, I'm going to go get a couple of beach towels." James jogged down to the main office and grabbed two towels off the top of the stack and then took Kate's hand and ran to the edge of a cliff that looked over a rocky outcrop on the beach. He put the towels down and sat, opening his arms and legs to her. Kate nestled into the space he provided, resting her back against his chest. He tightened his arms around her when she shivered again. A few minutes later, the sun peeked over the hills, illuminating the sky with a myriad of colors. The sun warmed them, and Kate stopped shivering but did not pull away. They ate the fruit and bread in the basket and talked about their plans for the day.

"There are about a dozen wineries around here, and the inn has bikes we can borrow if you want to explore the coast. There are also tide pools all around here." James pulled out his phone and did a quick search. "Low tide will be just before one this afternoon."

"Let's go for a ride, explore a bit, find the best beach for tide pools and have a picnic."

After dropping off the towels and basket at their bungalow, they walked hand in hand back to the main house. "We'd like to borrow two bikes." James handed over his car keys as collateral. "Do you have any suggestions for good tide pools?"

The woman behind the desk pulled out a map of the area. "Bates beach is really close and great, especially this time of year."

"More wildlife?" Kate suggested.

She shook her head. "No, it's too cold for the nudists, so you should have the place to yourself."

Kate laughed and thanked her for her help.

After a few minutes, he and Kate both found bikes that fit them.

"Remember. I haven't ridden a bike in a while, so you have to promise not to dust me." Kate straddled the bike and stared at him.

James smiled. "I promise. I'm not going anywhere without you."

They followed the boulevard for the better part of four hours. As they rode past a bakery, the smell of freshly baked bread was more than either of them could resist.

"Why don't we buy a loaf of bread and then make turkey sandwiches for a picnic on the beach?" Kate got off her bike and rubbed her ass.

James nodded and waited for her while she went into the bakery.

"I had them slice it for us." Kate held up a brown paper sack.

At their bungalow, Kate assembled sandwiches while James put together the rest of the supplies.

"Okay, we're all ready." She handed him a stack of containers.

Bates beach was deserted, except for a family who had come out for low tide. James handed Kate the pile of food while he spread the towels on the sand. She opened the container and handed him a sandwich. Sweet and savory flavors filled his mouth. "What's on this?"

"Turkey, cranberry relish, and gravy. The bread is awesome."

"Almost as good as yours. This sandwich is amazing." He took another bite. "This needs to go on your menu too."

"Oh, am I serving sandwiches at my hypothetical bakery?" Her eyes danced.

"You have to. It could be a bakery café couldn't it?"

"I suppose." Kate looked out at the soft receding waves. "I'm glad you like it. I made you two."

James rubbed his hands together and dug into the container for his second sandwich. Just when he thought he couldn't eat anymore, Kate pulled out two pieces of apple pie.

He groaned. "I didn't know you brought pie. I'm full."

"We could always eat it after we explore the tide pools. Let it warm up in the sun a little."

James nodded and stood, offering a hand to pull her up. Kate kicked her shoes and socks off and rolled up her pants. He followed her lead and when they were finished, she wound her fingers through his. When they approached the tide pools, the family nodded and James started to pull away from her until he remembered where they were. It was going to take some getting used to. He and Kate laughed and held onto each other tighter.

They walked around the perimeter of the pools, balancing carefully on the slippery rocks. The air was filled with the smell of kelp warmed by the sun.

"Oo, an anemone." Kate grinned as she brushed the silky tentacles with a piece of driftwood. Suddenly, her head snapped to the other side of the pool and she was up and running. "Come back here."

"Kate? What are you doing?"

She crouched by a crevice and carefully moved her hands until she was holding a crab barely bigger than a quarter. "Isn't it beautiful?" She pinched it gently by the back of its body. Its claws flailed for a moment, and then it relaxed. "I learned not to get near the claws, even on little guys like him, and if you hold still after you catch them, they calm down." She brought the crab over to James and let him inspect it. "Do you want to hold it?"

James shook his head. "I've been pinched by one before. It's not fun."

Kate bent over and gently put the crab in the same crevice where she found it. She picked up a variety of algae and named them all. "If I had come to UC Santa Barbara, I probably would've been a marine biologist. I love the ocean."

James chuckled. "You mentioned."

By the time they were done exploring, the sun had warmed their towels and the pie. They sat, facing each other, and ate in silence. Everything was perfect. The pie was just as delicious as it was yesterday, and James told Kate again how much he enjoyed it. He loved the way she blushed when he complimented her.

They had the beach to themselves now, and when James pulled Kate into his arms, she snuggled against his body. He sighed and smiled as he stroked her hair.

"Thank you for this weekend."

"I was just thinking that. It's so wonderful to be here with you." James squeezed her tighter against him.

The silence between them filled with the soft sound of crashing waves and seabirds squawking. As the sun started to set, Kate shivered.

"Come on, let's go. I believe a winery is waiting for us."

They packed up their things and went back to their bungalow. He couldn't help but noticed Kate rubbing her ass when she got off her bike. He would have to help massage it later. "Sore?"

She eyed the bike warily. "Yeah, I think I better stick to walking or driving for a while."

"Why don't we walk tonight? I'll take the bikes back." James kissed her before he left to return the bikes. When he came back, Kate was wearing a dress. She looked amazing. "Should I change too?"

"Nope. You look great. I just wanted to change out of my pants since they were crusty with sea water." She smoothed out her dress. "Is it too much?"

"You look perfect," he said and offered his arm.

As they walked, James could feel the heat from her body against his. After a few minutes, they came to a short white brick wall. "This is it."

The tables outside were filled with people chatting and drinking wine. Kate leaned closer to him and whispered, "I've never been to a winery before."

"Don't worry. All you have to do is drink." James winked.

"Welcome to the Smith and Sons Winery. Here is a menu, I'll give you a moment to look it over." The hostess smiled at them and disappeared behind a tall counter.

They decided on a few wines to try, and after the third one, Kate's eyes lit up. "I like this one."

"Would you like a bottle?" The hostess offered, holding up a bottle of Riesling.

Kate sipped again and licked her lips. "Mm. Do you like it, James?"

"Yes, we'll take a bottle. And I'd also like a bottle of this Syrah."

By the time they left, Kate's cheeks were a lovely shade of pink, and she was leaning heavily on him. "Are you hungry?"

Kate shook her head, smiling. "Nope."

Once they were back in the bungalow, he started the fire and opened the bottle of Riesling. He sat on the couch next to her, and as they drank, they talked.

"Do you like your job?"

James smiled. "Most of the time. I really enjoy teaching, and I'm getting better at keeping up with grading."

Kate giggled. "You're a really good teacher."

He put a finger to her lips. On vacation, he didn't want the reminder that he was her professor.

She pried her lips away. "I mean it."

"Well, you're a really good cook."

"I guess we're both good at something."

He sighed and thought about his job. "It's getting a little easier. The first few weeks were rough."

Kate shook her head. "I can't imagine."

"The worst part is, here I am, trying to keep my head above water, and Lloyd is going on about getting on the right track for tenure."

"Without tenure, you have no job security, right?"

"Right. But, come on. Give me a chance to get settled."

Kate frowned and took another drink. "He's right though. You've been working so hard for this position, what's a little more work?"

"Shush, you're not allowed to be a voice of reason."

"No?"

James shook his head. "You're supposed to offer your sympathy."

"No sympathy here. I believe that if you want tenure, you have to work for it."

"Believe me, I want tenure. I want to be one of those professors who's been there so long they don't give a shit anymore."

Kate laughed. "I've been thinking about that. I think you'll always give a shit, but you'll get tenure. It'll take a lot of hard work and a lot of sacrifices, but it'll happen. I can see it in your eyes. You're driven."

James scoffed. "Look who's talking. I've never met anyone so motivated and determined before."

"I guess that's why I feel so comfortable around you. Because we're the same person." Kate finished her glass and filled it again.

"I think that might be the wine talking. I'm cutting you off." James reached for her glass but she smacked his hand away.

"Don't take my wine. It's delicious." She took another sip and closed her eyes.

James got up and went to the kitchen. He filled a plate with leftovers from Thanksgiving and brought it back to her. "Eat something so you don't get sick."

"Mm, turkey." Kate finished her second glass as she ate. Before too much longer, she leaned over, resting her head on his lap.

He brushed her hair out of her face and drew lazy circles on her neck. Her breathing started to even out.

"I'm so glad you got to come with me this weekend."

"Mm." She smiled slightly.

"You are so beautiful."

That time, she didn't say anything and her smile was frozen on her peaceful face.

"I love spending time with you." He lifted her limp hand to his lips and kissed it. "Actually, it's not just spending time with you." He took a deep breath and said the words he'd been longing to say. "I love *you*."

Chapter Twenty

The sun poured through the windows next to the bed, making Kate's eyes ache. She was still wearing the dress she changed into last night. James slept next to her in bed. He was also dressed in the clothes he'd worn yesterday. The longer her eyes were open, the longer she wished they weren't.

Kate stumbled into the bathroom and filled the tub. She opened the medicine cabinet and sighed when she discovered a small bottle of ibuprofen. Once the tub was filled most of the way, she dropped her clothes on the floor and stepped in. With her eyes closed, the throbbing in her head subsided. A while later, the bathroom door opened. She smiled at James and then promptly shut her eyes again.

"Headache?" James sat on the edge of the tub.

"You could say that." She rubbed her temples. "Sorry I fell asleep last night. One moment we were talking, and the next I was waking up in bed."

"What do you remember?" James touched her hands and took over massaging the sides of her face.

"We were talking about your job and tenure, and I don't re-member anything else." Kate shook her head. "Why'd you let me drink so much wine?"

"I didn't let you do anything. I tried to cut you off and you smacked me." He pouted.

Kate grimaced. "Sorry. I don't remember hitting you."

James smiled. "It's okay, it was just a tap."

"Do you want to join me?"

James shifted away from her slightly. "I'd love to, but I need to use the toilet first." His face flushed.

"I'll turn the water on, and you close the curtain. I can also hum if that would make you feel more comfortable."

James chuckled as he closed the curtain. "Thanks, but I think I'll be okay with the curtain closed and the water running."

A minute later, James opened the curtain, turned the water off, and turned on the jets. Kate sat up and scooted forward, making room behind her in the tub. The water swirled around her legs and splashed against her ribs. As James stepped in, the water rose to her breasts.

Once his legs were stretched out, Kate snuggled back against him. "I want one of these." James put his hands back on her temples and began to rub again. "That feels so good. Between you and the painkillers I took, my headache is all but gone."

"Good. Can I take you out for breakfast?"

"That sounds great. Can we go somewhere that serves waffles?"

"I'll take you to my favorite café. They have waffles."

Eventually, Kate's stomach growled, which was, along with her pruney fingers, enough motivation to leave the tub and get dressed.

"I used to come here all the time when I lived here." James held the door for her, escorting her into the café. They sat across from each other at a booth in the corner.

"How long did you live here?"

"Five years."

Kate's mouth hung open. "In all that time, you only went to tide pools a few times?"

James laughed. "I was getting my Ph.D. and teaching labs. I didn't have time to go to the beach." He handed her a menu. "Hey look. Waffles."

After they ordered, Kate turned her attention back to him. "I just don't understand how you could live so close to the ocean but never go."

James shrugged. "I was driven. That's what you said last night. You can't fault me for something you were claiming was a virtue a few hours ago."

"There's nothing wrong with being driven, but you have to stop and smell the roses every now and then. Or in this case, stop and chase crabs." She laughed and scrunched up her nose. "Nope, that doesn't sound as good. No wonder it's not a saying."

"Maybe I should've stopped and smelled the crabs?"

Kate burst out laughing and put her hand in his, giving it a squeeze. "That's even worse. You should quit while you're ahead."

Suddenly their conversation halted as a man walked up to the table. Kate's stomach growled again at the thought of a steaming waffle covered in strawberries and cream, but when she looked at the man's hands, they were empty. She frowned and then looked at James.

"Dr. Baker."

Kate's heart raced and she pulled her hand out of James's. Although she didn't recognize him, he must've been someone from the university, and now they were both finished. Why wasn't James panicking?

The man smiled and shook James's hand.

"Frank, it's so good to see you." James was smiling.

"How long has it been? A year?"

"Yeah, about that." James looked at Kate. "Sorry. Frank this is my, um, this is Kate."

Kate let out the breath she had been holding and willed her heart to stop pounding. She pushed her hand toward him. "Hi."

"Frank and I were teaching assistants together at UC Santa Barbara," James added.

Frank shook her hand and grinned. "Now I see why you didn't look me up when you got into town. You've been busy." He wiggled his eyebrows. "So, are you here for the holidays? Last I heard you got a job at Bowman State."

James nodded. "Yes, we came up for the break."

"Oh? Do you work for the university too?" Frank looked at Kate again.

Kate smiled. "Yes, but not for much longer. I'm going to open a bakery." It was the closest she had come to telling James the truth. She could imagine the excited look on his face after she signed the contract and told him all about it for real.

"She makes the most amazing lemon bars." He grinned at her and then turned his attention to the server who was coming toward them with a platter of food.

Frank glanced over his shoulder. "I'll get out of your hair so you can enjoy breakfast."

"Thanks for stopping to say hi." James smiled.

"It was so good to see you again, and it was really nice to meet you, Kate." Frank shook her hand again.

"It was nice to meet you too, Frank." Kate waved to him as he left.

The server filled the table with plates and left them to eat in peace.

"How's your waffle?"

Kate took a bite. "Heavenly."

"I bet you make good waffles. Perhaps you should add them to your menu."

Kate laughed.

"Right along with French toast." James grinned.

FULL FROM BREAKFAST, Kate lounged on the couch in front of the fire. She was tired again. "Do we have to go anywhere today?"

James sat down next to her and pulled her head into his lap. "We can do whatever you want."

"I vote for staying here all day." She closed her eyes. When she opened them again, the sun had moved. "Did I fall asleep?"

"For about an hour. I didn't want to wake you."

Kate sat up and stretched. "Thanks for that. I feel much better. You're so good to me."

James shrugged. "Are you hungry?"

"Very," she said as she opened his pants. "Oh, you mean for food? Not yet. You?"

"I can wait."

THEY SPENT SUNDAY MORNING on the beach walking hand in hand. "I'm going to miss this."

"Me too." Kate squeezed his hand and wished they never had to leave. "What time do we need to go?"

"Check out is noon, but we don't have to leave Santa Barbara until you're ready."

"I don't want to go back. If we go back, I can't do this." She turned and kissed him. When she pulled away, his eyes were still closed and his lips were pulled into a smile. The blissful look on his face melted her heart. It was at that moment she knew she had fallen in love with him. Her breath caught in her throat.

"Are you okay?" His forehead creased with worry.

"What? Why?" Had she said something out loud?

"You're not breathing. What just happened?"

She looked down at their fingers, which were still intertwined. She loved him. But falling in love wasn't part of her plans. Their relationship was based on having fun and lots of sex. It wasn't supposed to be anywhere near love. Love complicated things. She pushed her feelings down to the pit of her stomach and swallowed hard. With a shrug, she said, "I don't know, just anxious about the rest of the semester I guess."

The wind whipped her hair across her face, sending a shiver down her spine. James caressed her cheek and pulled her snug against his side before they started walking again. "Me too."

After they checked out, they spent the rest of the afternoon on the beach. Every moment was spent with their hands interlocked. They finally left when the sun went down, bringing with it a chilly November evening.

The ocean passed in a blur of black and gray out her window as they drove home. "Do you want me to drop you off at your dorm?"

"No, I'll walk from your apartment." Saying goodbye was going to be difficult enough but having to do it without one last hug would probably kill her. Everything had been so easy in Santa Barbara, but now they were back to the real world, a world where they had to keep their relationship a secret for the next three weeks.

All she had to do was wait. Once they didn't have to keep everything secret, she could tell him the truth about her feelings. Her heart skipped a beat.

"Thank you for this weekend. It was really lovely." Kate kissed him as he leaned in the doorway of his apartment. He invited her in, but she knew it would be too tempting to stay, so she declined. He had work to do.

"Thank you for going with me, and for having dinner with my family. I'm glad you had a good time. I did too." He pulled her into a tight embrace. "Can we have dinner tomorrow night?"

"That would be great. See you tomorrow."

Out of breath from the walk across the street, Kate collapsed onto her bed. She dumped the contents of her backpack onto the blanket and sorted through the clothes until she found her phone. It chimed as it came to life. There were two messages.

"Hi Kate, it's me," Meg's voice sang. "Just wanted to wish you a happy Thanksgiving and let you know Emily says you're a poopy pants for not coming this year. Really what it comes down to is we miss your pie, aaaaand your smiling face. Hope you're having fun. Call me when you get home. Bye."

Kate laughed and moved on to the next message.

"Kate, it's Lisa from Golden Realty. I'm sure you're traveling for the holiday, but I wanted to let you know I have your contract in my office. Give me a call as soon as you can and we'll set up a time when you can come and look it over."

The message went on for another minute giving her detailed directions to the office. She took a deep breath and dialed.

"Lisa? I just got your message. Sorry to call you so late on a Sunday."

"No worries. I've been waiting to hear back from you. Did you have a good weekend?"

"Yes, I did. Thanks for asking. So, the contract is ready?"

"You bet. I have it at the office. When can you come to sign it?"

"Tomorrow, after I get out of class," she said, "I should be able to be there by two o'clock. Will that work for you?"

"I'll be in the office until five, so that'll be perfect. You'll need to bring your deposit."

"Got it. I'll see you tomorrow." She flew down the stairs and leaned on Meg's door and knocked frantically.

"I'm coming." Meg pulled open the door and smiled. "Kate. Quick come in and tell me all about your weekend."

Kate shook her head and took a deep breath. "No. First I'm going to tell you about the bakery. I just talked to Lisa. She has my contract all drawn up. I'm going to sign tomorrow."

Meg hugged her and they both squealed. "Awesome news." After the excitement wore off, she said, "Now tell me about your weekend."

As she recounted the events of the last four days she didn't share everything. Meg heard about the beach, wine tasting, and bike riding, but Kate couldn't bring herself to share the biggest event of all. The fact that she was in love with James would have to stay a secret until she could be with him like that again, out in the open for everyone to see.

Monday morning couldn't come fast enough, and as she went from class to class, Kate's excitement grew. She was finally going to tell James about her bakery. Once she had the keys in her hands, nothing could stop her from sharing her news with him.

Between classes, she made her way to the chemistry office. It was time to make things right with Dr. Moore and let go of some of her guilt. She smiled at Carrie. "Is Dr. Moore in?"

Carrie nodded. "You know he is. Everything okay?"

Kate swallowed hard and nodded. "Everything is great, but I need to talk to him. I'll tell you in a minute." After knocking on the door, she stepped inside the office and closed it behind her.

"Hello, Kate. What can I do for you?" Dr. Moore took his reading glasses off and put them on the desk so he could look at her.

Sitting in the chair opposite him, she sighed. "I wanted to talk to you about the lab job you arranged for me."

"At Analytics Inc. Yes?"

"As much as I appreciate your help, I've decided to go a different route with my degree." Each word was difficult to force out of her lips, but when she was done, she felt better. Finally, she had told someone the truth, even if it wasn't the whole truth.

"You," Dr. Moore tilted his head, "don't want the job?"

"I have something else lined up. Something wonderful. I'm sorry for the short notice. I just found out last night. It's been eating me up." She couldn't look at him.

"There's no need to feel bad. I understand. You are such a bright young woman, I'm sure you will succeed at anything you put your time and energy into."

"You're really not mad?"

"That you've found a job that's wonderful? Heavens, no. I appreciate you letting me know. I'll find another student to fill the position. Don't worry."

Kate relaxed and smiled. "Thank you for being so understanding. There are a lot of students in the majors' room right now if you want to start your search."

Dr. Moore laughed. "An excellent idea. Good luck."

"Thank you again. For everything."

They walked out of the office together, but while Dr. Moore went out, presumably to the majors' room, Kate stayed behind and talked with Carrie.

"I'm not taking the job he lined up for me. I'm going to open a bakery," she whispered. The whole truth.

"Really?" Carrie's eyes went wide.

"Yes, but don't tell anyone." More than the fear of failure, Kate worried about what Dr. Moore would think if he knew she was using her degree to cook. "It's not up and running or anything, I just thought he should know I'm not taking the lab job."

Carrie hugged her and mimed locking her lips. "Your secret is safe with me."

Time seemed to slow down the closer it got to two o'clock, probably because Kate was watching the second hand move during biochemistry. The moment James was done lecturing, Kate flashed him a smile and bolted for the door.

"KATE, COME ON BACK." Lisa shook her hand and then led her back to her office. A tidy pile of papers sat in the center of her glossy desk. "Those are for you."

They sat side by side and went through the contract together. Lisa explained every step and when they were done, they traded a check for the keys.

"Do I need to wait until December first?" Kate held her breath.

"Mr. Crane told me you could move in now since it's only a few days early."

Kate thanked her a dozen times before heading home.

Her cheeks ached from smiling as she dialed James. It went straight to voicemail, so she hung up. She didn't want to share her news in a message. She wanted to surprise him, and she wouldn't have to wait much longer to see him in person. They already planned on dinner, all she had to do was change the venue.

A plan formed in her head, and she got moving so everything would work out. By the time she gathered supplies from her dorm and went shopping, it was four o'clock. Her hands shook as she put the key in the lock. The latch clicked and then Kate was standing inside her new bakery.

She worked for nearly two hours, and when she left everything was in place. The table was set and dinner was in the warming oven.

On her way to James's apartment, he sent her a text.

"We need to talk."

"I'm on my way." She texted back.

Too impatient to walk, she took the stairs two at a time. James waited for her outside his apartment. All the joy inside her died the second she saw his face.

Chapter Twenty-One

Sleep did not come easy Sunday night. After spending three nights with Kate, James couldn't stand his cold, empty bed. If only she had stayed, or better yet if they had never come home. Everything was perfect in Santa Barbara. But his job wasn't there. How was he supposed to work when he couldn't stop thinking of her? The next five months were going to kill him.

That's how long it was going to be before they could be together openly. Time hung over his head like a gray cloud. The only silver lining was the thought that they might be able to go away again. Perhaps they could go over Christmas break.

The brisk ride into work didn't do much to wake him the next morning. The grogginess that came from a terrible night of sleep lingered no matter how many cups of coffee he drank. Maybe if he saw her before class, he would feel better.

James carried his biochemistry notes with him and made his way to the chemistry majors' room, where the tables were filled with students and books. Until that moment, he had only walked by the room, and as he stood in the doorway hoping to see Kate, someone waved, inviting him in.

"Dr. B. Over here."

James peered around the piles of books and found the source of the voice. It was Angelica.

"I've never seen you in here before." She smiled at him and patted the chair next to her. "Are you looking for someone?"

With his notes tucked under his arm, he leaned on the back of the chair and smiled at the other students who were sharing her table. James shook his head. "No, just waiting for the copier and thought I'd have a look around."

"I'm glad you did." She wound her hair around her finger. "Can I ask you a question about my exam?" Before he had a chance to respond, she reached inside her backpack. "I missed five points on this formula, and I was wondering if I could make it up. Somehow." She put her hand on top of his.

He was in the process of pulling his hand away when someone touched his shoulder.

"James, may I have a word?" Lloyd's stare was cold and his lips were set in a firm line.

James held up his notes. "I'm on my way to biochemistry. Can it wait?"

Lloyd narrowed his eyes. "I suppose. I'll expect you after class."

James swallowed hard. His boss still had a way of making him shake in his boots. After Lloyd left, Angelica followed James to the classroom, chatting the whole way about her Thanksgiving break.

As the students filtered in, he smiled at Kate. She gave him a casual wave before talking to Tim. They spoke in hurried and hushed voices and Tim hugged her before James began lecturing. Kate barely took any notes and when he dismissed them, she ran out of the room without a backward glance.

The unpleasant task of going to see Lloyd loomed over his head as he made his way to the main office, but he couldn't put it off much longer since he was anxious to know why Lloyd was so obviously upset.

Lloyd's office was open, and he was sitting behind his desk. When James stepped inside, Lloyd looked up. "Please close the door."

With a hesitant step, James closed the door and sat in the chair opposite him. Lloyd got up and sat on the edge of the desk in front of James, towering over him. He held a binder in his hands.

"Do you know what this is?"

James shrugged. "A binder?"

"It is the university's Faculty Handbook. I believe you have a copy."

"Yes, I got one during my orientation."

Lloyd flipped through the pages, stopping on a page marked with a yellow sticky note. "Are you familiar with article APM zero one five?" Lloyd's words pinned James to his chair.

"Can't say I am."

Whatever Lloyd was talking about, he was dead serious. "Let me educate you. Zero one five is part of the Faculty Code of Conduct. I am especially interested in reading Part Two: Professional Responsibilities, Ethical Principles, and Unacceptable Faculty Conduct."

Fuck. James understood with perfect clarity what this meeting was about. Lloyd knew about Kate, and now he was going to lose his job. All the air left his lungs.

As if on cue, his phone vibrated in his pocket. It was Kate. He silenced it and hoped like hell Lloyd hadn't noticed.

"I'm glad I have your attention." Lloyd took a deep breath and positioned his reading glasses on the end of his nose. "And I quote..."

James listened to Lloyd drone on and on about the pedagogical relationship between faculty and students, and how important it is to keep the students safe from inappropriate relationships. Of course, he had read the handbook before, but the words had never made him nauseated. Until now.

Lloyd took another deep breath and went on. "I think number six on the Types of Unacceptable Conduct list is the most pertinent to your situation..." The words spilled out of his mouth, one after another, forcing James deeper into his seat.

There it was: romantic or sexual relationships. He was finished. Doomed. James gripped the arms of the chair and jumped when Lloyd slapped the binder shut. Lloyd stared at him, obviously waiting for him to do or say something. He needed to buy time and find out exactly what Lloyd knew. Even though he wanted to run, he straightened his back and attempted to keep his voice as even as possible. "What are you trying to say, Lloyd?" His fingertips turned white as he held onto the chair.

"I thought it was pretty clear. I'm accusing you of having an affair with one of your students."

Blood pounded in his ears, deafening him. "Based on what evidence?" James's voice wavered.

"Don't treat me like a fool." Lloyd pounded the heel of his hand on his desk. "I see the way she looks at you and touches you. I know all about the study groups." When he said the last two words, his face scrunched up in disdain.

James frowned. He and Kate had been so careful. "What are you talking about?"

"Angelica." Each syllable of her name was accompanied by Lloyd's fist hitting his desk.

The breath he had been holding left his lungs. "I can assure you I have only had completely professional conduct with Angelica. If you are implying she fosters feelings toward me, I cannot stress enough I have no interest in her and have no intention of reciprocating them, nor have I in the past."

Lloyd narrowed his eyes. "You expect me to believe nothing is going on between you?"

James held his hands up. "Honestly."

Lloyd started pacing next to his desk. "Believe me, I see the attraction. You're young, successful, and handsome. I swear if you're lying to me." He spun to face James again. "I will report you to the Faculty Senate for disciplinary actions so fast it'll make your head spin."

"Lloyd, nothing is going on between Angelica and me."

"Then why were you so nervous? You turned as pale as a ghost when I read from the manual."

"Anyone would be nervous sitting across from you while you read out of the Faculty Handbook." James swallowed hard.

"Consider this a warning. If I find any reason to believe you're breaking the rules of conduct, you can say goodbye to your position here. I'll be watching you."

James nodded. His heart jumped with every word and panic settled deep inside him. He walked back to his office in a daze. His hands were shaking and he couldn't catch his breath.

Everything Lloyd said was true, except the name of the student, and it was only a matter of time before he found out the truth. Something had to be done.

James knew exactly what he needed to do, but he didn't like it. If he avoided Kate for the next five months he could save them both the pain headed their way. Perhaps she would be too busy with her life to notice if he disappeared. He dismissed that idea and faced reality. She deserved honesty. They needed to talk.

He could hear her running up the steps as he stood in the open door.

"What's wrong?" Kate tried to touch his face but he pulled away.

"Lloyd knows. He knows something is going on, he just had the wrong person."

Kate frowned. "Wait. What? The wrong person?"

James sighed and his shoulders fell forward as he leaned against the door jamb. "This afternoon, after biochemistry, he demanded a meeting. He read me the goddamn Faculty Manual section on unacceptable conduct and sexual relationships with students. He knows."

"Oh James. I'm so sorry. Did you get fired?"

"No, because he thought I was having sex with Angelica so I could deny it up and down."

"Angelica's not quiet about her crush on you." Kate wrapped her fingers through his and gave him a hopeful smile. "Then everything is okay. We're safe. We only have a few more weeks."

James tugged out of her grasp. The hurt on her face sliced through his heart. "It's only a matter of time. If not now, it'll be next semester. I'll lose my job. Everything. No one will hire me after he's through with me. We can't—"

"We can wait until after I graduate."

"No, we can't." Putting her life on hold for him was too much to ask.

Kate blinked and stared at him with eerily calm eyes. "So, this is the part where you tell me we're done." She nodded. "I understand. I was stupid to think I could have this."

"No. You're not—"

"Don't. Just don't." She shook her head, squeezing her eyes shut. When she opened them, her lashes were rimmed with tears.

He clenched his jaw and his head was pounding with the effort of holding his emotions in place. He wanted to hold her, to comfort her, but when he reached out to her she backed away, and then she was running again. Her feet hit one stair after another, and the space between was filled with quiet sobs.

Even when he could no longer hear her running, the sobs persisted.

They were coming from him.

THE WINDOWS OF KATE'S car fogged with her breath and her forehead rubbed against the steering wheel with each sob. It was supposed to be a good day. The greatest day. The day she finally got to tell James that her bakery was real. She had spent the better part of the afternoon cooking and setting up a makeshift bed in her new apartment. All for nothing. Her knuckles turned white as she gripped the steering wheel.

After taking a deep ragged breath, Kate started her car and drove back to her bakery. The smell of dinner waiting in the oven did nothing to rouse her appetite. She turned everything off, passed the table set for two, and dragged herself upstairs.

The unlit candles were a painful reminder of the night that could've been, so she shoved them all into a cupboard and sat down. The pile of blankets and pillows on the floor welcomed her exhausted body. Eventually, she ran out of tears and fell asleep.

The alarm on her phone woke her the next morning. Her eyes were swollen and ached when she opened them. She was supposed to work in the office today. Right down the hall from James. A sob choked her. She couldn't run the risk of seeing him.

After taking a few deep breaths, she called Carrie. "Hi, it's Kate."

"Hiya Kate, you don't sound so good. Are you sick?"

"No, not sick, but I can't come into work this week. I'm so sorry." Kate was on the verge of crying again.

"Hey." Carrie soothed her through the phone. "Don't worry about it. Is everything okay at the bakery?" she whispered.

"It's going to be okay, I'm just a little overwhelmed. I have more than I can handle right now. I'm so sorry, Carrie. I don't want to leave you high and dry." Kate sniffed and wiped her nose. It wasn't the bakery at all. It was James, but no one could know he'd broken her heart.

"It's quiet around here. Next week might get a little busy, but I have plenty of time to find help. Really Kate, don't you worry about me. Take care of yourself, okay?"

"Thank you. I'll be okay." If only she could believe the lie.

"Just promise you'll come to see me before graduation, okay?"

Kate could hear the smile in her voice. "I promise."

Her conversation with Carrie solved one of her problems. She still had to deal with facing James in class for the next week and a half. Tim might be willing to help, but he would have to know what happened. Meg would also want to know, so she texted them both and had them meet her at the bakery an hour later.

Meg and Tim came in together, right on time, with smiles plastered to their faces. They were obviously not prepared for the cloud of sadness that surrounded her. Neither of them spoke. They only hugged her and waited for her to tell them what happened.

"James and I broke up last night." Kate took a deep breath and forced herself to move on before she cried again. "Dr. Moore accused him of having an affair with a student and threatened to fire him. What could he do?"

"He could've chosen you." Meg touched her hand.

"He's worked for years for this job, I never wanted to come between him and his goals. The worst part is that he didn't want to wait for me to graduate." A tear ran down her cheek.

"Oh Katie, I'm so sorry." Tim wiped her cheek. "You love him, don't you?"

Kate bit her lip and nodded. "I never told him though. I also never told him about any of this." She swept her hands around the empty dining area of her bakery. "I was going to tell him last night." Tears started streaming down her cheeks again as the pain resurfaced.

"What can we do to help?" Meg and Tim both leaned across the table ready for directions.

"I need to move out of the dorms. I can't stand the thought of being so close to him."

"Done." Meg nodded.

"What about class?" Tim frowned.

"I was hoping you might help me, Tim. If you could take notes, I'll copy them and study on my own."

"I can't take notes for lab. I also can't do those labs by myself."

Kate shrugged. "I'll think of something. Don't worry, Tim, I'm not going to abandon you, even if it means having to see him. There are only two more labs. I think I could probably handle that." The thought of seeing him made her want to puke, but she couldn't leave Tim.

"When are you going to open?" Meg looked at the paper-covered windows.

"The fifteenth."

"That's your graduation day." Tim gaped at her.

"So? My parents aren't able to come, and as long as I can celebrate with you guys, I'll be good. I can't stand the thought of walking. He'll be there. Plus, I could sell pies and stuff for holiday parties." She sighed. "I still need to post a help wanted ad."

"I could always work for you over the break if you want," Meg offered.

"Thanks, Meg. That would be so great. I was worried about being able to find someone on such short notice."

Tim looked at the table. "I'm going home the day after you open, so I won't be able to help."

"Hey, I wasn't expecting any help, don't worry about it." She pointed her finger at him. "You did promise to go shopping with me for restaurant supplies though. Are you still up for it? I also need to find another oven."

He clapped his hands together and nodded. "Yes."

"You'll need furniture for your apartment too."

"Starting with a bed. I slept on the floor last night, and it was horrible." The floor wasn't as horrible as the emptiness.

"I can do it now." Meg smiled.

Tim checked his watch. "I have class at eleven, but I'll come back right after so we can get started." He stood and pulled Kate into a hug. "I'll be back."

Meg got up too. "While we wait for him, we can get some of your stuff out of the dorms. Do you have any boxes?"

Kate shook her head and then an idea popped in. "Brandie might though. She runs the bookstore next door."

"Well then, let's ask Brandie."

After a few quick introductions, Brandie handed over several boxes and Meg and Kate drove separately to their dorms.

"I think we should leave the bedding intact just in case you can't get a mattress delivered for a few days. You should also leave a few outfits here." Meg flipped through Kate's closet.

Kate came up next to her and tossed clothing onto the bed. "There. Now we can pack the rest."

Meg filled her arms and lifted, pulling half the contents out of the closet at once. "No sense in taking them off their hangers and folding them, right?" She draped them inside a large box.

They packed one box after another, collecting almost everything from the small room. It took three trips to their cars and then they were on their way back to the bakery.

"These stairs are killing me." Meg leaned against the wall and took a deep breath. "Please tell me you're going to pay for delivery service for furniture."

"I'm going to have to. My car isn't big enough for a bed or a couch."

"Good." She smiled and finished the trek up the stairs.

Tim arrived while Meg and Kate were just finishing unpacking.

"Is this all your stuff?" Tim looked around at the handful of boxes on the counters and floors.

"I don't own much. This is mostly clothes and books. The cooking supplies are down in the kitchen already."

"I suggest we go shop for furniture and then hit the restaurant supply store." Tim motioned for the door and ushered his friends downstairs. "But before we do anything, we're going to lunch. I'm driving, so just point me in the right direction."

The day passed quickly, and by the time the sun went down, Tim's trunk was heavy with boxes of flatware, plates, bowls, serving trays, a few pots and pans, and sheets for her new bed.

Kate sat in the passenger seat, looking at the receipts in her hands. "I can't believe I spent thousands of dollars in less than five hours."

Meg gave her shoulder a reassuring pat. "Yeah, but your apartment will be furnished and you'll be able to serve food at your bakery. I still can't believe they're going to deliver your furniture tomorrow night."

"Thank you for going out with me. Let me make you dinner." Being alone meant thinking of James and she couldn't do that to herself.

Tim grinned. "I can't say no to that. We'll unpack while you cook."

Later that night, as she unlocked her dorm room to go to sleep, James's key caught her eye. Her life was about to start, but all she wanted to do was go back in time. Moving out was supposed to be a joyous occasion. It was the last night she would spend in an overpriced building full of noisy students and communal showers. But as she squinted across the road toward James's dark apartment, sorrow tugged at her. Two days ago, when she thought of her future, he was a part of it. Now, she was on her own.

She sat on the edge of her bed and cried.

Chapter Twenty-Two

Tuesday afternoon, James took a pile of papers to Carrie's office. "Is Miss Rhodes coming in today?" It was a risky move, but he had to know.

Carrie frowned. "No. I'm afraid she won't. She called me this morning and explained she had a, uh, personal crisis. With only two weeks left, I told her not to worry about coming in. I sure will miss her though, she was the most competent assistant I ever had."

"Oh." He clutched the papers to his chest.

"I can help if you need." She nodded to the papers.

James shook his head. "No, you'll be busy enough without her. I can take care of these on my own."

Worry still creased her forehead. "Well, all right, but if you change your mind, you give me a holler."

He paced the floor in his office. He wanted to puke. Kate was having a personal crisis, and he had caused it.

Her text was still on his phone.

I'm on my way.

Sobs racked his chest as he thought of everything he had lost.

On Wednesday, as James waited for everyone to get to class, the heaviness in his heart took a firm hold as he realized Kate wasn't coming. It was obvious by the way Tim looked at him that he knew everything, which meant Tim could've reported him if he was planning to. At this point, James had nothing to lose by asking him, so after class, he pulled him aside.

"Where's Kate?"

"She's asked me to take notes for her for the last five classes." Tim narrowed his eyes. "And you damn well better not give her an Unofficial Withdrawal. She's completed far more than sixty percent of this class."

James exhaled. "Attendance isn't required for class, but it is for lab. Will you please tell her I'll have a sub for the last two labs?"

"Yes. I'll tell her." Tim gave him a long look before he left.

KATE CLEANED THE SHINY counter for the tenth time as she waited for Tim to deliver biochemistry notes. It was the first class she missed all semester.

"He's going to have a sub in lab," Tim blurted out.

"What?" Kate's mouth hung open

"I know. It shocked me too. He said you couldn't miss, so he said he'd have a sub for the last two labs."

Kate blinked the tears out of her eyes. "Okay then, I guess that solves that problem. How was class?"

"Okay. He asked about you."

Kate squeezed her eyes shut, her voice cracked when she spoke. "Thanks for taking notes and bringing them to me. I made cookies."

"You don't have to make me cookies every time I help you."

"Yes, I do. It's the only way I can thank you. Plus, I need another favor." She turned and looked up at the walls. "Would you help me decorate the walls tomorrow? The white is so stark, and I'd love to add a little personality to it. I want to draw the chemical structures of sucrose, fructose, and other food-related molecules."

"You can count on me."

Kate copied Tim's notes meticulously before he left, and while she was reading her biochemistry book and going over everything, the delivery truck from the furniture store pulled up outside.

A burly man wearing a black back brace came in, holding a clipboard. "Are you Kate Rhodes?"

Kate nodded.

"We have your delivery. Can you show me where it's going before I have the guys move it in?"

Kate led him upstairs and explained where she wanted each piece of furniture. An hour later, her apartment had a couch, kitchen table, chairs, a dresser, and a queen-size bed. The bed took up most of the small bedroom, but it was worth it. It was definitely a step up from the twin in her dorm.

Before the delivery truck driver left, Kate loaded a to-go box with cookies as a thank you for working so hard. The three men were happy to take them, and after taking a bite, they all agreed they would be stopping by once the bakery opened.

The new sheets were still warm and fluffy from the Laundromat when she tugged them over her new mattress. She smiled for the first time in days. It was a fresh start, and despite how much her heart still hurt, holding onto the pain would only slow her down. She didn't have time to grieve anymore. She had a bakery to open.

AFTER THEIR GAME OF racquetball, James and Sam worked side-by-side in the research lab. "Sam, can I ask a favor?"

"Shoot."

"Would you be willing to sub for my biochem lab for the next two Fridays? Lab runs from two to five in the afternoon."

"What have you got going on that you can't make it?"

"I fucked up, Sam."

"Do you want to talk about it?"

"How much do you know?" James rubbed his temples.

"Bits and pieces. It doesn't take a genius to figure out your mystery girlfriend is mysterious for a reason. I started figuring it out a couple of weeks ago when you showed up with a new serve that only Coach Winters knows. She's a student, isn't she?"

"She's not my girlfriend anymore," he whispered into his hands as he buried his face in his palms.

"Hey." His voice was as soft as his touch. "I personally think the handbook is outdated. Consensual relationships are just that. Consensual. I know you well enough to know you understand the importance of your position here and know you would always place your students and your job ahead of your personal interests."

"Thanks, you're a lot more compassionate than Lloyd. So, can you do it?"

Sam held out his hand. "Give me the manual so I know what I'm getting myself into." He looked it over and nodded. "I can do this. No worries. You want me to collect their notebooks after the last lab?"

"Yes."

"Can I ask a question?"

James nodded and held his breath.

"If she means this much to you, can't you just wait until she graduates?"

James squeezed his eyes shut. "I've already asked too much, I couldn't ask her to put her life on hold for the next five months."

"May isn't as far away as you think."

VANILLIN, CAFFEINE, albumin, oleic acid, sodium bicarbonate, sodium chloride, theobromine, gluten, and citric acid joined the sucrose and fructose structures on the walls of Kate's bakery. Each one featured the chemical formula under it.

"Thanks again, Tim."

"No problem."

"I talked to the sign company today. They're going to have my sign ready by next week. Do you want to see what it'll look like?" Kate opened her notebook and showed him her sketch. "They're going to put a sucrose structure on either side of the words Sweet Chemistry. Oh, and my extra oven is going to be installed in a couple of days."

"It's going to look awesome. You need to put a sign in the window saying what you're going to serve and when you'll open. You know, to stir up some excitement."

Kate made notes in her notebook. "Good idea. Look, I got an open sign and a bell for the front door today."

"You're on your way, Katie." Tim hugged her.

Between classes on Friday, Kate made a stop at the dorms. As she did a final sweep of the room and stripped the bed, she found James's shirt tucked under her pillow. Instead of stopping to grieve, yet again, she balled it up with her bedding and shoved it into her laundry bag. She would have to deal with it at some point, but not right then.

That afternoon, she waited until the very last minute to slip into lab. She gave a quick explanation of her absence to her classmates. It wasn't the full truth, but she couldn't risk James finding out about her bakery.

True to his word James had a substitute in lab. It was Dr. Bellevue. Kate knew him from a class she had taken last year, and also from the stories James had told her. Perhaps he knew about her too, but she didn't interact with him enough to find out.

"WELL, HOW DID IT GO?" James shifted on his feet.

"Fine. I saw quite a few of my old students."

"I hope they didn't give you a hard time."

"Well, Angelica did, but only because she wanted to see you. Was she the one who—?"

James frowned. "No. Not even a little bit. She has a crush on me." He cringed.

"I'd be careful with that one." Sam let out a slow whistle. "Are you doing all right?"

"I guess." James shrugged. "I miss her, but I can't talk to her."

"That's rough. I don't know where I'd be without Terri."

"It feels like part of me is missing without her."

"That sounds like love."

"Maybe." James looked away.

Saturday, James went to his balcony. He had been using the binoculars Kate had given him to try and see her, but it was always too dark to see anything. But during the middle of the day, enough light spilled in her room for him to see clearly that it was empty.

"SHE'S GONE." JAMES rested head rest against the table at his brother's house Sunday night.

"What do you mean she's gone? Gone where?" David asked.

"She moved, I guess. Her room is empty."

Heather frowned. "How do you know her room is empty if you haven't talked to her in nearly a week?"

James and David looked at each other. "Long story." James sighed. "She hasn't been coming to class or work either."

"Did she drop out?"

James shook his head. "No. Tim's been taking notes for her, and I asked Sam to teach lab so she would come. She did, but I didn't get to see her."

Heather put her hand on top of his. "You can't blame her, can you?"

"Kate was the best thing that ever happened to me. I want to be with her, but I can't right now. I really want to talk to her to make sure she's okay."

Heather shook her head. "You need to give her time."

Time had been the problem from the beginning, always reminding him that he couldn't have her until May. The moment they were free to see each other couldn't come soon enough, but what if she didn't want him after everything? He had no way to know.

ANGELICA VISITED JAMES'S office after class on Monday. "Dr. B, can you come to our last study group?"

"Not if it's at your house. I don't think it's a good idea to associate with students outside of the university setting."

"What if we had it in the majors' room? Would that be okay? It just wouldn't be the same without you." Angelica reached out to touch him.

"Sure." James dodged away from her and crossed his arms over his chest. "If you set up a study group in the majors' room, I'll be there." He looked down the hall and noticed Lloyd was eavesdropping. After Angelica left, Lloyd gave James a satisfied nod.

On his way into his office the next morning, he heard Carrie talking to someone. It was another woman's voice. James stopped dead in his tracks, leaned his bike against the wall, and hurried in. The metal studs on the bottom of his shoes clacked against the floor.

"Hi Dr. Baker, have you met Christine? She's my new Kate." Carrie pointed to the woman perched on the edge of the seat in the back room.

His shoulders fell as he forced a smile. "No, I haven't. Nice to meet you, Christine."

James paced his office. Calling Kate would only make things worse. Time. She needed time. If he talked to her, he would hurt her again. The memory of her face, contorted with sadness, was enough to bring him to tears. He couldn't do that to her.

Sam and James talked again as they walked back from their last racquetball game of the semester. "You still need me to cover for you on Friday?"

James nodded and thanked him for his help.

Kate didn't show up to class on Friday, but just like last week, she came to lab, did her work, and handed in her lab notebook, which was the only physical connection James had to her. Her voice echoed through his head as he read her words. No matter how much he searched for something meaningful, some sort of hidden message, the only things he found were procedures and results from lab.

The university was not a typical destination for James on a weekend, but he went to work anyway. Almost the entire biochemistry class was waiting for him in the majors' room. Kate was the only one absent.

"DID YOU GET TO SEE her this week?" Heather asked before they sat down for dinner Sunday night.

James shook his head. "No. But she has to come on Monday for the final, so maybe I'll get a chance to talk to her then. I just don't know what I'm going to do if she won't talk to me."

David cleared his throat. "Hey I hate to interrupt, but I talked to Mom today. They're coming for dinner on Christmas Eve."

James sighed. "Great. Just what I need." His mom would've loved Kate.

Heather tickled Miles's foot, making him giggle. "Don't worry, Miles is a perfect Grandma and Grandpa attention grabber. They won't even notice you're here."

BY THE TIME KATE WALKED in to take her biochemistry final Monday afternoon, she had studied more than ever before. She kept her eyes on the desk in front of her while James addressed the class, letting them know their grades would be posted online by Friday.

Kate made the mistake of looking into his eyes when she handed in her exam.

His face was drawn and he mouthed the words, "I'm sorry."

Even though she managed to hold it together for the last two hours, tears welled in her eyes. She dropped her test and ran. The only comfort she could rely on was she wouldn't have to see him anymore and be reminded of what she'd lost.

After her last final on Thursday, she snuck into the main office to visit Carrie. "I'm so sorry to disappear on you. I hope you were all right."

Carrie hugged her. "I told you not to worry about me. I found a sophomore who was able to start right away, and she'll be coming back next semester."

Kate reached into her backpack and pulled out a container of cookies. "These are for you. You can share if you want, but I made them for you. I'm opening on Saturday, so you should stop by some time if you can." She scribbled the address of the bakery on a sticky note.

"I will for sure." Carrie frowned. "Wait. Saturday is graduation."

"I'm not going to walk. My parents can't make it and I would rather get to work. Can you take me off the list? No need to read my name if I'm not going to be there." Winter graduation was tiny compared to spring. Maybe she would walk in May when her family could be there.

"I'll take care of it."

"Thanks for being so good to me. I am very thankful to have worked with you."

"I'm going to miss you, Kate."

"I'm going to miss you too." Kate hugged her.

"Don't be a stranger."

AT ONE POINT WHILE he was grading, James took a break and visited Carrie in her office.

"You look tired. Would you like a cookie?" Carrie raised her eyebrows and smiled. "You should say yes, they're really good."

James nodded and then took a bite. It was divine. "Did you make them?"

Carrie let out a short laugh. "No. I don't bake. Kate brought them to me. You're lucky I'm sharing with you."

The piece of cookie he had just swallowed got stuck in his throat and his eyes filled with tears and he choked.

"Are you okay?"

James swallowed hard and cleared his throat. "Yeah, it just went down wrong. Thanks for sharing with me. I should get back to work."

"Oh, I'm supposed to remind you," Carrie called out. "Winter graduation commencement is on Saturday, and Lloyd wants as many faculty members as possible there."

James nodded. "Let him know I'll be there." He was willing to do whatever it took to get on Lloyd's good side, even if meant sitting through a two-hour graduation wearing a ridiculously heavy black gown covered in patches of blue and gold velvet.

FRIDAY NIGHT, WHEN Meg, Tim, and Kate were celebrating their grades, everything in the bakery was ready and waiting to open.

"I can't believe I'm going to open a bakery in the morning. Thanks for all your work getting the place ready. I couldn't have done it without you."

"I'm really proud of you Katie." Tim hugged her.

"That's what friends are for," Meg added.

Kate had a hard time sleeping that night. She must've checked her clock a dozen times, and when it finally read four, she couldn't wait anymore.

Although Meg wasn't an early riser, she showed up at seven, just like she promised.

Kate handed her an apron that matched hers. "This is yours. I love you, Meg. I hope you know that."

"I know. I know." Meg grinned at her. "Can I have a muffin? They smell so good."

The muffins had just come out of the oven and the aroma of lemon filled the room. When Meg started the espresso machine, the bitter fragrance of coffee brewing joined in. "It smells like a restaurant in here," Meg said with a mouthful of muffin.

"Then I guess it's time to open the doors." Kate flipped the sign on the door.

She held her breath and went over her what-if list of possible failures. The list had been building for some time. In the beginning, it was two questions: what if she didn't get the contract and, what if she didn't get the loan? But now she focused on the real question: what if no one came? What if she had wasted all her time and money for nothing?

The steady stream of customers did wonders to assuage her fears. People came. They bought things. They smiled and promised to come back. Kate's business was a success.

Completely exhausted at the end of the day, Meg and Kate sat side-by-side on stools in front of the bar. Kate counted money from the till. She sold almost everything she made that day.

"Same time tomorrow?" Meg yawned.

"Yep, seven o'clock."

"Congrats on your first day."

Kate locked the door behind her and wiped down the counters one more time before heading up to her apartment. She dialed her mom and dad. They talked about work and the holidays and her parents made a plan to visit after the business slowed down. Knowing they were coming for a visit after the New Year gave her something to look forward to. At least they didn't know about James. Pretending he didn't exist would be a welcome distraction. If she could just get through the next couple of weeks without thinking about him every waking moment.

Chapter Twenty-Three

Christmas Eve approached quickly, and after making dozens of pies and platters of cookies, Kate closed the doors and prepared for her trip with Meg.

Meg invited her to come home with her, just like every year, and together, they made the drive to Meg's parents' house in San Diego.

Although Meg's family welcomed her and surrounded her with love, it wasn't the same as what could've been. Somewhere along the way, she'd planned to spend the holidays with James, and the disappointment of crushed dreams caught up with her.

Alone in Meg's old room, Kate buried her face in a pillow and cried.

A quiet knock drew Kate's attention to where Meg was standing. "My mom's getting ready to serve the pie we brought if you want to join us."

Kate wiped her cheeks and sniffed. "Okay, I'll be down in a bit."

Instead of turning to leave, Meg came and sat next to her on the edge of her bed. "Are you okay?"

"I miss him." A sob shook her body. "I'm sorry. It's Christmas Eve, and we're supposed to be spending time with your family. I don't understand how I can still feel so miserable, it's been weeks."

"You haven't had time to grieve. It's okay, Kate. You're entitled to be sad. Your life has been incredibly full, and this is the first real day off you've had."

Tears streamed down Kate's cheeks. "I had it all planned out. James and I were supposed to have a life together," she said and buried her face in the pillow again.

"Hey, I know things didn't turn out the way you wanted, but your life is really great. He's missing out and I bet you anything he knows it."

Kate laughed through her tears. "Thanks for trying to make me feel better."

Meg shrugged. "I'm a good friend. What can I say?" She rubbed Kate's back. "What do you say? Are you ready for pie? Because we should probably hurry before Emily eats it all."

"Yeah, let's go get some pie." Kate hugged her friend. "I'm going home in the morning. I think I've had enough time off, especially since all I'm doing is thinking of him."

"I'd like to stay a few more days if you think you'll be okay in the bakery alone."

"I'll be fine. My new helper starts in a couple of days. You should stay, but I need to get back to work since it seems to be the only thing keeping me sane. Enjoy your family, and what's left of your vacation. Thank you for getting me through the holidays. You're a great friend."

"You would do the same for me."

Kate narrowed her eyes. "I'm not sure I'll be able to help in a law firm, but when you start yours, I'll be there with muffins."

"Deal." Meg offered her hand. "I'll be sure to remind you of that in ten or fifteen years."

Kate left early the next morning. As soon as she unlocked the doors of her bakery, she realized why she was so relieved to be there. It was the only place that was just hers. It was incredibly peaceful. She had worked hard and gotten exactly what she wanted and there were no other variables contributing to the outcome. Relationships were different; they were dangerous. And while opening a bakery seemed like a risky move, it wasn't anything like the risks she took with James. She had unknowingly given him her heart and she wasn't sure if she would ever get it back.

BEFORE CHRISTMAS, JAMES spent a lot of time in his office preparing for the next semester. His teaching load would be more demanding, and he didn't want to get caught unprepared.

During the break, Lloyd came into his office. "I want to apologize for overreacting about Angelica. The last thing I want is for a faculty member in my department to be tarnished by something as sordid as an affair with a student. A disciplinary action goes on my record too, as something that happened on my watch, and the dean is less forgiving than I am."

James grimaced. "I'm sorry too. I should've known spending time with students outside of school isn't a good idea. I've learned my lesson."

Lloyd gave him a brisk nod. "I want you to succeed here. I'm glad we got that all straightened out. I hope you have a good break."

"Thanks, Lloyd, you too."

Christmas Eve was going to be just like every other year. James was alone, that was nothing new. Dinner with his brother and his family was supposed to be the silver lining, but as he sat outside David and Heather's house, his heart raced. Kate was supposed to be there with him. How was he going to face his parents alone?

In the kitchen, James handed Heather a pan of lemon bars. "For dessert."

"When did you learn how to cook?" His mom narrowed her eyes.

"Good to see you too, Mom." James hugged her.

"You didn't answer me." She put her hand on her hip.

"It's actually not that hard. A, um, friend of mine gave me a few lessons."

"Did you bring your *friend* to dinner?" She looked past him and frowned when she realized no one was following him.

"Carol, can you put Miles in his highchair? Dinner's ready." Heather winked at James.

David and their dad talked about business during dinner, and more than once, David had to remind him he was running the business now. James kept his mouth shut until his dad turned his attention to him.

"So, what about you? How's teaching?" His dad asked with mock excitement.

The night was almost over. All he had to do was ignore the snide comments for another few hours. It wasn't worth the fight. "Great, thanks for asking. I really like Bowman State. It's a great community. One of my colleagues introduced me to the provost. We play racquetball together."

"Is that supposed to impress me?" His dad took a sip of his beer and rolled his eyes.

"Joe, that's enough," his mom said under her breath.

"That's up to you, Dad." James pushed away from the table. "I'm going to get started on the dishes. Thank you for dinner, Heather. It was wonderful. As always."

An argument between his parents erupted the second he was in the kitchen. James sighed. It just wasn't Christmas without his dad being a dick. Last year, he succumbed to his dad's goading and got into a shouting match with him, so this year he vowed to keep his mouth shut.

Things would've been different if Kate were there. His dad would be polite and the hole inside of James's heart would be gone. Why did everything have to go to shit?

"Sorry Dad's such a jerk. I think he misses working." David draped a towel over his arms, getting ready to help do the dishes.

"Dad's always been like that. Work has nothing to do with it."

"I'm impressed you could walk away."

"I've already lost so much. I can't afford to give him anything."

By the time the dishes were done, everyone pretended nothing had happened. It was better that way, so they all sat in the living room together and exchanged presents. The lemon bars were a huge hit, but they didn't taste as good as the ones he'd made with Kate.

Just as Heather predicted, Miles was the center of attention and even made his dad smile. Miles managed to keep the peace for more than two hours, and then as his mom was crawling around on the floor with Miles, she paused briefly and looked at James. "When are you going to give me one of these?"

James's mouth went dry and his stomach churned.

"He'd have to get a girlfriend first. Unless he's not interested. James, do you like girls or boys?" His dad sneered at him, waiting for the fight.

"Joe, we talked about this. Be nice. I'm sorry, James. Your father has had too much to drink."

"It's okay, Mom. It's getting late and I have an early morning." James stood to leave and no one rushed to stop him. He hugged everyone except his dad. David and Heather both apologized, and Heather assured him she would get his pan back to him on Sunday after dinner.

Alone in his apartment, his thoughts turned to Kate again. Maybe he should've quit his job and made a life with her. That certainly would have made his parents happy. But he wanted it all. He wanted his dream job *and* Kate, but it was obviously not going to happen, and the sooner he accepted it, the sooner he could move on.

The next evening over a cup of coffee, James flipped through the pile of biochemistry tests that hadn't been picked up before the break. Now that he had recorded her grade, he knew which one hers was. Her score didn't surprise him since he already knew she was brilliant. The paper slid under his fingers, revealing the spot on the table with the scratch from her belt.

How was he supposed to move on when everything around him reminded him of her? He couldn't stay in his apartment anymore. He grabbed the bag holding the present David gave him last night and got in his car. An errand would be the perfect distraction.

James drove to a shopping area near the university where he waited in the long gift exchange line. He had never been to that part of town, even though it was only a few blocks from the university. As he walked down the street, he passed a corner market and a bookstore and nearly tripped over a sandwich board advertising the daily special: lemon bars. Even away from his apartment, everything reminded him of her. His stomach growled and his mouth watered. Maybe he should've eaten dinner.

The bell chimed over his head and when he stepped inside, his mouth hung open. Painted all over the walls, were incredibly delicate chemical structures of sugar, flour, baking soda, salt, chocolate, coffee, vanilla, eggs, butter, and lemon juice. The long counter in front of him was dotted with glass domes containing a variety of baked goods.

A rustling sound came from the kitchen, followed by a familiar voice. "I'll be right with you."

Chapter Twenty-Four

In her bakery, surrounded by recipes Kate could forget about her past and focus on the present. While making lemon bars that day, she wanted to linger on the bittersweet memories she had of James, but because she was working alone, she forced herself to put on a happy face and help customers.

As she was finishing up preparing for the next morning, the bell over her door chimed. Covered with cookie dough, she headed to the sink and called out, "I'll be right with you."

She smiled and walked out of the kitchen. "What can I help you wi—?" Her mouth froze mid-sentence as the man strolling in front of the counter turned to face her.

It was James.

They stared at each other for what seemed like an hour. Kate clutched the counter and tried to talk, but her words got stuck in her throat. There was no way to forget about the past when it confronted her in person.

James seemed to be having a similar problem and finally cleared his throat. "What are you doing here?"

Kate snapped out of her trance. "This is my bakery."

"Yours?"

She pointed to her pink apron that read: $C_{12}H_{22}O_{11}$. "I own it. I tried to tell you, that night." A tear streaked down her cheek. "The night you—" Ripped her heart out of her chest and stomped on it.

James looked around with his mouth hanging open. "It's so amazing. All that time when you had meetings and stuff going on, it was this, wasn't it?"

"Yeah, I didn't want to say anything in case my contract or loan fell through, you know?" Kate wiped her cheek and sniffed. Why did he care about any of it? Nothing in her life mattered to him. The pounding in her chest hurt.

"How do you have time for this?"

"I have all the time in the world."

"But what are you going to do in January?"

Kate shrugged. "Work just like I do now." What was so special about January?

James frowned and tilted his head. "What about school?"

"I graduated. On the fifteenth." Another tear fell down her face. A sharp pain dug into her heart. All he had to do was wait another two weeks and they could've been together, but he didn't want to wait. He was done with her.

"No." He shook his head. "No. I was at winter commencement. You weren't there. No one called your name. No one told me."

She frowned. They had talked about graduation, hadn't they? "What did you expect? For me to walk across the stage and make a fool of myself? I didn't have anyone to invite, so I opened my bakery instead." Tears flowed freely now. She hated how pathetic her life sounded. "What do you want?"

"What?"

"Why are you here? Did you come to ruin my day, or what?" Anger had taken over and she gripped the counter hard enough that her fingers began to hurt. "You made it very clear what was important in your life and I didn't make the cut."

"But, I, I didn't know," he stuttered. "I thought I had to wait until May. That wouldn't have been fair."

"I would've waited," she shouted. Two weeks or five months? What's the difference when you love someone?

He squeezed his eyes shut. "I ruined everything."

"Yeah, you did."

"I should've asked what you wanted." When he opened his eyes, his lashes were coated with tears.

"Yeah, you should have." Some of the anger slipped out of her and tingles spread through her hands as feeling returned.

"I'm so sorry." He pressed the heels of his palms into his eyes.

"I thought you didn't want me." Sorrow filled her heart.

"That couldn't be further from the truth." He took a step toward her. "I've missed you so much my body aches."

She wiped her eyes. "I missed you too."

"You moved."

Kate nodded. "I have an apartment upstairs." She pointed to the unmarked door.

"I wanted to call you."

"You should have."

"I didn't know what to say."

"Sorry is a good place to start." She took a long shaky breath.

"I'm sorry. I'm sorry for not listening. I'm sorry for assuming I knew what you wanted. I'm sorry I didn't wait." He looked around again. "And I'm sorry I missed all this."

It was more than a good start. He seemed to mean every word. "Meg and Tim really pulled through."

When James smiled, Kate's heart melted. She had missed that most of all.

"It's all because of you, you know. I need to thank you."

"For what?" James frowned.

"For encouraging me to open a bakery. And helping me make the menu," she added with a smile. Every one of his suggestions was written in her planning notebook.

"You told me it wasn't a new idea."

She shook her head. "No, it wasn't, but you gave it power. Importance. I wouldn't have had the confidence without you."

"You can do anything you set your mind to." He smiled again, and then he shook his head. "I'm so sorry I'm such a fucking idiot."

"No, you're not." She came around the end of the counter and stood in front of him. "I don't fall in love with idiots." She put her hand on his shoulder and rejoiced in the feel of his body under her fingertips.

He blinked tears out of his eyes and cradled her face between his hands. "I've loved you for so long but didn't know how to tell you."

Kate's body shook as a ragged sigh escaped her throat. "I love you, James."

The moment their lips met, the past was forgotten. They held onto each other as they kissed and when they finally pulled apart, James sighed. "I thought I lost you. I don't want to lose you again."

"I'm not going anywhere." Kate went to the entrance, flipped the sign, and clicked the lock into place. She pulled her apron off and dropped it onto the counter then held her hand out to him and led him to the door to her apartment. "Not without you."

The End

PLEASE HELP MY CAREER by posting an honest review wherever you purchased this book.

If you want to be kept up to date on new releases and sales, join here: https://mailchi.mp/2c5919ac4fe9/septemberwrites[1]

About the Author

September Roberts writes romance erotica in a variety of genres. Whether it's paranormal, new adult, or contemporary, you'll always get the happy ever after you've come to expect from her. She creates true-to-life romance, smart characters, strong heroines, intimate scenes, and plenty of humor.

She grew up exploring the western United States. Her love of nature began at an early age as she explored the Rocky Mountains, the Mojave Desert, California beaches, and pristine glacier lakes. While she was getting her degree in botany, she met the love of her life. She took a break from being a science nerd so she could write romance stories that she would want to read. Stories with love, humor, hot sex, and always a happy ever after.

Preview of In Your Shoes

Turn the page for a special preview of September Roberts's next novel, *In Your Shoes*

MARRIAGE IS HARD ENOUGH in your own body.

On the verge of divorce, Scott Erickson will do anything he can to save his marriage. After years of growing apart, Nicole isn't so sure it's worth saving, especially when she finds pictures of Scott with another woman. With the help of a marriage counselor, they attempt to communicate with each other, but each appointment is worse than the last until, finally, during a hypnotherapy session, they switch bodies.

Faced with challenges neither of them is equipped to handle, they both must learn to survive in their new roles and unfamiliar bodies, but is there a way to switch back? And if so, can their marriage be restored after they've walked in each other's shoes?

Chapter One

The sun had set an hour ago. Scott was late. Again.

The headlights of his car swept through the trees lining the street in his neighborhood. Another day gone working too hard at his shitty job.

Almost home. All he wanted was to sit down, have a nice meal, and maybe watch a little TV, but as he pulled into his driveway, something fluttered by the side of the car. Scott shifted into park, turned the key, and squinted through the windshield. A pair of underwear landed in front of his face on the large plane of glass—*his* underwear.

When he stepped out of the car, he frowned and then ducked as a shoe whizzed past his ear and then another.

"What the hell is going on?" he muttered as he walked up the curving sidewalk toward the front door, stooping to collect the debris covering his lawn and driveway on his way. With his arms full, he struggled to get inside. Dropping his things on the front porch, he opened the door slowly. The sound coming from upstairs made his heart race.

An angry rant spilled filled the house and assaulted him. It was unlike anything he'd ever heard.

Moving carefully up the stairs, he paused outside their bedroom. With his back pressed against the wall, he listened to

Nicole, half crying and half screaming. Nothing made sense. The string of sounds embodied anger and sorrow.

Forgetting his frustration with their new lawn ornaments, Scott pushed the door open. Half the drawers from the dresser had been yanked out and dumped on the floor, and a heap of hangers and his clothes decorated the closet floor. Well, at least the clothes that hadn't made it out the window yet. As if on cue, Nicole grabbed a handful of socks and threw them as hard as she could. They sailed through the dimly lit yard.

"Nicole? What's going on? Where's Hanna?"

Nicole's eyes widened as she spun to face him. Mascara streaked her cheeks. With her lips pressed together, she shook her head. "You have a lot of nerve showing up here."

"What's going on?" He frowned and took a step inside the room.

Nicole's finger thrust out in front of her. Dried blood clung to her skin. "You know damn well what's going on."

"Listen, I'm sorry I'm late. The Danson project—"

"Don't lie to me." Fresh tears ran down her face.

"Sweetie, I—"

"Don't you *sweetie* me." If she wasn't screaming before, she was now. "I saw the pictures. Get out."

"Pictures? What are you talking about?" The last pictures he'd taken with his phone were of a property on the west side of town. An empty lot. "Why don't we just calm down and talk about this?"

"No," she screeched. "I'm not going to calm down." The muscles in her jaw clenched tight.

With his hands in front of him, he took a step toward her. "I think if we just take a deep breath—"

She squeezed her eyes shut and shook her head. "How dare you." The next time she spoke her words came out as a growl. "Get. Out."

To make her point, she started throwing clothes at him. Scott dodged to the side just as a metal hanger hit the door.

"Get out." A rack full of belts directed at his torso accompanied her words. They hit the wall just outside their bedroom, gouging the paint and landing on the hall floor with a dull thud.

Scott backed away from her. "Where am I supposed to go?" The question was more to himself than anything, but Nicole heard him.

Through their open bedroom door, she screamed, "I don't give a crap where you go. Why don't you call your *girlfriend*? I'm sure she'd be happy to have you over."

A pair of shoes came flying down the hall. Scott didn't get out of the way in time, and one of them connected squarely with his chest.

Girlfriend? He'd clearly missed something, and as much as he wanted to find out what had made Nicole so angry, he knew her well enough to let her cool off.

It took twenty minutes for Nicole to finish tossing his clothes out the window and another ten for him to pick them up off the lawn and dump them unceremoniously in the back seat of his car.

Just as Scott fished the last pair of socks out of the shrubs, Nicole stormed through the house, turning off the lights as she went, submerging the yard into near darkness. The lock on the front door clicked into place, followed by Nicole's muffled sobs.

Over the past few years, he and Nicole had plenty of fights, but nothing like this. Most of their arguments ended with one of them sleeping on the couch. Usually him. It was clear that wasn't an option this time. Neither was sleeping in his car since he wasn't dressed for the chilly spring evening.

That only left one possibility. He would have to stay with his brother. If Luke would have him.

"ARE YOU SURE SHE SAID, girlfriend?" Luke took a sip of his beer and raised an eyebrow.

"Yes. I'm sure. I don't know what the hell is going on."

Luke shook his head. "There's no talking to 'em when they get like that. Best to just wait it out a bit. I'm sure this will all smooth over in a couple of days."

Scott cradled his head in his hands.

"Don't worry about it. Drink your beer. Beer makes everything better." Luke patted his back. "Listen, I have an empty closet in the workout room. You can hang all your stuff up if you want to and the couch is all yours for as long as you need it. Nicole just needs time, that's all."

"Thanks, Luke."

"You did the same for me when Nina kicked me out. That's what brothers do."

They worked together to unload Scott's car, taking armfuls of clothes inside. "I just don't get it. Why would she think I cheated on her?"

Luke shrugged and looked at the ground. "Maybe she thinks it runs in the family. Anyway, I'll go get you a few hangers."

"Why do you need a workout room, anyway? I thought you had a gym membership," Scott called across the hall to his brother's room.

Luke stood in the doorway with a dozen hangers. "I do. The gym is a great place to meet women. But you know how I feel about other people's sweat. Speaking of, if you're going to use my equipment, you have to wipe it down. Otherwise, it might be grounds for eviction."

Scott inhaled sharply. "Ooh, harsh."

They shared a laugh, helping ease a little tension out of Scott's body. Luke was right. Nicole just needed a little time.

Chapter Two

Nicole had been sitting by the front door crying for an hour when someone knocked. After wiping her cheeks and nose, she stood and opened the door to her best friend.

Jennifer pulled her face away from the glass in one quick movement. "Jeez. You scared me." She sighed and hugged Nicole. "Didn't go well, I take it?"

Nicole shook her head and hiccupped. It always happened when she cried. "No."

"Do you want to talk about it?" Jennifer put her arm around Nicole and led her to the kitchen.

They sat side-by-side on the stools in front of the cooking island in the middle of the immaculate room. If it had been a typical night, Nicole would still be cleaning up after a meal she had spent hours making. A meal Scott would most likely miss. But she hadn't made dinner. She had kicked out her cheating husband instead.

"How much did you see?" Another hiccup.

Jennifer laughed. "Scott picking up his clothes off the lawn. He had to fish a pair of boxers out of the shrubs between our houses. You have a good throwing arm."

Nicole cracked a smile.

"What did he say? Did he admit to it?"

"No, but he didn't deny it either. I was so mad, and he kept telling me to take a deep breath. To calm down." Nicole clenched her jaw. "I hate when he does that."

"Did you tell him everything? About the pictures of Amber and him?"

Nicole nodded, and fresh tears sprang out of her eyes. "He said, 'What pictures?' And then he looked at me like I'm crazy. Does he think I'm stupid? How could he lie right to my face?"

"I'm so sorry." Jennifer rubbed Nicole's back.

"Thanks for letting Hanna come over. If she had been here, she'd never forgive me for talking to her dad like that."

"Psh. Hanna needs to learn Scott isn't perfect. I'm glad I could help. She and Ashley went to the basement to watch a movie and she didn't hear anything."

"Thank you." Nicole rested her head on Jennifer's shoulder. "I don't know what I'd do without you."

"You'd still be in the dark. That's for sure. The only reason I knew anything was because Amber is my friend on The Network." Jennifer rolled her eyes. "Every time I see her post something, I feel so old. I used to change her diapers. Twenty years ago. Now I'm just some creepy old lady who likes her posts."

"You're not old. Thirty-six is not old. Don't forget, I'm a year older than you." Nicole crossed her arms over her chest and nodded. "And thank goodness you saw those pictures. I feel like such a fool. He's out there, parading around with a twenty-one-year-old woman."

"Well, she's not hiding it either. You saw the pictures."

A sob racked Nicole's body. "Amber probably gives him everything he wants. Everything he needs."

"Hey." Jennifer started rubbing circles on Nicole's back again.

"He's probably with her right now. I told him to go to her—" Another sob cut her off.

"Don't think about that. That's not helpful."

They sat like that for a while, Nicole crying and Jennifer comforting her.

"Thank you again. I guess I should go get Hanna. School night." There would be no time to dwell on what happened with Scott. Every day seemed to be busier than the last, especially with the school play just six weeks away.

"She's welcome to stay over, but I know how you feel about sleepovers on school nights. At the very least, let me take her in the morning. That way you won't be rushed to get to work."

Nicole nodded. New sessions at the yoga studio would start tomorrow.

"Why don't you just go to bed and I'll send Hanna home? Get some rest."

It seemed like a good idea, but no matter how hard Nicole tried, she couldn't fall asleep. The front door opened and closed at one point, followed by the thunderous stomps of Hanna's feet. How a fifteen-year-old girl could make so much noise baffled her. Hanna went right to the bathroom and took a shower and then went to her room.

Nicole sighed. It would be better for everyone if she didn't have to see Hanna for a while. Eventually, a fitful sleep claimed her, but she woke several times during the night covered with sweat, images of Amber and Scott together filled her brain.

"YOU'RE HERE EARLY." Nina's smile faded. "What's wrong?"

"Scott, he—" Nicole pushed the heels of her palms against her eyes, trying to stop the tears. "I kicked him out last night."

"What happened?" Nina narrowed her eyes.

"I saw pictures of him with a woman he works with," she whispered.

"Oh, Nicole. I know how much that hurts. You think everything is fine, and then you realize it's not. I still can't figure out what happened with Luke, even after all this time. I loved him so much, but it wasn't enough. It's so frustrating. Are you holding up okay?"

"I don't know. I'm numb. I didn't sleep well last night. I woke before my alarm this morning, so I decided to come in early."

"How's Hanna taking the news?"

Nicole looked at the ground. "I haven't told her yet."

"You mean she didn't notice?" Nina scoffed.

"How would she? Scott goes for a run before she gets up and doesn't get home until dinnertime. If he bothers to show up at all." Nicole's chin trembled. "Now I know why he was always late."

Nina tucked her blond hair behind her ears. "Do me a favor."

"Sure."

"Forget about him. At least while you're here. This is your space. Don't let him in."

Nicole squared her shoulders and straightened her back. "Okay. I'll try."

"Good. Now take a deep breath." Nina smiled when Nicole complied. "Perfect. Do you want to hit something?"

"Yes, please."

Nina and Nicole laughed. "Luke's the reason I had a punching bag installed. You're welcome to use it."

By the time Nicole's ten o'clock class started, she had drained most of her excess energy. Since it was her first class of the session, she spent most of her class talking while she demonstrated the basic yoga moves. After an early lunch, she waited for her noon class, which always drew a big crowd of people on their lunch breaks.

All eyes followed her as she walked to the front of the nearly full class.

"Welcome to N2 Studios. This is Beginning Yoga, and I'm your instructor, Nicole Erickson."

The students greeted her with a few hellos, and as she glanced around the room, one face stood out above the rest. Rodney York, Scott's boss. When his eyes swept up and down her body, her skin crawled. After a quick smile, she went on with the basic introduction to the class.

At the end of the hour, Rodney came up to her, and before she could pull away, he hugged her and kissed her cheek, just like he did every time he saw her at work parties. "My girl. I'm really looking forward to this class. Carol's been nagging me to do something to relax, so I thought this would be the perfect thing. And what better person to take it from?"

A tight smile spread across Nicole's face. There was nothing worse than being called my girl. It was personal, possessive, and demeaning all at once. "I hope you get what you want out of class."

"I hope so too." Rodney gaped at her breasts.

Nicole cleared her throat, started rolling up her mat, and pointed to the door, hoping he would take the hint. "Great. I'll see you Thursday." Before leaving, he winked at her and all she could think about was his poor wife. Cheating husbands seemed to be trending.

Nina walked in and closed the door after Rodney left. "Do you know that guy?" she asked as she scrunched her face.

"Kind of. He's Scott's boss. He hits on me at every Christmas party. This ought to be a fun session."

Nina grimaced. "You want me to reassign you?"

"Nah, I'll be fine. I can handle a creep." Nicole took a drink from her water bottle. "How's Holly working out?" Nicole and Nina had opened the studio together, but she didn't feel like much of a partner since she had such limited hours there. Nina always consulted her on new hires and new classes but handled everything else herself. Nina had always been dedicated and driven to succeed.

"Great. She's teaching Warrior Woman. The ladies love it. Lots of yelling and kicking. Maybe you should take it. The new session starts tomorrow at five." Nina wiggled her eyebrows.

"I can't. Hanna has soccer practice Wednesday nights."

Nina sighed. "Between your hours here, volunteering at her school, taking classes, and running around to all her activities, I don't think you have more than five minutes to yourself in a day."

Nicole shrugged. "I'm used to it by now. Speaking of, I need to run. I can't volunteer in yoga pants and a tank top. Hanna would die."

While Nicole stopped at home to change, she noticed the gouge in the wall outside her bedroom. Bitter memories of the previous night threatened to turn her into a blubbering fool again, but no one needed to see her like that. As she drove, she put their fight out of her mind. Outside the school, she parked in the same spot she always used and went straight to the main office.

Preoccupied, the secretary nodded as Nicole checked herself into the school's system. The halls bustled with students running from one class to the next. A few of the theater kids walked down the hall with her.

"Hi, Mrs. E. What are we going to work on today?" Braxton lisped through his retainer.

Nicole shrugged. "Whatever John, I mean, Mr. Gotchberg, wants us to do."

They slipped into the back of the theater just as John began directing the students.

John clapped his hands twice, silencing the noisy teenagers. "Listen up, people. We have six weeks to get our acts together and make this thing happen. I expect to see each and every one of you here at rehearsal after school." With another clap, he said, "Places." John jumped off the stage and walked over to Nicole. "Thank you for volunteering. I'm not sure I tell you enough how much I appreciate having adult help around here."

Nicole chuckled. "You tell me every time I'm here."

"Well then, I guess you know."

Nicole walked with him as he made his way to the fourth row. "What would you like me to do today?"

"Help with lines, costumes, props, you name it. These kids need help. A lot of help."

Nicole nodded and turned to leave.

"Nicole? Are you okay? You look sad." John frowned.

"I'll be all right. Thanks, John." Nicole couldn't discuss her fight with Scott with a room full of students within earshot, especially with Hanna standing nearby.

Nicole ushered the students around, getting them in position for the opening scene. As part of the stage crew, Hanna worked quietly in the background on the set, positioning props as the actors went through the motions and lines. Braxton painted the set, and Nicole had to point out more than once when paint dripped on the stage. By the end of the hour, she knew why he was so distracted. He couldn't keep his eyes off Hanna.

As the students left for their last class, the theater quieted. John grabbed a stack of notes and said goodbye before he left.

"I'm going to finish painting the set. I'll see you at rehearsal after school." Alone in the room, Nicole worked without distraction for the next hour. She had just finished one of the corner posts when the final bell of the day rang and Hanna came back for after-school rehearsal.

"What were you and Mr. G talking about?" Hanna popped her gum and then wound it around her finger.

"Hanna, I've told you before. Gum is in your mouth or in the garbage. You have to the count of three."

Hanna rolled her eyes. "Whatever."

"One, two," Nicole raised an eyebrow and waited for Hanna to obey before she got to three. Nicole had spent far too much time removing gum out of Hanna's hair and clothing to watch her play with it.

Hanna smacked her gum again. "Why did you get paint all over the place?"

Nicole frowned. Obviously, she'd missed a spot when she cleaned the floor. "I didn't. Braxton did." As soon as she said his name, her frown morphed into a smile. "He's a nice kid. He's a freshman too, right?"

"I guess. We have English together."

"I think he likes you," Nicole whispered.

"*Mom*." Hanna's cheeks went red. They both turned as the rest of the students lumbered through the theater. "Shh."

Nicole pretended to zip her lips shut, but Hanna's cheeks still burned. Ah, to be a high school student again. Despite the fragile state of her marriage, she didn't feel the need to warn her daughter about falling in love with the wrong boy and ruining her life. Hanna would have plenty of time to figure things out before that would happen.

While the actors fumbled through their lines, Nicole's pocket vibrated. Turning away from everyone, she pulled her phone out and stared at a text from Scott.

We need to talk.

Nicole's jaw clenched, and tears welled in her eyes as she replied.

"I have nothing to say. Stay away from me."

Scott didn't respond.

Nicole took a deep breath, wiped her eyes, and plastered a smile on her face before she faced the students working nearby. Luckily, she had plenty of work to do without having to be around anyone else.

As Nicole and Hanna walked through the empty school halls later that evening, Nicole checked out of the system and pulled her keys out of her purse. "What do you want for dinner tonight?"

"Spaghetti. It's Dad's favorite."

Nicole cleared her throat and got into the car. "Your dad won't be joining us for dinner tonight."

Hanna plopped into the passenger seat and frowned. "Is he working late again?"

"Actually, he'll be out of town for a while. Some big project." Nicole focused on getting her keys in the ignition, afraid the truth would spill out of her mouth if she looked at Hanna.

"Huh. That's weird. Wasn't he just out of town?"

Nicole narrowed her eyes as she thought about it. Maybe he'd been at Amber's house last time. "That's what I thought, too. Do you still want spaghetti?"

"Sure. Whatever." Hanna picked paint out of her fingernail. "Can I go over to Ashley's?"

"Do you have any homework?"

Hanna flicked a piece of dried paint on the floor mat of the car. "No."

"Well then, that's fine with me. I'll call when dinner's ready." Nicole pulled into the garage, and Hanna left the second she turned the car off.

The silence in the house unnerved her. Scott's absence made the house feel empty for some reason, even though he'd been gone a lot lately. It was different knowing he wouldn't come home. Sitting at his spot at the table, she put her head on his placemat and cried. What if she'd made a mistake kicking him out? What if she'd been wrong about Amber? But the pictures were plain as day, so how could she be wrong? There was only one explanation: he was cheating on her. End of story.

How could she come back from that kind of betrayal? It didn't matter how much she did around the house or how much she did for their daughter. It wasn't enough for him. Maybe it never had been.

Made in the USA
Columbia, SC
26 July 2018